THE ENCHANTED
GARDEN CAFE

ABIGAIL DRAKE

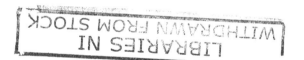

Edited By Lara Parker

Cover Art By Najla Qamber

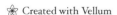 Created with Vellum

*To South Side Vinni, who started this whole adventure
by asking a young singer and a kid with a guitar
to host an acoustic show one Saturday night.*

*And to Kathleen, who still laughs about how
a few hours spent in a smoothie bar turned into a novel.*

CHAPTER 1

FALLING IN LOVE IS LIKE BAKING. RESULTS
MAY VARY WITH EXPERIENCE. - AUNT
FRANCESCA

I opened the box and stepped back, tripping over a pile of Himalayan wind chimes I'd left lying behind me on the floor of the shop. They clanked in a discordant melody as I untangled them from my feet.

"What the heck?" I asked, ignoring the chimes and focusing on the parcel that had arrived in the mail earlier that morning. Tiny stone phalluses in various shades of gray filled the container to the brim. Checking the return address, I noticed the shipping cost and wanted to cry. Most of our inventory budget for the entire month had been used to mail this one small box halfway around the world.

"Mom, what exactly did you order from Inuyama, Japan?"

My mother popped her head around the corner, a bright smile on her face. "Did they finally arrive, Fiona? I've been waiting for ages."

"For stone penises?"

Why was I even surprised? This wasn't the first time something like this had happened, and it probably wouldn't be the last. My mother, Claire de Lune Campbell, had never been the master of impulse control, and she had a history of making very poor decisions. She'd been born Claire Campbell and added the "de Lune" in, what I can only guess, was a moment of pot-induced inspiration. The pot no longer played a part in her life, but the total inability to make common-sense decisions remained.

Mom picked up one of the stone penises, a happy twinkle in her eye. "Aren't they lovely?"

On the outside, Mom and I looked alike. The same blonde hair, the same blue eyes, the same stubborn tilt to our chins, but there the resemblance ended. Mom was as happy and bright as a butterfly landing on a flower, and she had the same level of fiscal responsibility. I stressed about everything, especially money, but I had good cause.

My mom owned and operated the Enchanted Garden Café, where we served food, coffee, and specially blended teas and sold unusual items in our small gift shop. Nestled in the middle of the South Side, the funky hippie district of Pittsburgh, it was the perfect spot for my mom but a constant source of anxiety for me.

I wiped sweat from my face and brushed off my clothing. Dust covered my T-shirt and shorts, and some kind of stone powder had fallen out of the box from Inuyama onto my tennis shoes. Mom, glowing in a dress made from recycled saris, didn't have a speck of dust on her, but she hadn't handled the phalluses.

Kate, the girl who worked behind the counter, came over to us, her blue eyes alight with curiosity. "I want to see them," she said. Mom handed her one, and she studied it closely, peering at it through the thick black frames of her retro hipster glasses. Her ebony hair was pulled off to the side in a low ponytail, and her colorful tattoos peeked through the crocheted black cardigan covering her pale skin. "At least they are anatomically correct. Look at those veins."

My cheeks grew warm, and Mom smiled, putting a cool hand against my face. "Aww, Fiona is blushing."

"No, I'm not. It's hot in here."

"Of course it is," she said, making me feel twelve instead of twenty-five, but it *was* hot for early June, and the air-conditioning was broken. Again. Even with all the windows open, it still felt stuffy.

I ignored her and picked up a penis. "What are these things anyway?"

She beamed at me with pure, unfiltered happiness. "Fertility charms from a little shrine in the mountains of Japan. They have a big festival there every year. I went once."

She sighed, most likely remembering happy times at the fertility festival, and went back to the kitchen. I looked at Kate and rolled my eyes, making her snicker, before getting back to work. The fertility charms came in all sizes and seemed handmade. I just wasn't sure how to sell them or where to display them in our shop.

A Victorian eyesore, the café was painted on the outside in what once had been a mix of bright pink and various shades of green. The pink had faded to a dull rose, and the green looked like the color of old limes just before they rotted. It needed work and a fresh coat of paint, but instead of doing so, we spent our money on phalluses from Japan. That was how things worked with my mother. No planning. No rhyme or reason. No logic. No rational thought.

The bell above the door tinkled, and I turned, a penis in each hand, as a stranger walked into the shop. I couldn't see his face at first because the sun was at his back, but he carried a guitar case. A sure sign of trouble.

"Hello," he said as he came closer.

He had straight dark hair that brushed his shoulders, brown eyes, and a goatee. He reminded me of a sexy, naughty French pirate, and I knew his kind well. Close to my age, he was definitely one of the artsy, flighty types who always hung out around my mom. I could spot them a mile away.

"Holy guacamole, if he were any hotter, I'd need new underwear," whispered Kate, taking off to the back of the shop and leaving me alone to greet the stranger.

"Hi."

For no reason at all, my cheeks grew so warm they pulsated. I needed to get the air conditioner fixed. Yet another item on my list of practical things we couldn't afford to get done.

Sexy French Pirate Man looked down and smiled. "Sorry to bother you. It looks like you have your hands full."

I'd almost forgotten about the penises. I quickly put my hands behind my back, a silly move since an open box of them sat right on the table in front of me.

Composing myself, I casually placed the phalluses on a shelf next to some potted herbs, hoping they'd be mistaken for some kind of garden sculpture. They did look a bit like worms from a distance. Up close, unfortunately, there was no disguising them.

Sexy French Pirate Man just stood there watching me. I found it extremely annoying. "Can I help you with something?" I snapped.

He looked like he was trying not to laugh. "I'm here to see Claire."

"Of course you are," I muttered under my breath. It took some effort to force a fake smile onto my face. "Hold on a second." I stuck my head into the kitchen and yelled, "Mom, someone wants to speak with you."

She walked out in her apron, wiping her hands. When she saw the stranger, her eyes lit up. "You must be Matthew. How good of you to come."

He smiled with genuine pleasure. "Hello, Claire."

She pulled him into a hug. My mother was a compulsive

hugger. She hugged everyone, even the mailman when he brought the mail every day. I preferred a handshake or maybe even just a nod.

"Matthew Monroe, this is my lovely daughter, Fiona."

"Mom. Please." Dirty, hot, and desperately in need of a shower, I felt far from lovely at the moment. I glared at her, but she ignored me.

"Matthew agreed to host acoustic night for the summer while Frankie is away. Isn't that wonderful?"

I stared at her in shock. Acoustic night, held every Saturday, was a pain in the neck. She made it a BYOB event, which meant we usually had drunk people in the back garden until well past midnight and a mess every Sunday morning.

The garden was normally a tranquil oasis, a place with crumbling brick walls, bright flowers, and a gurgling fountain in the center. Mom, in typical Claire Campbell fashion, thought the fountain possessed magical properties and was somehow connected to a mystical underground spring mentioned in ancient prophecies. My theory? The water probably came directly from the muddy Monongahela River just down the street.

Either way, the garden was a big moneymaker for us. Every Sunday, ladies wearing fancy hats and white gloves came in droves, traveling for miles in their expensive cars for the chance to nibble on tiny cucumber sandwiches and drink my mom's famous teas. They also liked to browse the shop and pick up little things, like books on natural remedies, jewelry made by local artists, and the occasional bong. We sold them as water pipes, but they knew what they were just as much as we did. The last thing those ladies would want to see, however, was vestiges left from a bunch of drunks at acoustic night. It would ruin the whole ambiance for them.

I hated acoustic night, but we'd managed to keep it under control as long as my mom's friend Frankie Quattrone hosted it. He was a tall, lean man with long curly hair and tiny glasses; people listened when he told them to get out or to stop smoking weed in front of the café. I doubted Matthew could do it. It would end up being complete chaos.

I struggled to remain calm. "I thought we planned to cancel acoustic night until Frankie came back."

Frankie was currently staying in an ashram in India. It never ceased to amaze me how many of my mom's friends stayed at ashrams. None of my other friends knew people who went to ashrams. They went to the beach or stayed in a cottage on a lake. Nice, predictable, normal ways to take a vacation. Ashrams weren't even on their radar.

Mom hugged Matthew's arm. "We did, but Frankie called and said Matthew would help out."

"Perfect."

Of course, she missed the sarcasm in my voice. She had no sarcasm sensor at all. "It *will* be perfect. Exactly what we need. It's been so stressful around here lately."

"What do you mean?" asked Matthew, his dark eyes immediately filled with concern. My mom had that effect on people. The top of her head barely hit his shoulder, and she looked like a tiny lost fairy. People naturally wanted to protect her. A few inches taller and a whole lot tougher, I didn't need protecting and made that clear.

"Mom, we shouldn't talk about this with strangers . . ."

"Oh, posh. Matthew isn't a stranger. He's one of us now. Aren't you, Matthew?"

Matthew nodded, so mesmerized I wanted to groan. "But this is a legal matter. We aren't supposed to discuss it."

I felt the panic rising in my chest, but Mom remained unconcerned. "We can trust Matthew." She lowered her voice. "A big corporation called Anderson Solutions is trying to buy up the whole block. They want to tear down all these beautiful little shops and build a giant, ugly parking garage."

"That's terrible," he said.

"I know," said Mom. "My aunt Francesca would be rolling in her grave right now if she had any idea what was going on. This was her house, you see. She left it to me when I found out I was pregnant with Fiona and had nowhere else to go, but the rest of the block is owned by a man named Mr. McAlister. He isn't well, poor dear. He's thinking about selling. And Anderson is doing what they can to intimidate us into selling, too, including filing a bunch of silly little complaints against us. Frankly speaking, I don't have the resources to keep up. Lawyers are expensive creatures."

I'd lost sleep over it for weeks. On one hand, the café felt like a noose around my neck, strangling me ever so slowly. On the other, it was my childhood home and our entire source of income. If Mom had to close the café, I didn't know what she'd do. She would never be able to find another job. The best she could hope for would be to buy another café and start from the ground up, but I wasn't sure how she'd manage it. She'd put too much of herself, body and soul, into the Enchanted Garden.

"They are," agreed Matthew. "Is there anything you can do?"

"There's a city council meeting in a few weeks, and that's why this is so important. Acoustic night is a big crowd pleaser and brings a lot of young people into the café. We need all the help and support we can get." Mom had to blink away tears. "Aunt Francesca was . . . well, she was magical. There is no other way to put it. Other than a few pieces of jewelry and a book of her favorite recipes, this café is all I have left of her. Losing it would be like losing her all over again. I'm not sure if I could bear it."

I'd never met my great-aunt, and I didn't care much about jewelry, but I'd grown pretty attached to her recipe book. A handwritten journal, with lots of odd notations and funny little quotes, it had been a constant source of inspiration for me. I'd found it hidden underneath the window seat by the big stained-glass window in the main room of the café when I was very small, and I'd learned to bake with it. And although I wasn't sure I agreed with my mother's conclusions about having Matthew play here all summer, she did have a point. We needed all the help we could get, or we could lose everything.

The bell above the door tinkled again, and in walked my boyfriend. Tall, blond, and perfect, Scott wore an expensive suit and tie and didn't seem to feel the summer heat. I stood on tiptoes to give him a kiss. As his lips brushed mine, he took one look at my hair and clothing and gave my ponytail a gentle tug.

"Fiona, we're going to be late . . ." His eyes widened when he noticed the box of stone phalluses. I hurriedly shut it and shoved it under a table.

"Two seconds," I said. "Promise."

Mom and I lived in the apartment above the shop, so I ran upstairs to my room, taking the steps two at a time. Hopping into the shower, I said a prayer that the hot water tank still worked and dressed as quickly as possible, donning a simple black sundress and pulling my hair into a tight bun at the nape of my neck. I put on a little lipstick, grabbed my purse, and ran downstairs. It was never a good idea to leave Scott alone too long with Mom.

Back in the shop, she was forcing Scott to taste her new tea, explaining to him why the phalluses would be such a huge hit. "They're part of our new fertility line. That tea is as well. I call it Fertile Myrtle."

Scott almost spat out the tea in his mouth, and Matthew bit his lip, probably an effort to keep from laughing at the horrified expression on Scott's face. "*What* did you give me?" Scott asked, his cheeks growing pink.

I grabbed his arm. "It's nothing, just herbal tea. We'd better go. We have reservations, right?"

As I pulled him outside, I saw my old friend Moses walking toward us, his gait uneven because of his bad leg. Scott glared at me, probably knowing what was coming, and I gave his hand an apologetic squeeze. "Just a second. Promise."

I jogged over to Moses, and his whole face lit up when he saw me. He had the most beautiful smile in the world, a slash of white in his dark face that made each person he bestowed it upon feel loved and important. "Baby girl. How nice to see you on this beautiful evening."

I kissed his weathered cheek. He carried a beat-up saxophone case in one hand. "Are you going to play at the café tonight?"

His dark eyes sparkled as he caressed the worn black leather. "You know I will. It's the best part of my week."

"I put some soup in the fridge for you, and there's fresh bread too. Make sure you eat. I mean it, Moses."

"You have a heart of gold like your mama," he said, leaning forward to whisper in my ear. "And you're far too good for that one over there."

Scott tapped his foot impatiently, but I ignored him, patting Moses on the shoulder. I felt his bones under the thin fabric of his meticulously ironed shirt, and it worried me. He'd been an adjunct professor at the university until he got sick last year, a job he loved but one that left him with no health insurance or pension. It made me furious. Moses deserved better.

"You don't think anyone is good enough for me. You never have."

He laughed, the sound rich and deep. "That is the honest truth, and I will not deny it."

"Go eat your soup." I gave him a wave goodbye and ran back to Scott.

He glanced at his watch. "If you are done socializing with the city's indigent population, can we please go?"

I frowned. "He isn't homeless. He's going through a rough patch."

"I'm sorry, Fi," he said, drawing me close. "I know you're protective of him, and I adore you for it. This isn't about Moses. Your mom . . ."

I squeezed his hand. "I understand. Trust me. So where are we going tonight?"

Sometimes changing the subject was better than having a discussion that could lead to an argument. Scott didn't like my mom, and I suspected the feeling was mutual. They both put on a brave front for my sake, though.

He smiled. "I made a few calls and got a table Le Mont. Nothing's too good for my girl."

He opened the door of his Jaguar for me, and I slipped in, relaxed and happy for the first time all day. Scott had that effect on me. Being around him made me feel calm and safe. Sometimes it seemed like he was the only thing I could count on, the one stable, normal element in my chaotic life. And I needed stable and normal. I'd never had it before. I'd never even come close.

Kate once said I spent so much time trying not to be my mom I had no idea who I truly was. She suggested meditation, journaling, and self-realization techniques, but I didn't need any of that. I had dreams and plans of my own, and I had Scott.

As the sun set over the river and we sped out of the South Side, I closed my eyes. As soon as I finished my last class in the fall, I planned to move out. I'd already talked to a friend who needed a roommate, so things were lining up. I just had to wait until everything was settled with Anderson Solutions and then find a way to tell Mom without breaking her heart.

CHAPTER 2

Scott forgot to mention his coworker, Harrison, would join us for dinner with his girlfriend, Mindy. Scott and Harrison worked together at Burgess and Garrett, a big real estate investment firm downtown, and Harrison was a bit of a drinker. As they waited at the bar for us, he already looked slightly toasted.

"Sorry we're late." Scott rolled his eyes and ordered a drink.

"Women." Harrison raised his glass in manly agreement.

Mindy fluttered her eyelashes. "But we're so worth the wait."

We'd gone out with Harrison and Mindy many times before, and I hadn't enjoyed it. Harrison, a stocky redhead with a thick neck, had an opinion about everything. Mindy, a bleach blonde with a fake tan, seemed to have no opinions at all.

The restaurant, elegant and expensive, sat high on Mount Washington and overlooked the entire sparkling city of Pittsburgh. The bright-red cable cars of the Duquesne Incline slowly moved up and down, connecting Mount Washington to the South Shore area below. Although the inclines had been created to take steelworkers to the mills in the morning and back home in the evening, now they were used mostly for tourists. I loved to watch them inch up and down the mountain, and I adored the view of the city from Le Mont. The three rivers joined together just below us, where the fountain of the Golden Triangle burst up into the air in a beacon of light. As a bonus, the Pirates were playing at PNC Park that night, which meant there would probably be fireworks later, and we were in the perfect spot to watch the show.

Scott and Harrison hadn't even noticed the view. They immediately got wrapped up in a conversation about work. Mindy gave me an awkward smile.

"How's work? Are you still waitressing?" she asked, taking another sip of wine. We'd gone over this before, many times, but Mindy had the short-term memory of a gnat.

"I'm getting my MBA, but I work for my mom part-time. She owns a café in the South Side."

Scott leaned forward with a smile. "It's where old hippies go before they die."

Harrison and Mindy laughed. I forced a smile onto my face. "Now, Scott . . ."

Scott held up a hand to stop me, enjoying himself. "You should have seen what Fiona was doing when I walked in. She was filling a shelf with stone schlongs."

Harrison almost choked on his drink. "Why?"

"Fertility charms." I picked up the menu and pretended extreme interest in the selections. "Imported from Japan."

"Her mom gave me fertility tea." Scott and Harrison laughed so hard their faces turned red, and Harrison had to wipe his eyes with his napkin. "She's a character. The tea was called Fertile Myrtle."

I didn't like the way he made fun of my mom, even if she

kind of deserved it. "She's famous for her teas, and the shop is one of the most popular places on the South Side."

"I love the South Side," said Mindy. "I've been to some fun bars there. We should go to your mom's place after dinner."

Imagining Harrison and Mindy at acoustic night made me cringe. "Or we could go to that nice place near Station Square with dueling pianos." Station Square, also located on the South Shore, was just an incline ride away. I tried to sound enthusiastic, and it worked.

"That would be awesome," said Mindy. Harrison and Scott launched back into their work discussion again. Mindy and I were stuck with each other. I tried to think of something to talk about as minutes ticked by.

"I love your dress."

A lie, but I'd gotten desperate. Her dress, so short I could almost see her panties, was an awful shade of green that looked like the sludge we sometimes had to clean out of the fountain at the Enchanted Garden.

"Thanks. I bought it at the new designer shop in Shady-side. Expensive, but worth every penny." She whispered how much it cost, an enormous sum that would have been enough to pay the shipping on that box of phalluses ten times over.

"Wow." The idea of spending that much on a dress made me ill.

"Harrison doesn't mind." She smiled. "He likes to buy me nice things. I'm sure Scott is the same way. You met in college, right?"

She'd heard this story before as well, but at least it was something to talk about. "I saw him on campus a few times, but we didn't meet until later."

I'd admired him from a distance. He'd been the student government president at the University of Pittsburgh and in a popular fraternity. I was the wide-eyed freshman who nearly swooned every time he smiled at me. He'd been my ideal, my dream man, for years. Even before I knew his name.

"I was a big, bad senior," said Scott with a wink. "And stupid. I should have asked you out years ago."

"How did you two finally end up together?" asked Mindy.

"He got lost a few months ago in the South Side and came into my mom's shop to ask for directions."

"I ended up asking her out instead," he said, kissing my hand.

"And the rest is history," said Harrison, raising his glass to us. "You two are perfect for each other."

For once, I agreed with Harrison. If I had a checklist of every single thing I wanted from a man, Scott met each requirement. Smart, handsome, and employed, he was not an artist or a musician or a stoner. He didn't believe in alternative medicine. He'd never been to a reiki therapist. He had no idea what ear coning was or why anyone would do it. He was perfect and normal in every way. My only concern came from the fact my mom didn't like him.

When I first started dating him, she'd gotten right to the point. "Do you think you could fall in love with him, Fi?"

I'd never said as much, even to Scott. "Why wouldn't I?"

Judging by the expression on her face, I assumed she could think of several reasons, but wisely, she didn't mention them. She chose a different tactic. "Is he good in the sack?"

"I am *not* going to talk to you about my sex life."

I had no sex life, and she probably knew it. Other than two boyfriends when I was an undergrad, neither of them exceptionally remarkable, I'd been too busy studying and working to have a serious relationship. When I met Scott, I thought he had potential, but every time we'd even gotten close to having sex, something went dramatically and horribly wrong.

Once, after a particularly romantic dinner and several

bottles of wine, Scott had gotten food poisoning. Another time, I broke out in hives. The last time, he tripped on his way into the bedroom and ended up at the ER with a badly sprained ankle.

I wasn't about to share this information with my mom, however. She'd say it was the universe's way of telling us we shouldn't be together. If so, the universe was wrong, and the less my mother knew about my relationship with Scott, the better.

He interrupted my thoughts, pulling me back to the fancy restaurant and the company of Harrison and Mindy. "So what do you want, Fiona?"

I stared at him blankly, and he laughed. "You've been looking at the menu since we sat down. What are you going to order?"

"I'm not sure."

The prices weren't listed, making me a little uncomfortable. Scott always insisted on paying, but I didn't want to take advantage. I went with vegetable pasta, certain it was one of the less expensive items.

We ate in a comfortable silence. Harrison and Scott drank heavily. I sipped on my glass of wine, and Mindy chugged hers. The evening would have been more enjoyable if I'd been drunk, but I was painfully sober and very tired. Even the fireworks didn't perk me up.

A dull headache took root, and when the others wanted to go to a bar for after-dinner drinks, I begged off and said I'd take a cab home. I knew one bar would turn into two and possibly three or four. Unlike Scott, Harrison, and Mindy, I had to work in the morning. Scott gave me a sweet, sloppy kiss and paid for the taxi.

I gave him a stern look. "Don't drive home. You're sloshed."

He kissed me again. "Sloshed? It's so cute how you're

always taking care of me. I love that about you, Fiona. I love everything about you, in fact. You know that, right?"

"Thank you, Scott." My standard answer. He'd been hinting around to telling me he loved me for weeks, usually when intoxicated, but I'd never quite been able to say it back.

Scott waved as I sped off in the taxi; he looked a little unsteady on his feet. Luckily, his apartment wasn't far away. He lived in an elegant downtown high-rise with big windows, shiny stainless-steel appliances, and a great view of the Monongahela River. After barhopping, he'd take a taxi home, sleep it off, and pick up his car in the morning, his usual routine. It didn't bother me, but I had no desire to join in.

The cab let me off right in front of the café. People sat at the small tables we'd set up on the sidewalk, and others hovered near the door, listening. It was quite a crowd, and as soon as the sound of the music reached my ears, I understood why.

Matthew sat on a barstool, strumming his guitar. Mom softly kept the beat with a set of bongos she had tucked between her legs. Moses played his saxophone, the sound twisting and winding though Matthew's music like an intricate quilt. A young woman with braided hair and skin that glowed in the candlelight belted out a soulful melody about love and loss and hope.

I stopped, as enthralled by the music as the others. The woman had a lovely voice, and Moses was a genius, but Matthew grabbed my attention and held it. His black shirt and jeans accentuated his sleek, muscular body. A necklace with a yin and yang symbol carved in wood hung on a leather cord around his neck. His dark hair brushed his shoulders, as soft and smooth as silk, and his elegant fingers flew skillfully over the guitar, making it moan and sing and cry with a hauntingly beautiful sound. I'd never heard anything like it, and Matthew was as mesmerizing as his music.

As soon as the song finished, Matthew's eyes met mine. I'd been caught watching him but couldn't look away. This time he didn't smile. He stared back at me, his expression as haunted and sad and beautiful as the song he'd played.

Mom came up and touched my arm. "Isn't he amazing?"

I nodded, not trusting myself to speak. I managed to pull my gaze away from Matthew with difficulty and turned to my mom.

"How's it going tonight?"

"Quite well," she said, giving me a worried look. "You're back early. Did something happen?"

I shook my head, trying to clear it. My headache was gone, but Matthew's music had put a spell on me. I felt foggy and strange.

"I had a little headache, but I'm fine now. I'll help in the kitchen. I'm sure Chad is going nuts."

On acoustic nights, my mom closed the kitchen for hot food, selling snacks and smoothies instead. She didn't have a license to sell alcohol, but she put a complimentary shot of vodka or rum in the smoothies if the customer wanted one. Most of them did. Some of them wanted the shots without the smoothies, so I had to be strict.

Chad Wallace, a college student, helped us out on acoustic night since Kate couldn't work evenings. He had his Afro tucked into a slouchy hat, and he wore an old "Free Mandela" T-shirt. There was a line about ten people long when I headed back, and he looked relieved to see me. "Thank goodness. It's been crazy here."

The kitchen was the most modern room in the house, a gourmet's dream, with top-of-the-line appliances and a marble slab for baking. We'd spent a great deal of time and money remodeling it, even turning a small butler's pantry into a room for my mom to mix her teas and herbal concoctions, but tonight the kitchen wasn't used for any of those things. It served as smoothie central.

I pulled on a white apron that said "Kiss the Cook" and set to work. Soon, the line dwindled down to a more manageable number. As we made the smoothies, I listened to Matthew play and I swayed to the music, sometimes singing along when I knew the words. Chad did the same.

"I don't remember it ever being this busy on a Saturday night," said Chad as he cleaned out the mixer. "It's the guitarist. He's great."

I frowned as I thought about it. He *was* great. Maybe even a little too great. That idea stuck in my head as we worked, and the more I thought about it, the more worried I became.

My mom gave the last call for smoothies, and we cleaned up the kitchen. We ended the night with a piña colada smoothie and a shot of rum for ourselves, and I made one for my mom and Matthew too. Moses never drank, so I made one for him without alcohol. I took off my apron and carried the smoothies to the main room.

It was packed, and I had to push my way through the crowd. Mom and Matthew chatted like old friends, so I set their smoothies aside and looked for Moses.

He winked when he saw me. "Thank you for the soup, Fiona. It was wonderful. It warmed my heart as much as it filled my belly."

"There's always a place set for you here, Moses."

I knew he'd never ask for anything. He had too much pride. I'd finally gotten him to the point where he accepted a cup of soup from me without trying to pay for it. I handed him a bag of cookies, and he grinned. "The cookie monster strikes again."

"Snickerdoodles. Your favorite. And I made a smoothie for you too."

I put it on the table next to him. He took a cookie out of the bag and moaned as the first taste of cinnamon and sugar hit his tongue. "You have magic in your fingertips, Fiona."

"You know how I feel about magic, Moses."

He laughed, taking a sip of his smoothie. "Having a mother who sees magic everywhere has made you into a cynic, young lady. Just because you can't see it, count it, or quantify it doesn't mean it isn't there. The way you bake, the way you create such wonderful things to eat, if that isn't magic, what is it?"

"High-quality ingredients and lots and lots of butter."

"Call it what you might, but it tastes like magic to me. Tonight was an evening to remember, but it's time for me to pack up my rusty old saxophone and head back home."

"I put your saxophone case next to the door to Mom's office so it wouldn't get trampled. It's a full house tonight." I gave him a hug. "Be careful out there, Moses."

He laughed. "The only things I have on me of any value are these cookies. Goodnight, baby girl, and thanks for always taking care of me."

"Goodnight, Moses."

I surveyed the room. Although crowded, the customers seemed to be having a nice time, and no one looked trashed. A good sign. I saw several people take flyers for our upcoming poetry nights, reiki sessions, and even for the tarot readings. Mom went back to the kitchen to help Chad close up, and I turned to Matthew.

"I hope you like piña colada." I took a sip. Cold, sweet, and tropical, it had a slight warm kick from the rum.

"My favorite," he said with a grin.

Charming. Another bad sign. No reason a charming, handsome, sexy-like-a-French-pirate, incredibly talented guitarist would host an acoustic night for free with the smoothie being his only payment. It didn't make sense. He could easily get a paying gig at any of the bars in the South Side.

"Have you seen the garden yet?" I asked.

Matthew shook his head. "I haven't."

I led him back to the garden. It was mostly deserted. We sat on a bench near the crumbling stone fountain, sipping our drinks. There was hardly any mess, no broken beer bottles or piles of vomit. No one had passed out on a bench or slept half-naked under a table. Everyone had thrown away their trash, and it looked like it had even been recycled. Other than a few random candy wrappers and empty glasses, it appeared I'd have little to do Sunday morning. I might even be able to sleep in.

"It's so nice back here," he said softly. "Did you do this?"

I looked around. When my mother had inherited the house from Aunt Francesca, the garden had been a completely different space. In old photos, I'd seen nothing but a patch of lushly manicured green lawn, surrounded by rosebushes, with just the fountain in the center.

The fountain looked ancient even then, and Mom suggested it might be older than the house itself. Of course, this played conveniently into her whole mystical spring theory, which I absolutely dismissed, but I had a feeling she might be right about the age of the fountain. It did seem pretty old.

Aunt Francesca was in those faded photos, too, wearing flowing organza dresses, with her blonde head tilted back in laughter as she held a glass of champagne or a cup of tea in her hands. She always seemed to be throwing a party, and even as a child, I'd been obsessed with the platters of deli-cious-looking foods shown in the pictures. She'd been like me, a baker, not a gardener, and it had taken the loving care of my mother to truly bring this place to life.

It really was a beautiful space now, with winding pathways, hanging plants, and eclectic artwork sprinkled through-out. The entire area wafted with the sweet aroma of flowers, some exotic and some as plain as black-eyed Susans and daisies. There were shady trees, colorful bushes, and room for ten good-size tables, which came in handy for our Sunday tea parties. The idea for those parties had come from Aunt Francesca's weekly soirees, but the plans for the garden had come entirely from my mother. She really was a horticultural genius.

I shook my head. "Mom is the one with the green thumb. I kill whatever I touch."

He reached out to touch the delicate, variegated leaf on a nearby bush, stroking it gently between his fingers. "So . . . how was your date tonight?"

I almost choked on my smoothie. "Fine. Thanks for inquiring, I guess. Look, there is something I want to ask you." I thought about being diplomatic but failed. "Why are you here?"

Matthew seemed confused. "You asked if I'd seen the garden, and I said I hadn't, and you brought me back here."

I narrowed my eyes at him. "I mean, why are you hosting acoustic night? You could play anywhere in town. Why here?"

Matthew leaned back on the bench, his eyes shuttered. "I owed Frankie a favor, and this was my way to pay up."

I couldn't imagine what kind of favor Matthew could owe Frankie and hoped it didn't involve drugs or anything illegal. If Matthew was in any kind of trouble, the lawyers chasing us would sniff it out, and it could be the last nail in the Enchanted Garden's coffin.

"Are you telling me the truth?"

Something strange flickered in Matthew's expression before he shook his head. "Why would I lie?"

As much as I tried to control it, I blinked back tears. The stress had been killing me, and there was no one I could share it with. Mom would tell me life would turn out as fate determined and give me a serenity charm. Scott would listen but point out everything my mom did wrong, a pointless exercise. I knew exactly what she was doing wrong but felt powerless to stop her.

He let out a sigh, probably getting a hint about my emotional turmoil from the look on my face. "I'm here as a favor to a friend. That's all."

"A pretty big favor."

"Frankie is a pretty good friend."

Folding my arms across my body, I frowned. Something felt off about Mr. Matthew Monroe. I was sure of it. But I knew Mom wouldn't listen. She refused to see anything but the best in people. I, on the other hand, had been naturally paranoid since birth.

As the fountain gurgled beside us and the twinkle lights sparkled in the trees, I stared at him. His face was partially shadowed, and his eyes were intense as he held my gaze. Other than the obvious fact he was very hot and extremely talented, I knew nothing else about him, and that made him dangerous.

"Trust me, Fiona," he said softly.

Just as he said the words, a scream pierced the calm of the night, making me leap to my feet. It came from the narrow, dark walkway between the café and the building next door, and another scream quickly followed the first. I ran toward the side door of the garden, not knowing what I would find when I got there, but I did know one thing for certain. The screams came from my mother.

CHAPTER 3

I opened the wooden door, fumbling with the latch. We used it only once a week or so, when removing trash after tea parties. Old and in disrepair, like everything else at the café, it stuck. I had to push against it with the full weight of my body to get it to open.

Matthew followed close behind as I stumbled through the door. I looked around in dread, my eyes scanning the dark passageway. The only light came from a single dim bulb above the side door to the kitchen. We used this space to store our garbage cans, but drunks often saw it as a convenient place to relieve themselves. It reeked of urine, beer, and rotting food.

I panicked, my heart pounding in my chest. The screaming had stopped, and a horrible silence filled the air. I was about to run back into the café and call the police when I saw my mother kneeling on the damp cobblestone walkway next to a pile of rags. She held her cell phone in her hands, and she sobbed as she requested an ambulance.

There is peace in that time right before you get bad news. In the moments before you see a car crash or an accident happen. Right before you hear words that will change your life forever. It's the last few seconds of blissful ignorance, like hovering on the edge of a cliff before you tumble over the side and into the dark abyss below. Even though the truth was in front of my eyes, I lingered in the space between not knowing and knowing until my mother hung up her phone and spoke. "It's Moses. He's hurt."

She put her hand gently on the pile of rags, and I saw the battered old saxophone case on the ground. My knees gave out, and I sank down next to her, numb. We were both useless, immobilized by fear and sorrow. It was Matthew who covered Moses with his jacket to keep him warm and did a quick assessment of his injuries using the flashlight on his cell phone. I couldn't move. I could only stare at the growing circle of red near Moses's head.

"There's so much blood," I said. "Why is there so much blood?"

"A head wound always bleeds a lot. The cut itself isn't huge, but we should apply pressure to it." The matter-of-fact tone in Matthew's voice kept me from losing it completely. Mom handed him her scarf. He wadded it up and held it to Moses's head, pressing gently on the wound. "What do you think happened?"

Mom looked around, her eyes hollow and sad. "I heard a noise. I thought maybe Mrs. Felix's cat had gotten into the garbage again. I don't know how long he's been here. We were so busy."

My teeth chattered as my body shook. "I told him to be careful. I should have walked him home. I should have taken better care of him."

Mom wrapped her arms around me, and I put my face into the curve of her neck like I had done when I was small. "You can't blame yourself, Fiona," she said. "There's no way you could have known."

I heard the logic in her words, but it didn't erase the guilt and pain that drifted like a dark shadow over my heart. When we heard the whine of the approaching ambulance, Matthew went to meet the EMTs.

"You ride with them, Claire," he said after they had stabilized Moses and loaded him onto a gurney. "I'll bring Fiona and meet you at the hospital."

I still wore my sundress, so I ran upstairs and changed quickly, grabbing a pair of yoga pants and a hoodie. I didn't bother looking in a mirror. I shoved my cell phone into my pocket, put on a pair of flip-flops, and slipped out the door and into the night with Matthew.

I barely remembered the cab ride to the hospital, but the bright lights and chaos of the ER on a Saturday night jolted me out of my stupor. As Matthew went to the front desk, I stood in the middle of the room, staring around at drunk college kids who'd been hurt in bar fights, crying babies who'd picked the worst possible time to get sick, and a woman who looked like she was in the middle of an asthma attack. Her daughter sat next to her, and when the daughter's eyes met mine, we both knew. We were in some special kind of hell.

Mom came out of a closed door with a big red sign above it that read "No Admittance." Her gaze searched for us in the crowded room. Matthew grabbed my hand and pulled me over to her. My feet moved, but my brain refused to function properly.

"They did an initial exam," she said, her white T-shirt dotted with Moses's blood. "They don't think he fell."

"Then what happened?" I asked.

Mom's hands were splattered with blood as well. She tried to wipe them on her shirt. "They think someone hit him on the head from behind. He still hasn't woken up. I don't know . . . I'd better go back."

She reached out to touch me but thought better of it,

with her bloodstained hands. Giving me a tight smile, she nodded at Matthew and slipped back behind the ER doors.

I could barely process what she'd told us. As I sat in the crowded room with Matthew, I felt frozen. His quiet, steady presence was the only thing keeping me calm.

Slowly, other people from the neighborhood trickled in as the news spread. Madame Lucinda, the owner of the Hocus Pocus Magic Shoppe, sat next to me and held my hand. She'd been Moses's friend for decades. She dabbed at her eyes with a handkerchief, the many rings on her fingers twinkling in the fluorescent lights of the ER. When a nurse came to let us know he'd been put in a room, Matthew, Madame Lucinda, and I walked down the long corridor together.

My feet stopped right outside his room, and I could go no farther. Madame Lucinda let go of my hand. She didn't push me to come with her. Mom stuck her head outside to check on me.

"He's going to be okay," she said, her face awash with relief and exhaustion.

"Who did this to him?" I asked.

"We have no idea. Poor, dear Moses."

As soon as she went back into the room, my teeth started to chatter again. Matthew put his arm around my shoulders, and I leaned against him, accepting comfort from a virtual stranger. I couldn't help it. I needed his support. My knees wobbled so badly I could barely stand.

"You should go see him," said Matthew, his voice soft. "It's always better than what you imagine."

"I have a pretty scary imagination." My cheek rested against his chest, and I felt the faint rumble of his laughter against my skin.

"I promise. It won't be as bad as you think."

He led me into Moses's room, and I realized Matthew had been both right and wrong at the same time. In some ways, it *was* better than I'd imagined. Bandages circled Moses's head, and his face looked swollen and bruised, but he was still Moses. My Moses. The man who'd helped me with math in middle school. The one who listened to my angst-filled tirades in high school. The one who understood me better than most people ever would. The same person but so tiny, old, and fragile in that big white hospital bed. A machine measured his heart rate, and an IV bag hung next to him, dripping fluids into his body. I reached for his hand, wanting to hold on to him, and his skin felt dry and cool to the touch.

A dark-haired nurse around my age came into the room and picked up his chart. She wore scrubs and a nametag with "Brenda Clark" in bold black letters.

"How's he doing?" I asked.

"He has a pretty serious concussion. His CAT scan looked good, but the doctor worried there might be some swelling in the brain. An injury like this can be traumatic for someone his age."

"When will he wake up?" The tears I'd been trying to contain slowly streamed down my face. Someone hurt him on purpose. Suddenly, nothing in my quiet little world felt safe or right anymore.

Nurse Brenda gave me a sympathetic smile as she adjusted Moses's IV and checked his vitals. "That isn't something I can answer. Rest is the best thing for him right now. The police are here. Do you mind if they ask you a few questions?"

The policemen waited right outside Moses's door. Officer Miller had a crew cut, a paunch, and a resigned air about him, like he'd seen a lot of nights like this one. The younger police-man, Officer Belfiore, had black hair and a cleft in his chin. He winked at Nurse Brenda as she walked by, but she ignored him. He sighed and wrote in his notebook as Officer Miller asked us questions.

"When did you last see Mr. Richards?"

We told them about acoustic night and the approximate time of the attack. We also gave them Moses's home address and promised to find the number for his sister who lived in Florida.

"He was a college professor at Duquesne until he got sick last year. Everyone loves him," I said. "I can't imagine why anyone would hurt him."

Office Miller shrugged. "We don't always know people as well as we think. We all have secrets, even Mr. Richards. But often these things are random. He may have walked into something he shouldn't have, or maybe he just got mugged."

"Right next to the *café*?" I asked. "He'd barely stepped out the door. It doesn't make sense."

The whole idea seemed hard to swallow. Other than a few incidents of petty theft and vandalism, there had never been serious issues anywhere near the café.

Officer Belfiore read my thoughts, his warm brown eyes kind. "Times are changing. The South Side isn't as safe as it used to be, and we've seen a real increase in drug-related crimes lately. This could be as simple as a junkie trying to take his money and Moses putting up a fight. We'd like to check out the crime scene tonight. If you're ready to go, we can give you a ride home in our squad car."

Nurse Brenda promised to call the minute Moses woke up, and Matthew took Madame Lucinda home. Mom and I rode in the police car in silence, arriving back at the café as the sky slowly lightened and the sun came up.

It didn't take long for the officers to figure out the assailant had hit Moses with Mom's large wooden scrub brush. They found it in the alley and bagged it as evidence.

"In the next few days, keep an eye out for anything unusual, like strangers hanging around the shop. Lock your doors. Be aware of your surroundings. The usual stuff."

Officer Belfiore gave us his card before leaving. We promised to call if we noticed anything.

Mom wouldn't allow me to help her clean up the blood. "My clothes are already ruined," she said. I knew she didn't want to add yet another terrible image to the ones already in my brain. For once, I didn't argue with her.

She cleaned outside with the door shut. I thought I heard her sobbing softly, but I didn't interrupt her. Instead, I paced around the kitchen, tidying things up. I froze when I saw a bag of crushed cookies on the floor.

"Moses's cookies," I said softly. I bent down to pick them up and noticed something odd. Two long black streaks led from my mom's office to the door. I frowned, trying to figure out what had caused them.

Mom came in looking pale and tired, her clothes filthy. I showed her the marks on the floor, and she shrugged. "Maybe I did it when I hauled the bucket out," she said, and it made sense. The bucket was old, and the wheels underneath it sometimes jammed up.

"I found these on the floor too," I said, showing her the cookies. "I gave them to Moses before he left."

She rubbed her eyes. "I don't know, Fiona. He probably dropped them on his way out."

Mom looked so tired I didn't press it. "Maybe," I said.

She nodded, a deep desolation in her eyes I'd never seen before, and went upstairs to take a long, hot shower. When she came back down, she seemed a bit more like herself. I made a big pot of herbal tea, and we sat in the kitchen sipping it.

"Do you think he'll be the same when he wakes up?" I asked.

She sighed. "I hope so."

Not the answer I'd wanted. Now that it looked like he would survive, I worried about brain damage and other long-term repercussions. I stared down at my tea, a lump forming in my throat. "Why would anyone hurt him?"

"I don't know, sweetheart." She got up and tidied the kitchen. "It was so crowded here last night. Did Scott drop you off? I thought I saw him, but it's always a mad rush at the end of the night. I couldn't be sure."

I shook my head. "No. I took a cab home. Scott went to a bar with his friends."

"I wish he would come by more often, especially to acoustic night. He might actually enjoy it. Last night was a blast, until . . ." She shook her head sadly and turned to me, drying her hands on a towel. "We need to focus on something positive. We should throw a party and invite Scotty and his friends."

"That's a terrible idea, and he hates to be called Scotty."

"I know, but it reminds me of *Star Trek*, and I always sort of had a thing for that chief engineer," she said with a smile.

"It reminds *me* of Mrs. Emerson's dog."

Mrs. Emerson lived across the street until she passed away a few years earlier. She had a little black Scottish terrier that humped everything it could reach. My old red sneakers had been one of his personal favorites.

"I remember *that* Scotty too," she said with a laugh. "But about the party, I want to do it. And it would cheer us up. We could hang Chinese lanterns in the garden and invite all our friends. It would be so much fun."

"We'll see," I said softly. I didn't want to disappoint her, but it had the potential to be a total disaster.

She understood, and her shoulders slumped. "He doesn't like me."

I put my arms around her and gave her a hug. "He doesn't know you."

A wisp of hair had come loose from my bun, and she

pushed it behind my ear. "I'll try harder, Fiona. I'm sorry. I can pretend to be normal."

I squeezed her again. "Normal is highly overrated." It was something Kate said all the time, and it made my mom smile.

"But it's what you want." She took a deep breath. "Does this mean I have to wear a bra?"

I laughed. "The bra isn't the problem."

Her face grew sad. "Then what is?"

"It's not you. He's a little uncomfortable around all of this."

I waved my hands around, encompassing the shop and the garden and the teas and the fertility charms. If I included the other things, like the monthly meetings the Wiccans held here and the posters about legalizing marijuana, it was a lot for the average person.

She straightened her shoulders. "I'll make him like me. It'll be my new project. He already loves you, and I love you, so we have that in common. He's a nice guy. It won't be too hard."

She had a look of steely determination in her eyes, and I had to rein her in. "Just be yourself. Everyone loves you."

She looked out the window at the fairy lights in the garden. "Everyone *does* love me except your boyfriend."

I rinsed out my teacup and put it away with a heavy heart. She was right.

CHAPTER 4

THERE IS NOTHING LIKE A PRETTY DRESS, SOME FANCY CAKE, AND A PARTY IN THE GARDEN. -AUNT FRANCESCA

I managed to take a nap, curling up on the soft cushions of the window seat, relieved I didn't have to clean the garden this particular Sunday morning. I awoke a few hours later, disoriented. It took me a moment to remember the events of the night before, but when I did, I sat up with a start. Mom was in the kitchen.

"Did the hospital call?"

She came to the doorway, stirring something in a bowl she balanced on her hip. "No, but Kate and Chad went to see him. They said he's resting peacefully."

Peacefully. Moses had never hurt another living soul by word or by deed in all the time I'd known him. He didn't deserve this. I stared around the quiet, sunny room with hollow eyes. I'd learned long ago life wasn't fair, but this was so much worse than fair or not fair. This seemed senseless and intentionally cruel.

When I looked at the grandfather clock in the corner of the room, I realized I'd slept much later than intended. I shuffled into the kitchen and grabbed a cup of coffee. "Why didn't you wake me up?"

"You needed to sleep. Last night was a terrible shock."

I frowned. "But . . ."

"Hush, Fi. Enjoy your coffee. You work too hard."

I carried my coffee back to the window seat, one of my favorite spots in the house. We kept most of our gift items in this room, and I'd spent many hours curled up here with my nose in a cookbook. I had an unhealthy addiction to anything by Julia Child, but my favorite cookbook was actually the well-worn journal full of recipes left behind by Aunt Francesca. Mom told me she'd been a magical cook, and insisted I'd inherited her aunt's talents. As much as I doubted either one of us had any magical cookie-baking ability, reading her journal felt like a visit with an old friend. We were kindred spirits, and I understood her somehow. If we ever had met, we would have liked each other very much.

I pulled the journal out, needing some time with Aunt Francesca and a chance to focus on something other than my worry about Moses. I also grabbed my copy of *Mastering the Art of French Cooking* by Julia Child and leafed through it until I calmed down. Julia Child always did that to me. My culinary anchor.

As I looked over a complicated and detailed recipe for puff pastry, the bell rang above our door and Matthew strolled in. I wasn't wearing a bra and awkwardly folded my arms across my chest. "What are you doing here?"

Mom seemed surprised at my tone. "Matt came to pick up his jacket. He left it here last night."

I guess I sounded a bit rude, but he didn't act bothered. We sat around the island in the kitchen, talking about the events of the night before and about Moses.

"I still can't believe it happened," said Mom.

The memory of Moses lying helpless in a pool of blood made the shaking start again. Needing to change the subject,

I turned to my mom. "We'd better get ready. We only have a few hours left before our guests start arriving."

"Oh, that's plenty of time," said Mom as she handed Matthew a steaming mug of coffee.

"What's going on today?" Matthew asked.

Mom's eyes sparkled. "Our afternoon tea party. It's so much fun."

"Anything I can do?"

I opened my mouth to tell him no, but she answered before I could speak. "Fiona could use some help setting up the buffet tables. Do you mind?"

"Of course not." Matthew took a sip of coffee and watched me over the rim of his mug, waiting for me to respond. He enjoyed this.

"I don't need any help," I said.

"Yes, you do." Mom smiled sweetly at me, but I could tell she didn't intend to back down. Great.

I rolled my eyes at her, acting like an annoyed teenager, but couldn't help it. She brought it out in me. "Fine. I'll get dressed," I said, stomping up the stairs.

After a shower, I took my sweet time getting ready. Matthew Monroe could wait. I didn't like the way my mother had pressured me into accepting his help or how he showed up here unannounced, and I still didn't trust him.

It was too early for Scott to be awake, but I sent him a text telling him about Moses. I felt oddly fragile, like the delicate wineglasses Mom kept on the top shelf of her china cabinet. One small bump and I might shatter into a million pieces. I wasn't used to feeling like this. I didn't like it. I needed to talk to Scott but was fairly certain he wouldn't be up for hours.

I tossed my phone onto the bed. The best way to get back to normal was to keep busy and work, and there was always plenty to do at the café. Hopefully I could distract myself and stop picturing Moses lying motionless on the ground.

I sighed and opened the door of the antique wardrobe in the corner of my room. We always wore dresses for Sunday afternoon tea. Today, I chose a pale blue vintage one with tiny white polka dots. It had a sweetheart neckline with spaghetti straps and fit tightly around my waist, flaring out above my knees. It showed a bit more cleavage than I usually displayed, but it was a safe choice for a garden party. I put on a touch of makeup, pulled my hair into a tight chignon, slipped on a pair of flats, and went back downstairs.

I hoped Matthew had given up and left but no such luck. He sat at the island, eating breakfast with Mom. Her eyes lit up when she saw me. "Oh. I love that dress. You look like Grace Kelly."

I doubted Matthew knew who Grace Kelly was, but he surprised me. "*High Society*. That's it exactly."

"Did you know Grace Kelly was a friend of Aunt Francesca's? I mean before she moved to Monaco and became a princess and everything."

I shook my head. "I had no idea."

"Aunt Francesca was quite the progressive. A single lady who traveled the world and had all kinds of adventures," she said with a wistful look in her eyes. "Sometimes I feel like she's still here. Looking over us. Don't you feel that way, Fiona?"

I couldn't tell her I didn't. That would seem cruel. Instead I just shrugged. "I guess so."

My mom, nonplussed, turned her radiant smile onto Matthew. "And do you know who you look like, Mr. Matthew Monroe?" she asked.

He wiggled his eyebrows. "Cary Grant?"

I shook my head. "No. He was in the original with

Katharine Hepburn. Not the remake," I said, getting a little flustered. "And you don't look like him. Not at all."

"Who do I look like?" he asked softly.

"A pirate," I answered before I could stop myself. He laughed.

"She's right," said Mom. "You do look like a pirate. Like that Orlando Blooms."

My eyes met Matthew's, and we shared a smile. She'd gotten the person right but not the name. "Bloom, not Blooms," I said.

She lifted her hands in defeat. "I'm a gardener. I can't help it. Go set up the tables, you two."

We put the long buffet tables on either side of the garden and covered them with pretty lace tablecloths. We'd come to an unspoken agreement not to talk about Moses anymore or what had happened the night before. I hung on by a tiny emotional thread. Surprisingly, Matthew proved to be extremely good company and very distracting. He lightened my mood, but I chalked it up to the fact it was a beautiful, sunny morning. At this point I operated on only a tiny bit of sleep and lots of coffee.

"Are you a student?" he asked as we straightened the cloths on the buffet tables. Mom brought out the linens for the individual tables, and we covered them as well.

"I graduated with a double major in accounting and finance a few years ago. I've been working on my MBA, and I'll finish next semester."

"Accounting, huh? Do you keep the books for your mom?"

I froze. "Why do you ask?"

Matthew looked surprised at my tone. "Just curious."

I handed him another tablecloth, and we spread it over a table. "I've been doing the books since I was ten."

I could take care of the taxes, too, but a sweet old man named Mr. Jenkins had done them for years. It didn't cost much, and I didn't have the heart to take the job away from him.

"That's a lot of responsibility."

I shrugged. "I like numbers. They make sense."

"Unlike people."

I stared right at him. "Some people."

Mom brought out the plates, and we worked together. We had the afternoon tea down to a science. It was a reservation-only event and always fully booked. Mom had worked in a teashop in England once during her misspent youth. She knew how to do it right.

We set each table with a fancy assortment of mismatched china and silverware. Mom made flower arrangements, and we put the vases full of fresh flowers in the center of each table. The elegant porcelain teapots were ready and waiting in the kitchen. Mom had already mixed up several varieties of tea and kept them warm in giant pots on the stove.

We loaded up the tables with a variety of finger sand-wiches and savory snacks. There were cheese boards with an assortment of English cheeses, slices of fresh apple, and mango chutney. Plates full of scones sat next to bowls of fresh cream and homemade jam. Tiny cakes decorated with edible flowers and miniature fruit tarts looked too good to eat. I was in charge of cookies and usually baked several different kinds. We set plates of those on each table as well.

"What are the teas today?" I asked as we put on the finishing touches.

"Earl Grey and an English Breakfast tea for the conserva-tives, a bright Orange Pekoe for the slightly adventurous, and my own Tea of Love for those who want to live on the wild side. It has cinnamon, spice, and everything nice in it."

"I'd like to try that one," said Matthew with a grin, and she handed each of us a cup.

I downed my tea, enjoying the complex flavors and the

delicious rush of warmth, and turned to Matthew. "Are you planning on staying?" I wasn't trying to be rude, but Matthew seemed to bring it out in me.

"Oh, please stay, Matt. It'll be fun," said Mom, taking his arm and misunderstanding why I'd asked the question in the first place.

"It's all women . . ." I began, but she interrupted me.

"Exactly. The tea ladies will love Matthew."

She was right. As the older ladies strolled into the shop in their floral dresses, hats, and gloves, Matthew charmed the silk stockings right off them. Most were in their seventies and eighties, but they shamelessly flirted and chatted with him, making him the star of the show. He kept the ladies entertained as we got them seated, and kindly agreed to play the guitar as they ate.

We put him on a stool in the back of the garden, and I had to admit it was a nice view. He'd pulled his dark hair back into a ponytail and wore a white shirt with the sleeves rolled up, which showed off his tanned forearms. He had the yin and yang necklace on again and several bracelets made of random bits of leather and string. He looked as tasty as the scones on the buffet table, if a person was into that whole sexy bohemian musician thing.

While he played, people stopped talking and listened. He had that effect. Even someone who knew nothing about music could tell from the minute Matthew touched the guitar he was something special.

He played older music that suited the crowd, and some of them hummed and sang along. He also played classical pieces, which came as a pleasant surprise and fit the mood of the tea party perfectly. The old ladies smiled, enjoying themselves.

Mom stood next to me. "He really is something, isn't he?"

I nodded but couldn't take my eyes off him. He did that to me when he played, and he was so focused on his music I could watch him unnoticed, a bonus. Unfortunately, it didn't last very long. He looked up and his eyes found mine, and suddenly it felt a little hard to breathe.

"This is a song I started working on last night. It isn't finished yet."

Matthew played, and the sounds of our fountain resonated in his song. As the music swelled, horrible sadness overtook me, and I realized that after last night and what happened to Moses, nothing would ever be the same again.

I put down my serving tray and left the garden. Mom gave me a worried glance, and I felt Matthew's puzzled gaze on my back, but I kept going. By the time I reached the interior of the shop, tears rolled down my cheeks. I forced myself to pull it together. We didn't have time for this today.

Mom followed me into the shop. "Are you all right?" I nodded, not trusting myself to speak. I'd dried my tears, but she could tell something was wrong. "You were crying."

I shook my head. "Something flew in my eye. A bug. Or dust. I'm fine."

She placed a gentle hand on my cheek. "You don't always have to be so strong, you know. You're allowed to cry and feel and have moments of weakness. The world won't fall apart without you holding it together."

A group of tea ladies, full of good food and tea, came in, ready to shop. One of them, a sweet, little old thing in a blue dress with a matching hat, approached us. "I'd like to buy some of that tea we had today. It was wonderful."

"The Tea of Love?" asked Mom with a warm smile. "I'll get some for you."

When Mom went to get the tea, Old Blue Hat pulled me aside. "I have to know, how does she do it?"

"What do you mean?"

"Her teas are incredible. I've never tasted anything like them. And they work."

"Work?" I frowned, confused.

"When I first started coming here, my joints ached constantly. She gave me a tea that took all the pain away. I can walk and bend and even do a little dancing." She demonstrated with a little wiggle of her hips. "And after she gave us the Elixir of Youth tea, I honestly feel ten years younger."

"That's nice," I said, not sure where this was going.

"Today's Tea of Love was fantastic. I feel . . . romantic. I know you must have had some too. I saw you cry when the nice young man played his guitar."

"I had dust in my eye. And a bug."

She looked unconvinced. "Your mom has some kind of special magic. I'm sure of it. I can spot someone with *the gift* a mile away."

I wanted to groan but controlled myself. "She knows a great deal about herbs, and some teas have anti-inflammatory properties . . ."

"Then how do you explain the inflammation to my libido? My Harry is going to be a happy man this evening."

The idea of Old Blue Hat and her husband getting it on was more than I could handle. I wanted to erase that image from my mind forever.

"And you have to admit he is a looker," she said.

"Who?" I hoped she wasn't talking about Harry. I didn't want to know what Harry looked like. The name was enough.

"The boy with the guitar. If I were forty or fifty years younger . . ." She fanned herself with a white-gloved hand.

Mom brought out the tea, and I rang up her order. We packaged the specialty teas in sheer silk bags tied with satin flowers like pretty little sachets.

I decided to clarify things. "There is nothing going on between the guitar guy and me. Nothing at all."

Old Blue Hat gave me a knowing wink. "It didn't look that way."

"I have a boyfriend, and I'm happy, so happy I can barely stand it."

"You're a lucky girl."

"Yes, I am. Thank you. Have a nice day." I forced a pleasant smile onto my face. Old Blue Hat meant no harm, but she annoyed me.

When I turned to restock the shelves, I slammed right into a wall of solid muscle. Matthew stood there with a strange expression on his face. "That guy last night was your boyfriend? The suit?"

"His *name* is Scott."

Matthew looked like he was about to speak, but one of the women came up with a stone phallus. "Is this a dildo?" she asked in her sweet little-old-lady voice.

Matthew choked back a laugh and walked away, leaving me to answer her question on my own. I found nothing humorous about the situation. "No, ma'am, it's a fertility charm."

"Oh," she said, comprehension dawning in her bright-blue eyes. "A *virility* charm. I'll take two."

Mom came to the counter, and I pulled her aside. "What did you put in their tea?"

She noticed the crowd gathering around the stone phalluses and grinned. "Cinnamon, spice, and everything nice. I told you that already. Have some more. It's delicious."

"No, thanks. We've all had enough."

We sold half our inventory of stone phalluses in one afternoon to a bunch of senior citizens. I wouldn't have been surprised if there was some kind of aphrodisiac or hallucinogen in Mom's tea. Another thing we could get into trouble for and yet another thing to worry about.

It wasn't until much later, long after the sun had set in the sky, when I finally went up to my room and had a chance to check my phone. I had a bunch of messages and missed calls, but Scott never texted me back, and oddly enough, I didn't even care. I had no desire to talk to anyone tonight, not even the boyfriend who supposedly made me so blissfully happy. I decided not to read into that. Not at all. Instead, I turned off my phone, set my alarm clock, and went straight to bed.

CHAPTER 5

Monday, my favorite day of the entire week, always felt like a fresh start. A new beginning. Since the shop was closed, I usually spent the day making cookies for the next tea party, relaxing, and hanging out with Mom.

I called the hospital while still in my room. There was no change in Moses's condition, and visiting hours wouldn't start for a few hours. I cradled the phone in my hand, knowing I couldn't do anything to help him right now. I had to be patient and wait.

The Monday newspaper contained the easiest crossword puzzle of the week, another great thing about Mondays. I planned to have a leisurely breakfast and a giant mug of coffee, finish the crossword, and spend the rest of the morning baking in my nice, quiet kitchen.

I already felt the summer heat filling the house, even with all the windows open, and it would get even warmer once the ovens started. I put on a white cami and a tiny pair of shorts and skipped down the steps, about to run out to get the paper, when I realized something odd. All the blinds were still closed, and the shop seemed dark. Mom normally awoke at dawn and always opened them as soon as she came downstairs. It had something to do with the sun god Ra and welcoming him into our house, or some such nonsense. She never, ever left the blinds closed. Something weird was going on.

I paused at the bottom of the steps. When I heard chanting and smelled something burning, I frowned and then grimaced. *Uh oh.* I knew that smell. It was incense, which only meant one thing.

I stuck my head into the front room and wished liquid bleach could have been poured directly into my eyes to erase what I'd seen. At least a dozen people had spread out their yoga mats, their bare bottoms rising high in the air in a downward-facing-dog position.

Naked yoga. Great. Just what I needed to deal with today.

"Mom?"

I didn't want the people doing yoga to turn around, but I had to get her attention somehow. Her head popped up in the front of the room. She was naked, too, of course. She waved and held up a finger.

"One second, Fiona."

They went from downward dog to plank and into cobra, and I got to see all of it. The entire sun salutation. Lucky me.

I kept my eyes directed at the ceiling as I waited. I'd just caught a glimpse of our accountant's seventy-year-old dingdong, not an experience I cared to repeat.

When they finally stood up, Mom looked over her shoulder at me, and I pointed to the kitchen with a stern expression on my face. She grabbed her robe and followed me inside.

"What was *that*?" I asked in a whispered hiss. "A bunch of sweaty naked people in the café. Are you freaking kidding me?"

She looked confused. "It's our yoga class."

"But they aren't wearing any clothing."

"It's hot."

I got a cup of coffee, needing to be completely awake for this discussion. "We can't have nude people exercising in our shop. We've discussed this before. We serve food here."

"You worry too much."

"You don't worry enough." Those words came out a little louder than intended, and Mom looked hurt.

"They have nowhere else to go, and we thought it would be good to come together and create some positive energy in the café after what happened to poor Moses."

"Couldn't you just burn some sage or something?"

"I already did that."

I took a long drink of coffee. Like an impulsive child when it came to making important decisions, Mom never considered anything beyond the needs of the moment.

"I thought we agreed we wouldn't hold yoga here until we got the air conditioner fixed," I said.

She jutted out her chin and folded her arms across her chest. She intended to be stubborn about this.

"Hence the naked yoga. A perfect solution."

I glared at her. "Not a solution, a mistake. Like ordering the penises and scheduling that stranger to play at acoustic night and all of the other things you do behind my back. You can't keep doing this. Anderson Solutions is trying to shut us down, and you're making it easier for them."

Tired of being the mature party in our relationship, I grabbed an apron, stuck it over my head, and pulled out cookie sheets, banging mixing bowls around as a way to vent my anger. She watched, tapping her foot. "Someone needs to switch to decaf."

I opened my mouth, about to respond, when I heard the

bell above the front door tinkle, and panic filled my chest. "Oh no. Were you expecting anyone?"

Mom shook her head, her eyes huge as she probably realized the same thing I did. Our yoga people were in Savasana, the corpse pose, by this time. To anyone unlucky enough to walk through the front door right at this moment, it would look like a bunch of naked people had crawled in and died on the floor of our shop.

We heard a startled, masculine gasp, and Mom bolted for the door in her Chinese silk robe. She came back into the kitchen dragging Matthew behind her, a big smile on her face.

"It's only Matthew," she said. "Nothing to worry about."

My shoulders sagged with relief, but then I got annoyed and scowled at Matthew. "Again? Are you planning to move in?"

He didn't look offended. In fact, he acted like he was trying not to laugh. When I gave him a puzzled look, he pointed to my apron. "Thanks for the warning," he said.

I'd been in such a snit I hadn't noticed which one I'd grabbed. We sold an assortment of funny aprons and kept the samples for ourselves. Today, mine was black and read "Kitchen Bitch" in white block letters.

"Ha ha ha. Hilarious."

I stood behind the large marble island in the center of our kitchen. The island had been a splurge but worth every penny. I rolled out pastries, kneaded dough, and baked to my heart's content on it. Mom called it my therapy, and today I definitely needed it.

Matthew gave me an assessing look. "Maybe you should do yoga too. You're very tense."

"You both should," said Mom. "It's wonderfully freeing."

For a minute, I imagined Matthew doing yoga naked, and immediately dropped the metal mixing bowl I'd just pulled out of the cupboard. It clattered to the floor, most likely snapping the yoga people right out of their deep, meditative state. I winced and put it in the sink, trying not to make eye contact with Matthew.

Mom ignored my clumsiness and gave him another sunny smile. "You're always welcome to join us, Matthew."

I muttered something under my breath about the department of health, but they ignored me. My phone rang, and I knew it was Scott. He usually called on his way to work, another adorably predictable thing about him. That and the fact he'd never, under any circumstances, do yoga.

I took my coffee and snuck out the back door and into the garden. "Did you get my messages?" I asked. "Someone attacked Moses. He's in the hospital."

He was silent for a second. "Moses? The old man with the saxophone?"

"Yes," I said as the emotions rose to the surface again. "Someone beat him up right outside the door to our kitchen. He's in a coma."

I had to squinch up my face to keep from crying, remembering the feeling of Moses's fragile bones when I'd touched his shoulder on acoustic night. He was entirely too breakable.

"Don't you keep that door locked?"

It seemed like an odd question. "We do, but Moses may have decided to slip out that way instead of going through the shop."

Scott cleared his throat. "People get mugged in that part of town all the time. It's a bad area."

"No, it isn't. Not right next to the café at least." I paused. "And Moses isn't *people*. He's my friend. He's also old, and he's been through so much already."

"Sorry, Fiona. You know how I feel about the South Side. It isn't safe."

I didn't want to get into it right now. "Did you stop by on Saturday night?"

"What are you talking about?"

"Mom said she thought she saw you when she was closing up." When he didn't respond, I continued, a little confused. "Never mind. She must have been mistaken. It was busy."

He sounded befuddled as well. "We went to a bar downtown but didn't stay long. I went home not long after you did, although I had more to drink than I realized."

"What do you mean?"

"I can't find my shoes."

"Your shoes?"

"My custom-made Johnson and Murphy's."

"The ones with your name printed inside?"

"Yes. Thank goodness I bought two pairs, but I can't understand what happened. I've looked all over the apartment. They aren't here. And the bar we went to must have been filthy. I got splattered with something gross and had to take in my suit to get dry-cleaned this morning."

He sounded upset, but it really was his own fault. And his night of drinking paled in comparison to the night I'd experienced. "Poor you."

He must have heard the hint of irritation in my voice. "Is everything okay?"

"Nothing is okay, Scott. Do you want to hear about my morning?"

I told him about the naked yoga, and he had the decency to get upset on my behalf. "She's breaking about a million health codes with that one."

"I know," I moaned. "But she won't listen to reason."

"Has she given any further thought to just selling the place?"

I sighed. "Not an option."

"Think about it. No more worries. No more dealing with your mom and all her craziness. You could lead a normal life."

A slightly hysterical giggle bubbled its way up my chest. "Normal is highly overrated."

"What did you say? I'm going through the tunnel, babe. I can't hear."

"Nothing. It's fine."

"Consider what I said. Your mom should be reasonable."

I hung up the phone. Mom was never reasonable, and now my Monday had been ruined. I was sick with worry about Moses, I hadn't done the crossword, and now I'd be baking at the hottest time of day. Matthew sat on a stool in the kitchen eating breakfast when I stomped back in. Mom had disappeared.

I pulled out ingredients to make chocolate crinkles. "Why are you here?"

He laughed. "You don't like me, do you?"

I shot him a look as I cracked eggs. "It's not that I don't like you. I'm not sure I trust you."

"Are you naturally distrustful, or is it just me?"

"I'm naturally *cautious*. I have to be."

"You need to relax. Enjoy the moment." Matthew took a sip of coffee and raised his mug to me. "I'm certainly enjoying this moment and this coffee. It's fabulous."

"It is. Mom makes the best coffee in the whole world."

"Whoa. Did we actually agree on something?"

I tried to frown at him and failed. "Don't get used to it."

He grinned, looking delectable once again. He wore an unbuttoned faded blue shirt with the sleeves rolled up and a white T-shirt beneath. His hair was in a ponytail, and he achieved the perfect level of scruffy without being messy. He had on khaki shorts instead of jeans and Converse sneakers. It was the first time I'd seen his knees. He had such nice-looking knees, which said a lot because most people had ugly knees, but nothing about Matthew was ugly.

"I'm not just here for the coffee. I wanted to see if you'd heard anything more about Moses. Do they have any leads?"

The tears threatened again. "The police think it's a random thing."

"Do you?"

I shook my head. "Someone has to know something."

"Let's ask around."

I looked at him in surprise. "You'd do that?"

"Of course."

I wavered between taking him up on his offer and telling him I didn't need his help. I decided to settle for middle ground.

"I'll think about it."

He stood up, putting his dishes in the sink. "Are you leaving?" I asked.

"Don't sound so hopeful. I told your mom I'd look at her PA system. She's had some issues."

"Oh. Thanks."

Matthew worked on the PA system as I baked. When he came back into the kitchen to wash up, I offered him more coffee and a plate of warm cookies. "This is a peace offering because this morning I was a . . ." I pointed to the words on my apron. "Kitchen Bitch" seemed pretty appropriate.

"Apology accepted," he said. He took a bite and moaned. "Fiona, you are a genius. A true artist. These are little chocolate balls of happiness."

"Balls of happiness. We could sell them with the fertility charms."

He laughed. "You do stock an eclectic bunch of items."

"A nice way to say 'weird.' Thank you. I hear it all the time, about the shop, about my life, about my mom . . ."

"Your mom isn't weird. She's unique."

"She's also irresponsible and pathologically impulsive," I said, and immediately wished I hadn't spoken. I normally didn't discuss her shortcomings with strangers.

"Maybe because you've always been the responsible one," he said.

In the middle of making gingersnaps, I stopped the mixer in midstir. "I'm an enabler?"

He pointed to the yin and yang symbol he wore around his neck. "There's always balance."

"If I were irresponsible, it would make my mom more responsible?" I shook my head. "It would never ever happen."

"Because you hold it all together?"

I nodded. "I have to."

"That sounds exhausting."

"It is."

"You can't control the universe, Fiona."

"I don't try to. Only my little corner of it." I held up my wooden spoon and pointed it at him. "I bet you have a tattoo of a Chinese character somewhere on your body. Am I right? Or is it a yin and yang symbol like your necklace?"

He looked affronted. "What makes you think I have a tattoo?"

"Your type *always* has a tattoo."

He took another long drink of coffee. "My type?"

I added the spices to the batter, making the room smelled like ginger, cinnamon, cloves, and allspice, and gave him a long, assessing look. "Musicians, artists, dreamers. You're all the same. You're gypsies. Free spirits. You don't like commitments, and you can't be counted on. Thanks to my mom, I've met a million people exactly like you."

I was mad at my mom, and Matthew happened to be a convenient scapegoat. I regretted my words as soon as I said them, but there was no taking them back. I squared my shoulders, preparing for Matthew to launch an angry, defensive, verbal assault, but he simply looked at me with those sad, dark eyes.

"Or maybe you're wrong about me. Maybe you're wrong about a lot of things."

"What do you mean?" I asked, not sure I wanted to hear the answer.

He came closer. His proximity disturbed me, but I couldn't move, not even when he brushed my cheek with the back of his fingers, removing a bit of flour from my face. "Maybe you need to figure it out," he said, walking out the door.

The rest of the day passed by more smoothly. I baked my cookies and went to the hospital to check on Moses. Nothing had changed. He was silent and still, but I held his hand anyway and told him about my day. He would have laughed about the naked yoga if he'd been awake, and he would have said something wise and philosophical about understanding my mom and loving her quirks and all. He couldn't talk, though, and I doubted he heard a word I said.

I kissed his cheek before I left. "Get better soon, Moses. I miss you."

I got back to the shop and had time for a quiet lunch in the garden with my crossword. Mom forgot she'd been upset, and we put together several batches of soup for the rest of the week. I also made cornbread for the vegetarian chili and sour cream biscuits for a hearty stew.

Try as I might, I couldn't get Matthew off my mind. I was embarrassed by how I acted. He'd been right about my apron choice today. I *had* been the kitchen bitch.

I thought about the way he touched my cheek, and it caused an odd flutter in my chest. I concluded I was a horrible person. I had a perfectly good boyfriend, someone I might actually be able to build a future with. I couldn't let myself get distracted by a handsome face and a pair of warm brown eyes. Matthew Monroe, through no fault of his own, was getting under my skin. He was like a nasty, infected splinter, and I needed to yank him out as soon as possible.

Scott came over after work with a bouquet of roses, and we sat in the garden eating chili and munching on cornbread. He removed his jacket, loosened his tie, and put a handkerchief embroidered with his initials on his knee. I bit my lip to keep from smiling at both the handkerchief and the row of initials. SAL. Scott Anthony Lipmann.

I loved the fact he carried around a linen handkerchief. It seemed adorably old-fashioned to me. I also loved the way he always looked perfectly pressed and polished, even in the heat of summer. He was solid and dependable in a way that melted my heart.

After we ate, he leaned back, and I snuggled up to him. He smelled like a mix of expensive spices from his cologne with a bit of starch from his dry cleaner. I inhaled deeply, my head on his shoulder.

Scott took my hand. "My parents want to meet you."

"When?" I sat up and put my hand on my chest, feeling oddly nervous. This had never come up before. Ever. And I wasn't sure about it. His parents lived an hour outside the city and owned a meatpacking plant. The irony Mom was a vegetarian was not lost on me.

Scott kissed the tip of my nose. "Don't worry, silly, they'll love you. How would Thursday work?"

Thursday was usually a quiet night, and this Thursday we'd scheduled a poetry reading. Mom wouldn't need my help. I'd just make sure Chad could cover the kitchen.

I nodded, still worried, and Scott smiled. "It'll be fine. Stop frowning." He massaged my shoulders, and I relaxed with a sigh. "Have you talked to your mom about selling this dump yet?"

I tensed up again immediately. "Dump?"

His hands grew still. "Sorry, but I noticed the paint peeling off the back, and you're going to need a new roof. This is a money pit."

I looked around at the bright flowers and the gurgling fountain. Scott was right; it did need repairs, but there was beauty here as well. I wished he saw what I did.

He put his hands on my cheeks. "I'm trying to help you because I love you." He leaned forward, brushing his lips against mine. The sun had begun to set, and the twinkle lights came on in the garden. Mom had gone to visit a friend, and the shop was quiet and dark.

I slid my hands around his waist, enjoying the feel of Scott's firm muscles under his white shirt. The kiss deepened, and I ran my hands across his back, wanting him closer.

"Where's your mom?" he asked, his lips working their way down my neck.

"Out. She'll be gone for hours," I said, unbuttoning his shirt.

I was about to grab his hand and pull him up to my room when the fountain made a loud, strange noise. We looked at it in surprise just as a stream of water shot out of the finial, drenching us completely.

"What the . . ." he said, but another stream of water shot out of the fountain and hit him directly in the face. He stood up and backed away as water dripped down his nose and all over his pristine suit.

I stared at the fountain, trying to figure out what happened. "It's never done this before," I said. Thankfully, it stopped spurting water. In fact, I couldn't even figure out where that stream of water had come from. It now gurgled softly, as normal, like nothing had happened.

"I'd better go," he said, wiping his face in disgust. "That water is filthy. I'll have to take this suit to the dry cleaner, or it'll be ruined as well. I'm still waiting for them to finish cleaning my other one. I'll be going to work in sweats if this keeps up."

I tried not to pout. Another case of coitus interruptus. After a long dry spell, I'd finally found Scott, someone I actually wanted to sleep with, but it seemed like nothing went right for us.

I kissed his damp cheek. "I'm sorry, Scott."

His blue eyes softened. "It isn't your fault. But think about what I said, Fiona. This place is a money pit. Your mom should get rid of it before something else happens. What if that fountain shoots water at an old lady during one of your tea parties and she falls? What if one of these walls finally collapses? Or the roof caves in? You're a sensible person. Surely you see my point."

I did, but it made no difference. After he left, I changed out of my damp clothing, got up on a ladder, and checked the fountain from every possible angle. I couldn't find anything, not a crack or even a hole in the solid, carved piece of stone. It made no sense.

"I was about to have sex," I muttered to the fountain as I folded up the ladder and carried it angrily away. "Thanks a bunch."

I heard a sound behind me, almost like the giggle of a small child. It made the hair stand up on the back of my neck. When I turned around slowly, my heart pounding in an erratic dance in my chest, no one was there. The garden was empty, and other than the gurgle of the fountain and the sounds of birds rustling in the trees, it was completely and absolutely silent.

CHAPTER 6

COOKING IS THE BEST KIND OF THERAPY.
-AUNT FRANCESCA

Tuesday, Mom hosted an all-day reiki therapy session. Usually, I went to the farmer's market in the morning and used the afternoon to run errands. Because we had a record number of people signed up for reiki this week, however, I planned to help with lunch preparations in the morning, sneak in a quick visit to Moses after we finished, and go to the market in the afternoon.

I enjoyed working in the shop, but the kitchen was my favorite place. I loved chopping and sifting and kneading. When the aroma of baking cookies filled the air and I smelled spices like cinnamon, nutmeg, or cloves, I felt happy and content. I couldn't cut a lemon without lifting it to my nose for a whiff of its bright, citrusy beauty, and there was nothing as satisfying as putting bread dough into an oiled bowl and coming back to see it doubled in size.

I needed a "Kitchen Witch" apron instead of "Kitchen Bitch" because this was the kind of magic I could believe in. It wasn't the magic Mom and her friends talked about, with omens, charms, and crystals. My magic was practical. Scientific. I mixed the right ingredients in the correct amounts and created something wonderful.

I planned my life this way, too, putting the right things together in the correct amounts to get the desired results. If I had a recipe, it would read, "Take four years of undergrad in a useful major. Add an MBA. Work hard. Stir in the right man, if desired, and enjoy a happy and successful life without ever worrying about things like peeling paint, broken air conditioners, leaky fountains, or irresponsible parents."

I sighed. Mom would never change, but at least I could control the other elements in my life. Any cook knows, to get the best outcome from a recipe, choose the highest-quality ingredients and buy only the best in kitchen supplies. That's what I'd done by choosing Scott. He was as reliable as a good copper pot.

I couldn't help out in the shop as much during school as I did over summer break, so my mom's best friend, Maggie, filled in the rest of year and also taught reiki therapy. I'd known her since the day I was born. In fact, she'd been in the delivery room when I popped out. I called her Auntie Mags, and although she spent most of the summer enjoying her brood of grandchildren, today was her reiki class.

I carried out some pitchers of ice-cold water infused with cucumber and mint, and Auntie Mags smiled. "Thank you, Fiona. You're always able to anticipate our needs before we even know them ourselves. It's a gift."

The people in the class nodded, although most of them had never met me. Auntie Mags had that way with people. She saw positive energy in every person she met and made them want to see good in others too.

Auntie Mags was a big lady, a few years older than my mom. She wore bright colors and flowing skirts and blouses. She towered over Mom and me, but she embraced her size the way she embraced all things in life, the good and the bad. She called herself "the last of the Amazons."

I turned to go back to the kitchen, but Auntie Mags stopped me. "Fiona, we need a volunteer. Would you help us?"

I froze. "That depends on what you want me to do."

She laughed. "Nothing scary. Just lie down on the floor so I can demonstrate to the others how to unblock a chakra."

I clutched my serving tray, still wet from the pitchers, to my chest. "I have to make the salads for lunch. Can't Mom do it?"

Auntie Mags shook her head. "She doesn't have any blockages. Her chakras flow perfectly."

Mom squeezed my arm. "I'll make the salads. Help your auntie Mags."

She took the tray, and I gave her a dirty look. "Thanks."

Auntie Mags patted the blanket in front of her, and I stretched out on the floor with my head next to her knees. The group of reiki practitioners surrounded me, making me nervous and a little claustrophobic.

Auntie Mags spoke, and the class hung on to her every word. "First, make the patient as comfortable as possible. Are you comfortable, Fiona?"

I felt far from it. Yet again, I'd allowed Mom and her lunatic friends to pull me into something crazy and stupid. Auntie Mags must have read my thoughts from the expression on my face. She gave me a wink, pursing her lips so she wouldn't smile.

"Good. Now, as you all know, reiki can be performed either by gently touching the body or by letting your hands hover just over it. Fiona, which method would you prefer?"

I shot her a dirty look, and she bit her lip to hold back a laugh. "I think she would prefer that we *not* touch her today. Let's begin. Close your eyes, Fiona."

She'd tricked me into doing this. She knew I didn't believe in chakras or energy fields or any of this nonsense and had avoided her and her reiki hands for a long time. But when Auntie Mags started to work, I felt a strange pulse of energy, and I wrinkled my brow in confusion.

"Relax, Fiona," whispered Auntie Mags.

I forced myself to do as she asked, but as soon as she resumed, I felt the same pulse of energy. Like a soft, low-pitched hum, it vibrated as it traveled through my body. It wasn't unpleasant. Just unexpected and strange.

Auntie Mags went from my head down to my throat. It was soothing, but when she got to my chest, she stopped.

"Oh my. Her heart chakra is completely blocked. Feel this."

Suddenly, a whole bunch of hands hovered over my body, and the hum intensified. A strange, heavy pressure built inside my chest.

My eyes flew open, and I pushed their hands away. "Stop. I don't like this." I tried to sit up but swayed, dizzy and disoriented. Something strange had just happened. Something I couldn't explain.

Auntie Mags put an arm around my shoulders to steady me. "Someone get Fiona a glass of water, please."

My hands shook, but the water made me feel slightly better. Auntie Mags studied my face with concern. "I'm so sorry, Fiona. I didn't know."

"You didn't know what?"

She pulled me into a gentle hug and whispered in my ear, "What you've been carrying in your heart. You poor little thing."

I got to my feet and took a deep breath. I felt thrown off but wasn't going to share that with a bunch of strangers. "I'm fine."

Auntie Mags rose to her feet, too, and spoke to the class. "We'll take a five-minute break. Please go out and enjoy the back garden. It's incredible."

The class went outside, and Auntie Mags took my hands in hers. Her skin looked very brown next to mine. With her long, dark curls streaked with gray, she looked a bit like a gypsy fortune-teller. Part of that may have been the brightly colored scarf she used to hold back her hair and the big silver hoops in her ears. The effect proved pretty exotic for a lady from Cleveland.

"I never would have let you volunteer if I'd known how bad it was."

I frowned. "What are you talking about?"

Auntie Mags made a tsking sound with her tongue. "You have possibly the worst blockage in a heart chakra I've ever seen. It's emotional, pumpkin. I think you've done it to yourself."

"How could I do that?" I laughed and tried to pull my hands away.

She wouldn't release me. "You can't control everything, angel. You've got to let it go."

I gave her hands a gentle squeeze and moved away from her, shaking my head. "I don't believe in magic or charms or crystals or fortune-telling or energy fields. If I can't see it, I don't want any part of it."

Her warm brown eyes were sad. "What about love, sweet Fiona? Do you believe in that?"

"I have a *boyfriend*," I said with emphasis.

"Well, you can't see love. You can't calculate it or qualify it or even understand it, and yet it is there. The most powerful, wonderful, magical thing in the universe."

I snorted. "I believe in more practical sorts of emotions, the kind you can depend on. The kind that won't use you and leave you all alone when you're pregnant and helpless."

My gaze flew to the kitchen. Mom was making the salads, humming along to some soft music playing on the radio. I was fairly certain she had not heard me.

"Is that what you think happened to your mom?" asked Auntie Mags, putting her hands on my shoulders. "Well, you're wrong, Fiona, but it isn't my story to tell. You'll have to ask her about it."

"I can't. I've tried. It makes her sad," I said softly.

She pulled me into a hug, enveloping me in her soft warmth. "When you're ready to know, she'll be ready to tell you. But for now, we have to talk about your heart."

I pulled back. "No, we don't."

Auntie Mags pushed me gently but firmly onto a cushy chair. "Yes, we do, and you're going to listen."

I crossed my legs and looked at my watch. "You have five minutes, or your reiki people will have to forage for nuts and berries in the garden."

She didn't look concerned. "Your mom is perfectly capable of making a few salads. It's *you* I'm worried about. You seem to have lost touch with your heart center."

My confusion must have been apparent. Auntie Mags sighed and sat down next to me. "The heart center is that glowing place inside your chest. When you close your eyes and relax, you can almost see it. Try."

I tapped my foot impatiently. "I don't have a glowing place inside my chest."

"We all do, Fiona. You just have to know how to access it. Humor me, okay?"

"If I do, will you let me get back to work?"

She nodded seriously. "Yes. Now close your eyes. Relax your neck, your shoulders, and your arms. Let the relaxation flow through your body until it's as limp as a rag doll."

I complied, mostly to make her leave me alone, but it felt good to sit still and let all the tension drain from my body.

Once Auntie Mags was apparently satisfied I'd followed her directions, she continued.

"Now breathe slowly in and out, never losing that relaxed state. On your next inhale, I want you to feel what's in the center of your chest."

Auntie Mags was right. It was like a small, glowing ball of energy. My chest felt strangely tight when picturing it, but not a scary tightness.

My eyes flew open, and Auntie Mags smiled. "You did it."

I stood, feeling like I'd had a long, peaceful nap instead of two minutes of quiet time. "I think that was the power of suggestion more than anything else."

She shrugged. "Believe what you will, but I know you found it. I hope you learn to use it."

"Thanks, Auntie Mags." She genuinely wanted to help me, and I knew it. It wasn't her fault I thought her chakras and energy fields were a little west of crazy.

Kate had come in and helped Mom pull the salads together and heat up the soups for the lunch crowd. "How is Auntie Mags?" she asked.

"Great, except she tried to unblock one of my chakras in a room full of people and made me touch my heart center."

Kate giggled. "You make it sound so dirty. I might have to try reiki one of these days."

"Oh, you should," said Mom as she mixed up a poppy-seed dressing for the strawberry, spinach, and pecan salads. "It's a way to connect with places in your body where no one has gone before."

She carried the dressing out into the garden. Kate and I looked at each other and burst out laughing.

"She kind of makes it sound like *Star Trek*," she said, wiping a tear away from her eye.

I agreed. "A pornographic sort of *Star Trek*. This is her

second *Star Trek* reference in as many days. I had no idea she was a Trekkie. And she mentioned out of the blue that Aunt Francesca had been friends with Grace Kelly."

Kate's eyes widened. "*The* Grace Kelly?"

"Yes," I said. "Add that to the list of fascinating facts about Francesca. I wonder if I'll ever know the real story."

"What do you mean?"

I leaned closer. "She never married, she had tons of money, and she hung around with famous people. Also, she had parties all the time. Her life seemed to be a constant celebration."

"That's wonderful. I want to be Aunt Francesca when I grow up."

"Me too," I said. "But I feel like there was something tragic about her too. Like she had a hole in her heart. Maybe I'm just reading into things, but don't you think she had sad eyes?"

I pointed to the black-and-white picture of Aunt Francesca that we kept on the wall in a silver frame. She was in this very kitchen, her hair perfectly coiffed and an apron covering what looked like a sequined ball gown. People surrounded her, watching her cook, all of them in formal dress and holding fancy drinks. She smiled at the camera, her delicate arms covered nearly up to the elbows in flour, and looked absolutely at ease, but she looked something else too.

Lonely. Or at least I'd always thought so.

"It might just be me," I said. "How could she not be happy? She had everything a woman could want, right?"

"Almost everything," said Kate with an oddly wistful little smile.

We both looked up when the bell on the front door of the shop tinkled and Chad came in. He froze as soon as he saw Kate. She inhaled sharply, her cheeks turning pink, and knocked a pile of neatly folded napkins onto the floor. He helped her pick them up, and I watched them closely. Something had changed between them. They'd been flirty for a while, and I had a feeling they finally hooked up. Judging by the way they acted, though, it must not have ended on a good note.

As they stared at each other, I realized this could get awkward. I held my breath and waited.

Kate fidgeted. Chad stroked his dark beard, a nervous habit. The air grew thick with sexual tension. Chad was getting his master's degree in philosophy and Kate just finished her PhD in poetry. If they did get involved, it was a relationship doomed to fail tragically and with lots of introspective musings.

"Hello, Kate." Chad's voice seemed an octave or two deeper than normal.

"Chad."

Kate acted incapable of forming a complete sentence, which made me roll my eyes. "I'd better take these salads out. Do you need anything, Chad?"

Normally, Chad didn't come in during the week. He pulled his soulful brown gaze away from Kate and turned to me. "Your mom asked me to help in the kitchen so you could go to the market."

I smiled at him. "Thanks, Chad."

If I left right away, I could see Moses and still might have a chance at getting some decent tomatoes and herbs from my favorite stall and even pies from the elderly Amish man who came every week. I handed Chad an apron from the bin, and he slipped it over his head. I had to stifle a laugh when I looked at his apron, which was black with the word "Stud" above a drawing of a muffin. Chad glanced down and grimaced.

"Nice," he said.

Mom swished back into the kitchen and stopped when she saw his apron. "Oh. We have to get more of those. They're adorable."

We'd ordered several of each style of apron, and wearing the samples seemed to boost sales. I had to admit the aprons were pretty funny.

Auntie Mags came into the kitchen and grinned at the miserable expression on Chad's face. "It's nothing to be shy about, Chad. If you've got it, flaunt it."

Kate slipped quietly out of the room. I followed her, grabbing my shopping basket and a few totes on the way.

She stared out the window with a melancholy expression. Even her Betty Boop tattoo looked a little droopy and sad.

I came up behind her. "Are you okay?"

She wiped away a tear. "I'm fine," she said with forced cheerfulness.

Terrible at this sort of thing, I wasn't sure how to help. "Do you need to talk . . . or something?"

Kate let out a shaky laugh and patted my hand. "Or something. I'm all right. I just need to write a little."

Whenever Kate had a problem, she wrote poetry. She was a wonderful poet, but since the demand for poets in today's competitive job market was a steady zero, she worked in our shop, took care of a nice little old lady in the evenings, and wrote whenever she could. Since the traffic in our shop was often extremely slow, she usually had a vast abundance of writing time.

I gave her a wave, but she didn't notice. She already scribbled frantically, her head bent over her notebook. Kate expressed her emotions so clearly and beautifully with her words. It gave her an outlet. Whenever I had emotional turmoil, I just baked excessively. It didn't solve anything, but at least it kept my thoughts and my hands busy.

A niggling thought formed in my mind that Auntie Mags

might be right about my blocked chakra and my heart center. There very well could be something seriously wrong with me. I didn't want to believe it but couldn't forget how it had felt when those people tried to unblock me. Not painful but uncomfortable and strange.

I thought about Auntie Mags as I sat by Moses's bed and wondered if she could unblock whatever kept him unconscious. I knew his brain needed time to heal, but I wanted to do something, anything to help. Maybe I should consider Matthew's offer. Working together, we might be able to figure out who did this to Moses and why.

Nurse Brenda came in and smiled when she saw me. "He's doing better today. His vitals are stronger, and he moved around a bit this morning. Nothing major, just shifting his legs and hands, but I think he's on the mend. We've reduced his meds. We just have to wait for him to wake up now."

"He looks so . . . still."

She put a hand on my arm. "There's no rushing it. We have to be patient and give him time."

As I left the hospital, the sun warmed my face. I wore a comfortable sundress in a pale blue that matched the sky. It felt good to be outside, and my heart seemed lighter after talking with Nurse Brenda. I almost skipped to the market. I put on sunglasses and thought about my heart center. I wanted to see if I could feel it again on my own.

I stopped walking, closed my eyes, relaxed my shoulders, and lifted my chin. It took only a second before I found it, a golden, flickering light, right in the center of my chest. A peaceful, secluded island of calm in the middle of the raging sea of humanity that was the South Side, and I'd never even known it existed.

It made wonder what other things I'd missed or refused to see. Maybe there was something to all this reiki nonsense. Maybe I'd been too quick to judge my mom, Auntie Mags, and all their crazy friends. Maybe this was what Matthew meant when he told me I was wrong about a lot of things. Maybe, just maybe, I'd been wrong about him too.

CHAPTER 7

THE TASTIEST MEAL IS ONE SHARED WITH A FRIEND. -AUNT FRANCESCA

My little moment of nirvana ended when a person slammed into me suddenly from behind. I flew forward, expecting to hit the pavement, but a strong set of arms caught me just in time. I lifted my head and found myself staring directly at a wooden yin and yang necklace on a nicely muscled and familiar chest.

"Watch where you're going." Matthew said to the man behind me as he pulled me close, cradling me in his arms, two angry spots of color on his cheeks.

"She stopped right in the middle of the sidewalk." The man who'd bumped into me wore a business suit and looked like he'd come to the South Side on his lunch break. I put a hand on Matthew's arm to make him settle down. He seemed ready to brawl.

"He's right, Matthew. I wasn't paying attention." I turned to the man. "My bad. Sorry."

The man walked away, muttering something about "damned hippies and stoners" under his breath. Matthew watched him leave, his expression furious.

"You can let go now."

Matthew glanced at me in surprise, like he didn't realize he still had me clutched to his side. I disengaged myself gently from his embrace, feeling a tinge of regret. There was something so warm and safe and *solid* about Matthew.

"Sorry," he said. "I didn't mean to—"

"Don't," I said, clearing my throat. "I'm the one who should apologize. I didn't mean what I said in the shop yesterday. I'm sorry, Matthew."

He gave me a serious nod. "Apology accepted."

"Wow. That was easy," I said with a laugh.

The sunshine on his face brought out gold and green flecks in his eyes. "It doesn't have to be complicated. You're under a lot of stress. I get it. And you were wrong about me. I *don't* have a tattoo of a Chinese character anywhere on my body."

He rolled up the sleeves of his dark T-shirt to show me his biceps and lifted it to show me his stomach. He had a six-pack but no tattoos. "See? Not a one."

I raised an eyebrow. "You could be hiding it." I blushed, imagining him wearing nothing but his yin and yang necklace.

Matthew came closer and gave me a naughty look. "I could prove it, if you'd like."

"No, thanks." I jumped away so fast I dropped my basket.

He grinned, catching it before it hit the ground. "Where are you going, Little Red Riding Hood?"

"The farmers' market. Want to come?"

He looked surprised I'd asked him to join me. I was a bit surprised myself.

"Did you just ask the big bad wolf on a date?" he asked, and I gaped at him. He had the ability to make me feel flustered all the time and seemed to know it. "I'm teasing you. I'd love to see the farmers' market."

"Good. There's a little old Amish guy whose wife makes the most delicious whoopie pies. I'll get you one. My treat."

He watched me with his steady dark eyes. "Show me the way."

We walked side by side, and I wondered if inviting him was the wrong thing to do. Even if buying whoopie pies for another guy seemed perfectly innocent, Scott might not see it that way.

Matthew, obviously unconcerned about the moral implications of whoopie pies, looked around at the chaos that made up the South Side. "This place is amazing," he said. "So colorful. So alive."

"Also run down and a little smelly. You aren't from around here, are you?"

He shook his head. "I'm from Philly. I came here for . . . a friend."

He hesitated before he said "friend," so I knew it was a girl. She was, no doubt, someone sexy and tall with long dark hair and a throaty laugh. She definitely had tattoos, and she knew exactly where Matthew's hidden tattoos were as well.

I hated her.

I cleared my throat, pushing the thought of Matthew's girlfriend out of my mind, and adopted a formal tour guide kind of pose. "Let me show you around. To your left, we have Pamela's, which makes the best pancakes in the whole wide world. Over there is Oram's. They sell cinnamon rolls as big as your head. They're fantastic."

We passed a guitar shop. "I've been there," he said with a grin. "As you may have guessed, and I've been to the record shop too. Is this the block they want to tear down?"

I nodded. "From the street the Enchanted Garden is on all the way down to the church."

The Enchanted Garden was on a side street, around the corner from the main strip, and signaled the beginning of the residential part of the South Side. Most of the buildings on the main street were several stories and made of stone or brick. The café was a little pink and green anomaly.

"These buildings are amazing." He pointed to the stone gargoyles that topped the used bookstore. "Look at the detail."

"Those gargoyles happen to be my friends, Fred and Wilma."

Matthew laughed. "The *Flintstones?*"

"Yep. They're beautiful and close to two hundred years old. The café is one of the newer buildings on this block, and it was built in 1850."

"And someone wants demolish all this?"

"Anderson Solutions calls it progress. The South Side needs more parking."

Matthew shook his head. "It isn't right."

"It's in the hands of Mr. McAlister at this point. If he decides to sell . . ."

"All hope is lost."

"Yes. And we'd lose the candy shop, too, which would be tragic." We stood in front of Yonky's Candy Emporium. I glanced in the window and let out a gasp. A handwritten sign in the window said, "Closing after forty sweet and wonderful years—all inventory must go."

I pushed open the door and stepped inside. Mr. Yonky stood behind the counter, his shoulders stooped. He seemed to have aged ten years since I'd seen him last.

"Fiona. I hoped you'd stop by." He straightened his glasses and attempted to smooth down his gray hair. Half-filled boxes littered the floor, and barely anything remained on the shelves.

"What happened?"

He let out a sigh. "Anderson Solutions. They gave me an offer I couldn't refuse."

Matthew stood next to me, staring into the empty glass display case. "What kind of an offer?" I asked.

Mr. Yonky let out a bitter laugh. "One that let me keep the shirt on my back and my house too. I got off lucky, I guess. They are not nice people, Fiona."

"I got that feeling. Is there anything I can do to help?"

He handed me a lollipop in a bright wrapper. "Keep fighting. You and your mom have decided to stand up to them, and I know a lot of others will stand with you. I had no choice. It was time for me to retire, and Mrs. Yonky wants to move to Florida anyway, but what they are doing is wrong."

I gave him a hug and went outside, feeling defeated. I stared down at the lollipop. It reminded me of my childhood, of days spent running to Mr. Yonky's with coins clutched in my hand, ready to spend my hard-earned allowance on a special treat. "I have to do something."

"You are. You're standing up to them, like Mr. Yonky said."

"But I didn't help *him*. To be in business so long and to go out like this . . ."

Matthew put a finger under my chin and tilted my head up until his eyes met mine. "You're doing what you can, Fiona. Don't give up hope."

"I'm trying, but I feel like the whole area is doomed. It's depressing."

"Not doomed. Not even close. I know you're sad about Mr. Yonky but look around. Most of the other businesses are doing well."

He was right. Only a few shops had darkened windows and "closed" signs on their doors. Most were busy and bustling with customers. "I guess it isn't *that* bad . . ."

"It's actually a vibrant and interesting place. But I am curious about a few things," he said with a twinkle in his eyes.

"First of all, are you going to eat that lolly or stare at it? Because it looks good."

I handed it to him. "Here. It's yours."

He unwrapped the lollipop and stuck it in his mouth as we walked. "Secondly, I need a recommendation. There are tons of restaurants here. What if I wanted to go somewhere nice, like on a date?"

I thought about the sexy girlfriend I'd imagined and tried not to scowl. "It depends. If you want to splurge, I'd go up there." I pointed to the restaurants perched on top of Mount Washington, high above the South Side. "Those are some of the best places in town, and the views are fantastic."

"I'll keep it in mind," he said. "Where do you like to go?"

"I'm easy." I pointed to Wicked Wienies, the hot dog shop across the street.

"Hot dogs? Aren't you a vegetarian?"

"No way. My mom is a vegetarian. I'm a carnivore."

"Shall I buy you a hot dog, Ms. Carnivore?"

"Let's go to the market first before they run out of everything; then we can eat."

The farmers' market was held twice a week in the church parking lot at the end of the block. Soon, my basket and totes were filled with fresh produce and some beautiful herbs. All the vendors loved Matthew. He even charmed old Mr. Yoder, my Amish whoopie pie supplier, who was slightly deaf and thought Matthew was my husband. I bought whoopie pies for us and several fruit pies for the shop.

"You're a charmer," I said as we walked away.

"People usually like me. You're kind of the exception to the rule." He gave me a wink, and I groaned.

"I told you I was sorry."

Matthew put a casual arm around my shoulders. "Water under the bridge," he said. "Did you have a chance to see Moses today?"

I nodded. I should have moved away from his embrace but didn't. "The nurse said he's doing better, but he hasn't woken up yet."

"It might take some time, Fiona."

"I know, but I miss him." I shifted the totes in my hands. Matthew carried the basket. "Were you serious about what you said? Do you want to work together and ask around?"

He didn't hesitate. "Yes."

"And do you still want a hot dog?"

"Uh, yes."

I tilted my head toward the hot dog shop. "Let's start there. They're open all night, and the whole South Side eats there. If anyone has been chatting about what happened to Moses, they would know."

Bob and his partner Bernie, the owners of Wicked Wienies, stood behind the counter, organizing the lunch rush. The irony of the fact that an openly gay couple owned a shop called Wicked Wienies was not lost on me, but I was so used to it I didn't think about it anymore. Bob called out a greeting, and Bernie waved me over to the end of the counter to chat. Older and a little on the chubby side with gray curly hair, he had on a purple T-shirt that said, "I Love Wienies!" As soon as I got close enough, he reached out and clasped my hand.

"I heard about Moses. Is he okay?"

I nodded, swallowing hard. "He's still unconscious, but everyone is . . . hopeful. Have you heard anything? About who might have done this?"

Bernie shook his head. "The whole South Side is talking about it, but no one knows a thing. Moses has a lot of friends, and I don't know of a single person who'd wish to do him harm. It's so strange."

Bob joined us. His T-shirt, also purple, said, "Eat More Wienies." I watched as Matthew tried to hold back a smile.

"It's Matthew's first time here," I said. "Be gentle with him, guys. No atomic chili today. Just wienies."

"You never forget your first wienie," said Bob seriously. "And sadly, we had to take the atomic chili off the menu. One of the cooks got it in his eye and nearly went blind."

He pointed over his shoulder at a cook in a white T-shirt wearing an eye patch. He gave us a cheery grin and waved his kitchen tongs at us. Bob shook his head sadly. "Poor guy. He's okay, though, better than Moses. I can't believe something like this could happen at the Enchanted Garden. What on earth is this place coming to? An old man getting beat up for no reason at all. How's your mom holding up, Fi?"

I blinked away tears. "She's fine. We're trying to figure out who could have done this. If you hear anything, will you let us know?"

"Of course we will," said Bernie. "But I have a funny feeling about this one."

"What do you mean?"

He gave Bob a long look. "Bob and I were talking about it this morning. If none of our customers has a clue about what happened, it can only mean one thing."

"What?"

Bob leaned forward so we could hear him above the din of the noisy restaurant. "It wasn't someone from the South Side who did it."

I nodded. I had a feeling Bob and Bernie were right.

We lunched on hot dogs with nonatomic chili, fresh-cut French fries, and milkshakes. I sipped my chocolate milkshake, trying to put the pieces of the puzzle together.

"You're deep in thought," said Matthew.

I wiped my mouth with my napkin. "I was thinking about what Bob said."

"That it wasn't someone from the South Side?"

"Yes." I let out a sigh. "Which is bad news. It'll be harder to figure it out if it isn't someone local."

He reached over to squeeze my hand. "Don't give up, Fiona. Someone has to know something."

I pulled my hand away, suddenly a little uncomfortable. "Thank you for lunch. Bernie sure knows his shakes, doesn't he?"

"Do you want to try some of mine?" he asked, holding up his strawberry milkshake. I hesitated only for a second.

"Yes."

"Good," he said, "because I wanted the chocolate but thought you'd be greedy about it."

I giggled, and we switched glasses. "Mmmm. This is good too."

"I bet you're one of those girls who never has to diet, aren't you?"

I used a spoon to scoop out a lump of strawberry. "I don't eat like this daily, but I don't diet. My mom doesn't either. I guess I got her genes."

"What about your dad?"

I leaned back in my seat. There were two options when this subject came up, honesty or avoidance. I chose honesty. "I've never met him."

I'd never discussed it with my mother, but I suspected my conception occurred on a whim created by a lot of pot, very few inhibitions, and the presence of a handsome stranger. I had no idea who my father was, but Mom had straightened herself out as soon as she found out she was pregnant, and she built the café and made a life for us here. Not exactly the life I would have chosen, but somehow it worked, for her at least.

Matthew studied my face with his steady, dark gaze. "Are you okay with that?"

"I don't have a choice." I glanced at my watch and slid out of the booth. "I should get going."

Matthew leaped to his feet and picked up my tote bags. I grabbed the basket.

"Did I offend you?" he asked.

I shook my head. "Not at all. It is what it is. I have my mom. I don't need anyone else."

"You're lucky."

Something in his voice told me he wasn't so fortunate, but I didn't want to ask about it in the middle of the hot dog shop. I forced a smile onto my face. "Can you help me carry this stuff home? I still owe you a whoopie pie."

He rubbed his washboard stomach and groaned. "Are you trying to fatten me up?"

I giggled, sounding like an obnoxious fourteen-year-old girl. I laughed at every single thing he said. I tried to stop but giggled again as we walked back into the shop. Kate, still scratching away in her notebook, looked up in surprise. Her eyes went from me to Matthew and back to me again, and my cheeks grew instantly warm.

"You remember Matthew, don't you, Kate?"

"Hi, Kate. Nice to see you again." He lifted the tote bags. "I'll bring these back to the kitchen."

"Thanks." Kate and I spoke in unison. As soon as he was out of earshot, she grabbed my arm.

"What the hell is going on?" she asked, her voice an urgent whisper. "Are you cheating on the Ken doll?"

Kate called Scott "the Ken doll" and me "psycho Barbie." She thought it was hilarious. I didn't. Mom had called Scott "Ken" twice by accident.

"We ran into each other and went to the market together. And we had lunch." I covered my mouth. "Oh my. You're right."

Kate nodded. "Sounds like a date to me."

I blinked. "I didn't mean for it to be . . ."

Mom came out of the kitchen and took the basket from my arm. She leaned down to get a whiff of the herbs. "This dill is divine, darling. And look at the chives."

"Did you hear about Yonky's? It's closing."

Mom nodded sadly. "I did. That poor man. And what a loss to our little community."

"I'll miss his lemon drops," said Kate. "And the way he always let children pick out something, even if they didn't have enough money."

"He's a kind man, and his goodness will be rewarded. Karma will take care of him, and karma will take care of those soulless people at Anderson too. We can't focus on it, though. We need to keep moving ahead." She glanced at Kate. "Did you tell her?"

Kate shook her head. I had a moment of panic, wondering what else might have broken, but Mom grinned.

"We sold almost all of the fertility charms. We only have half a dozen left. And a bunch of girls came in from one of the sororities at the university and bought all of our stardust necklaces."

"They did?" The stardust necklaces were small, corked glass bottles filled with glitter that we hung on black leather cords. We'd put them together for next to nothing. It had been Kate's idea. "Way to go, Kate," I said.

"It's marvelous news. We can get the air conditioner fixed now. Marty said he'd stop by later today."

Marty, a retired mechanic and the sweetest old man in the world, did all the handyman jobs for us we couldn't do ourselves. We kept him busy. A house as old as ours existed in a constant state of disrepair.

Mom went back into the kitchen. I heard her talking with Matthew and Chad. Kate gave me a squinty-eyed look. "What are you going to do about Matthew?"

I gave her a squinty-eyed look right back. "What are you going to do about Chad?"

We stood there, in the middle of a squinty-eyed standoff, when Matthew stuck his head through the door.

"Whoopie pie anyone?"

CHAPTER 8

BREAKFAST IN BED IS THE KINDEST SORT OF LUXURY. -AUNT FRANCESCA

"Good morning, sunshine."

Mom carried a tray laden with breakfast foods and put it on the table next to my bed. She had on faded jeans and a delicate white blouse made of tiny ribbons and lace. I'd found the blouse for her at a thrift shop, and it made her look even more dainty and fragile than usual.

Rubbing my eyes, I looked at the clock. I'd slept in, something that never happened. "Oh no."

"Oh yes." She sat down on the side of my bed and brushed the hair out of my eyes. "You've been working too hard. You needed to rest, but I feel like there's more to it than that. What's going on, Fiona?"

"Nothing."

I covered my face with my pillow. I'd been up half the night wondering if lunch with Matthew equaled a date, worrying about what might happen if Scott found out, and remembering the way Matthew's eyes crinkled in the corners when he laughed and the way he kept seeking an excuse to touch me throughout the day. A random brush of an elbow. His hand on my lower back as we walked along the crowded sidewalk. His arm hung loosely around my shoulders. It was almost as if he couldn't stop himself, like he craved contact with my skin. I kind of craved contact with his skin, too, especially when I recalled how he'd yanked up his shirt to show me his tattoo-free abdomen. It's no wonder I couldn't sleep.

Mom pulled the pillow away. I could tell she was trying not to laugh at the expression on my face. "I know you well enough to know that it isn't 'nothing,' but I'll wait until you are ready to talk to me about it. You should know, however, I've been there myself, darling."

I picked up a croissant and nibbled on it. "What do you mean?"

As the sunlight hit her face, I realized, once again, that she was a remarkably beautiful woman. A bit of gray now threaded its way through her hair, and some fine lines etched themselves around her eyes, but otherwise she didn't look old enough to be my mom.

She wiped her hands on her apron, a faraway look in her eyes. "You probably don't know this, but when I was in college, I got engaged."

I blinked in surprise. "To be married?"

She nodded. "His name was William, and my parents adored him, but he was all wrong for me. It took me a while to understand that, but as soon as I did, I broke it off."

"How did you know?" I asked softly. I put some jam on my knife and slathered it on my croissant, wondering where this revelation had come and why she'd brought it up now. "What made you realize he wasn't the one for you?"

She gave me a sad, little smile. "Because I met the right man. The only man for me. Your father."

I almost choked. "My *father*?"

"Yes. We Campbell women seem to be doomed to the same fate."

"What do you mean?"

She shrugged. "It happened to Aunt Francesca. You know that story, right?"

"No, I don't."

She blinked, surprised. "Oh. I thought I'd told you. She was engaged to a steel baron, you see, one of the wealthiest men in Pittsburgh. He begged her to set a date, but she hesitated. She wanted to live her own life a bit before settling down, and he was a bit of an adventurer as well. I guess he understood, and he was willing to wait for her."

"What happened?"

"Well, he decided to go on an Arctic expedition. He wanted to marry Aunt Francesca before he left, but she brushed him off again. She told him they had plenty of time, but she had a secret. While he was away, she organized a huge wedding, the biggest people around here had ever seen. She reserved a church, planned out an amazing menu, and bought an elegant dress, made with Irish lace so delicate it looked like part of a spider's web. She made the cake herself, of course. She was a baker, after all. And on the day he was supposed to return, everything was finally ready. But sadly, he never came."

"Oh no," I said. "He met someone else?"

She shook her head. "He got sick while on the expedition and died. They weren't able to bring him back home. Aunt Francesca didn't even have a body to bury."

I put a hand over my heart, thinking about the photo of Aunt Francesca and her sad, lonely eyes. "What did she do?"

She cupped my face in her hands. "She threw a party in his memory and invited everyone she knew. She wore her lovely gown made of Irish lace, cried over him at the church she'd reserved for their wedding, and then set out with one intention. To celebrate his life and the love they shared in the best way she knew how. By not letting another moment go to waste."

"That's terrible," I said, reaching for a tissue. "Heartbreaking. She never met anyone else?"

"No," said my mom with a faraway look in her eyes. "Campbell women never do, it seems. It was like that for me with your father. All it took was one kiss for me to know it was very different from what I felt for my fiancé. Something magical. And the sex . . ."

I held up a hand to stop her. "Please, don't go there."

She laughed. "Okay, my little Puritan. The truth of the matter is that kisses can be enjoyable with just about anyone, but when you kiss the right person, it goes so far beyond that. It's powerful and raw, and the desire can be overwhelming and almost frightening, but it's also something sacred. Predestined. At least that's how it was with your father."

"But he left you." The words came out of my mouth before I could stop them, and I gasped. "I'm so sorry. I shouldn't have said that."

She patted my hand. "Don't apologize for speaking the truth. He may have been the one for me, but I may not have been the one for him. I guess we'll never know."

I slid to the side of the bed to sit next to her, putting my head on her shoulder. "Who was he?" I didn't want to make her sad but needed to know and had never found the courage to ask before.

"His name was Simon, and I met him at an ashram in Rishikesh."

I rolled my eyes. "Of course you did."

"We had two perfect months together, and then it was over, and he was gone."

"What happened?"

She rested her head on top of mine. "I figured out I was pregnant."

I swallowed hard. "He left you because of me?"

She turned to me in surprise. "Oh no. Simon didn't know about you. He also didn't know I was engaged. I had to go home and tell William I couldn't marry him. It was the right thing to do, but I asked Simon to meet me in a café before I left. I wanted to tell him the truth."

"What did he say?"

"It was kind of the same thing that happened to Aunt Francesca, in a way. He didn't show up. I waited for hours, but he never came." She played with one of the ribbons on her blouse. "He must have gone back to Belgium. He always hated goodbyes."

"He was Belgian?"

"Yes." She tweaked my nose. "I guess that's why you like chocolate so much. And waffles."

"You never saw him again?" I swallowed hard. "It's so unfair."

Mom sighed. "I hadn't been honest with him. I pretended to be into free love, but truth be told, I wanted Simon all for myself, and losing him almost broke my heart."

"What did you do?"

"I went back home and told William. He wanted to get married and pretend you were his, but I couldn't do it. William was a good, decent person, but Simon was my soul mate."

I shook my head. "He deserted you. Soul mates, if they exist at all, wouldn't desert you." I brushed away the hot, bitter tears that ran down my face.

"It wasn't like that, darling. Loving Simon was the most wonderful thing that ever happened to me, until you came along, of course."

I rested my head on her shoulder, inhaling her sweet, warm scent. She patted my back, comforting me, even though I should have been the one comforting her.

"Did you ever try to find him?" I asked.

She shook her head. "I didn't even know his last name. It seemed so unimportant at the time. He didn't know mine either. He called me 'Claire de Lune.' I made that my real name after my parents kicked me out. It made me feel stronger somehow. Less alone."

"I'm sorry, Mom." I'd thought I'd known her so well, but really I didn't know her at all.

She pinned her clear-blue eyes on me. "I'm not. I experienced real, true love, Fiona, and eventually I had you. I wouldn't change a single thing."

"Aren't you even curious about him?"

A brief shadow flickered across her face, like a cloud covering the sun on a bright summer day, and then it was gone. "I only hope he's happy. But it was because of karma we met the first time, and it's up to karma if we meet again."

I wanted to yell but controlled myself. "Or you could try to look him up."

"Without knowing his last name? And what would I do if I found him?"

"Contact him. Ask him why he didn't show up. Tell him about me."

My voice shook, and she pulled me into her arms. "I didn't want to upset you, but I felt it was the right time to share this with you. I don't regret anything, but the thing I am most proud of is the fact I didn't marry William. I considered it, mind you. I was scared, and it would have been the easy way out. William would have taken care of me. I could have continued living the pampered, spoiled life I'd grown accustomed to, but I couldn't do it."

"What happened to William?"

She smiled. "He married a friend of mine from high school. They have three children and are very happy together. I get a card from them every Christmas."

"Has there been anyone else you loved since Simon?"

She shook her head. "I've tried, but it was like being given grape juice after you'd had fine wine." She shuddered. "No point."

"Aren't you lonely?"

She squeezed my hand. "I have you, my friends, and this wonderful shop. Sometimes, I even feel like darling Aunt Francesca is still here, floating around somewhere, looking after me. How could I be lonely?"

She went downstairs, and I stayed in bed a long time, staring at the ceiling. I heard her chatting with Kate and knew they were getting things ready for the lunch crowd. Normally, I'd rush downstairs to help them, but today I needed time to think.

This morning's conversation had been an obvious attempt to get me to reevaluate my relationship with Scott. I had to admit I felt a strange sort of attraction to Matthew, but it was meaningless. My mom didn't understand Scott *was* the right person for me. Matthew was merely a bump in the road. A blip on the radar. A burr under my saddle. A snake in my boot.

And I didn't believe in the curse of the Campbell women. And who said a person was only destined to love once in a lifetime? The whole idea was ridiculous.

I got up to change. An excessive use of unrelated cowboy references meant I was overthinking things.

My phone rang. "Tarnation," I muttered. It was Scott.

"I was just thinking about you," I said as I hugged the phone against my ear. I had been thinking about him. Sort of. "I, uh, miss you."

"Aw. Sweet. Work is crazy busy. I only have a minute, but I wanted to hear your voice. I miss you too."

"Should I bring anything to your parents' house tomorrow?"

Scott chuckled. "No. They just want to meet you. I talk about you all the time, you know."

"You do?"

"Of course I do. I told you not to worry. They'll love you. I've got to go. Harrison is calling. Did your mom decide what to do yet?"

I frowned. "About what?"

He let out an exasperated sigh. "About the café. She's going to sell, isn't she? I could help her crunch numbers, if you'd like."

"She isn't selling the café, Scott."

There was silence on the other end of the line. For a second, I thought we'd been disconnected. "But she's considering it, right?"

"No. We've been over this before." I wanted to know why he asked, but he seemed distracted.

"Harrison keeps calling. He's been driving me nuts lately. Sorry, hon. I'd better take this."

He hung up, and I felt a little let down by the whole conversation. I'd never even had a chance to tell him about my father, and once again we'd gotten into a pointless discussion about the café.

Nothing was on the schedule for today, which was a relief. I visited Moses and helped Mom and Kate with lunch, but my mind kept going back to what my mom and I talked about that morning. I finally had a name for my father and knew something about him. I'd always thought it had been a one-night stand, only because mom said they didn't have much time together. I'd assumed that meant hours, not weeks.

I went out to spend some time in the garden. It always made me feel more at peace. Mom followed, carrying a tray with two steaming cups of coffee. We sat quietly side by side, both lost in thought.

"What did he look like?" I asked.

She took a sip of coffee, a little smile playing on her lips. "He had dark hair and green eyes, and he was very tall. You look like me, but I see bits of him in you. You have his dimple in your cheek and his smile."

I touched my cheek, like trying to feel a connection to my father through my dimple. Ridiculous. "Thanks for telling me, Mom."

"It was too painful to talk about it before, but now I sensed . . ." Her eyes scanned the garden, and she let out a wistful sigh. "It was the right time. Don't make a mistake that will mess up your whole life, Fiona. Don't be like Aunt Francesca. Don't be like me."

I stared straight ahead, watching as the fountain bubbled and gurgled up its pseudomagical water. "I won't."

CHAPTER 9

YOU ARE WHAT YOU EAT, SO DON'T BE CHEAP,
FAST, FAKE, OR EASY. -AUNT FRANCESCA

Getting ready to meet Scott's parents made me a nervous wreck. I couldn't decide what to wear, and discarded clothes soon piled up high on my bed. I finally chose a navy-blue vintage Dior dress I'd found at Second Hand Sally's down the street. Sally, a former NFL star who traded in her cleats for pumps a long time ago, had excellent taste in clothing, and she always put the best things aside for me as soon as they came in.

"I saw this and thought, 'Simple, classy, elegant. It screams Fiona.' I knew you'd love it," she said. I got up on my tiptoes to kiss her cheek.

"You're the best," I said, patting her face gently. "And you need to shave. You're all pinchy."

Sally batted her false eyelashes at me. She had on Chanel and was a six-foot-five-inch vision in pale pink. "My new beau likes me scruffy. It's so ridiculous what we do for love."

I understood exactly what she meant. My hands shook as I slipped on the beautiful dress. It fit like a glove and instantly made me feel better. A pair of navy-blue pumps and pearl earrings that had belonged to Aunt Francesca completed the outfit. I pulled my hair into a tight chignon, put on a touch of mascara and lipstick, and grabbed a navy-and-cream striped clutch I'd also found at Sally's. We were still in the midst of a rare summer cold snap, so I borrowed a pashmina scarf from Mom. I attributed the cold snap entirely to the fact we'd just paid hundreds of dollars to fix our air conditioner.

When I walked downstairs, Kate and Mom clapped, and Mom handed me a bouquet of flowers she'd put together for Scott's mom. "You look beautiful, darling," she said.

I smiled shyly. "Sally strikes again."

Kate nodded. "Sally is a genius. I got my boa there."

Kate wore her usual black, this time a strapless corset top, but she now had a black feathered boa wrapped around her neck. She looked fantastic. Chad evidently thought so too. He walked into the shop and took one look at Kate, and his jaw dropped. He stood there silently staring at her until Kate's cheeks grew pink from embarrassment.

"And Chad is speechless. A rare thing indeed," said Mom, and the spell was broken.

"I've got to go," murmured Kate as she grabbed her bag.

"I should get to work," said Chad at the same time.

Kate gave me a peck on the cheek. "Have fun tonight," she said. "And don't be nervous. They're going to love you."

I felt a little queasy. "Are you sure about that?"

Kate squeezed my hand. "If they don't, they're idiots who don't deserve you." That didn't make me feel better.

"Where's Fiona going?" asked Chad.

"To meet Scotty's, I mean *Scott*'s, parents," said Mom.

Chad's eyes found Kate's. "Must be nice."

Kate made a sound a little like a growl. Mom ignored it. "I'm sure they are lovely . . ." She tried to come up with the right word but didn't succeed. "Meatpackers." She looked pleased with herself. I rolled my eyes.

Chad laughed, but then his face got still. "You're joking, right?"

"Sadly, no," said Mom, "but I'm sure they're nice."

"But . . . but . . . but . . . but . . ." Chad was so upset he got stuck on the first word and couldn't move on.

"I know, Chad." I came to his rescue. "You're all vegetarians. I realize that, but most people are not. They eat meat. Scott's parents simply provide a service, much like we all do."

Chad muttered something that sounded like "unevolved, unethical barbarians" and stomped back into the kitchen to get ready for the poetry reading. Kate watched him go.

"Give him some tea. That'll make him feel better," she said.

Mom gave Kate an assessing look. "It might."

Kate's cheeks turned pink again. "I've got to go. See you tomorrow." Usually she stayed for the poetry readings, but tonight she rushed out the door.

I watched her leave. "Call me crazy, but I think love is in the air."

Mom grinned. "That's it, Fiona."

I didn't like that grin. I knew it well. "That's what?"

"The name of the tea I'll make for Sunday. Love Is in the Air. The ladies will adore it."

"We have to talk about your tea. We don't need a bunch of sex-hungry seniors on our hands. What exactly are you putting in it?"

The bell above the door rang, and Scott walked in, looking perfect as always. His neatly cut hair curled over his collar in a way I found sexy. His blue eyes were bright, and his suit didn't have a single wrinkle.

"Oh, look. It's the Ken doll," Mom said softly. I elbowed her and walked over to give Scott a hug. He smelled wonderful, like starch and soap and expensive cologne.

He kissed my cheek, careful to avoid my lipstick. "Are you ready?"

I nodded, feeling a nervous flutter in my chest, and waved goodbye to Mom. She bit her lower lip. She was nervous too.

It turned out I had nothing major to worry about. Scott's parents were nice and welcomed me graciously into their home. They lived in a giant colonial positioned very prettily among the rolling hills just outside of a town called Butler. I didn't see much of the actual town itself, but I enjoyed the quiet beauty of the country and the drive on long, scenic, winding roads that led past farms and forests. It was nice here and completely the opposite of what I'd grown used to living in the South Side.

"It's so quiet," I said.

"I know," he said with a smile. "Don't you love it?"

Scott's mother, blonde and slightly chubby, had a broad, sweet face and an infectious laugh. His father was a taller, grayer version of Scott. The meal his mother prepared relied heavily on steak, frozen vegetables, and processed cheese, and their taste in wine was abysmal, but I liked his parents, and they seemed to like me too. They were an average family, what I'd always wanted, but to my great surprise, I found them . . . boring. Mr. Lipmann talked about two subjects: his health and his time spent playing football a million years ago in college. Mrs. Lipmann talked about one subject only. Scott. By the end of the night, I could barely keep my eyes open.

Just when I thought the meal would never end, Mrs. Lipmann stood up and led me into the formal sitting room. "So the menfolk can talk," she said.

Images of Scott and Mr. Lipmann drinking port liquor and smoking pipes filled my head, and I held back a giggle. No port for me, however. She handed me a cup of coffee. *Instant* coffee. I did my best to drink it without making a face.

Photos of Scott covered the walls like a shrine. Scott as a

chubby baby. Scott with a gap between his teeth in second grade. Scott in several photos with a curvy, attractive redhead.

"Oh. That's Brittany." Mrs. Lipmann stood next to me and used a tissue to remove a smudge from the glass. "Her parents are our best friends. They live just down the road."

"How nice," I said, not sure how to respond. He'd never mentioned Brittany to me, and some of the photos looked recent. Very recent. In one photo, he had on the same suit he wore tonight.

Mrs. Lipmann seemed to read my thoughts. "They broke up a few months ago. We always assumed they'd end up together. We even bought an extra parcel of land linking our property to her parents' property. We thought someday they'd build a house and raise their children there. Join the garden club and volunteer at different social functions. You know what I mean. Now they aren't together anymore, so I guess some other lucky girl will snatch up her spot." She gave me a wink, and suddenly I felt a cold wave of panic seize me. I didn't want Brittany's spot, and I didn't want to build a house next door to the Lipmanns. She continued, oblivious. "There is the business to run too."

"The meatpacking plant?" I asked as the wave of panic I'd felt reached tsunami levels.

"Mr. Lipmann is getting too old to handle all the stress of it himself. I know Scott likes his job in the city, but it's time for him to come home and take some of the responsibility off his father's shoulders. He's sowed his wild oats long enough."

I couldn't tell if she meant I was his wild oats in this analogy or not, but I certainly hadn't been sowed. Not recently at least and definitely not by Scott.

"I'm sure he'll do the right thing." A generic response but the best I could come up with.

She patted my hand. "I know he will."

Scott stuck his head in the door. "Are you two done gossiping about me yet?"

Mrs. Lipmann giggled, her laugh not quite as infectious as earlier. I gave him a feeble smile and glanced at my watch. "It's getting late, Scott."

He rolled his eyes. "And you have to work tomorrow. Making granola muffins for homeless hippies or something. I know, I know. We'd better get going."

He kissed his mother and shook his dad's hand. "Remember what we talked about, son," said Mr. Lipmann.

Scott gave him a tight smile. "Like you'd ever let me forget?"

"What was that about?" I asked as we climbed into the car.

He shrugged. "Nothing. Family stuff. My dad wants me to help out more with his business."

"Your mom said something to me about it too."

"It's not going to happen. Not right now at least. I'm too busy, and I love working for Burgess and Garrett. Big things are happening there, and I'm excited to be a part of it."

I let out a little sigh of relief. "Good for you, Scott." *Good for me too.*

He linked his hand with mine. "I knew you'd get on well with my mom. She's a hoot. My dad's a great guy, too, and I could tell they both really liked you."

I nodded, distracted. I couldn't get a good read on Mrs. Lipmann. She may have just been chatty and conversational, but I felt like she had an agenda, and I was an unexpected complication.

"They were both very . . . nice," I said, stifling a yawn. "Sorry. We've been busy at the café lately. I'm kind of worn out."

"You work too hard." He brought my hand to his lips,

never taking his eyes off the road, and kissed my fingers one by one. "Can't you imagine us like them someday?"

"Like who?"

"My parents. A big house in the country. A bunch of kids . . ."

"Oh. Wow."

Suddenly, I felt claustrophobic, like the car closed in on me. I pulled my hand back to my lap and took deep, slow yoga breaths as I tried to calm myself down. The reaction was a physical, visceral sort of thing, and it took me by surprise.

Scott didn't seem to notice I was one step away from jumping out of the car and making a run for my life. He smiled at me, reaching for my hand again.

"What size ring do you wear?"

"Huh?"

He laughed, caressing my left ring finger. "You have to know why I'm asking . . ."

"No. I don't." I sounded harsher than I'd intended, but that was because I choked out the words over the wall of pure, raw terror filling my chest.

He got quiet and let go of my hand. "Maybe we should talk about this later."

I turned my face and noticed with a sense of relief the lights of the city as they rushed past my window. We were almost home, but my hands remained clenched into little fists on my lap. I didn't understand what had just happened, and I felt a little out of control, which frightened me.

"Maybe that's a good idea," I said, my voice small and unsteady in the quiet interior of the car. "Let's talk about it later."

When we arrived back at the café, he opened the car door for me and helped me out.

I saw the hurt in his eyes. I'd hoped to avoid a discussion, but Scott, it seemed, couldn't let it go.

"What's wrong, Fiona? Tell me. Please."

I stared up at him. In the moonlight, he looked like a lost statue of Adonis wandering the streets of the South Side. But Adonis didn't belong here, and neither did Scott.

"When did you and Brittany break up? Judging by the photos all over your parents' house, it seems like it happened recently, yet you've never so much as mentioned her existence."

He ran a distracted hand through his hair. "She was my high school sweetheart. When we broke up, my parents took it pretty hard."

"But you still didn't answer my question. When exactly did it happen?"

He shoved his hands deep into the pockets of his pants. "A few weeks before I walked into your shop and fell head over heels for you."

I pursed my lips, folding my arms across my chest. "I'm a rebound?"

He reached for me, putting his hands on my upper arms, his eyes searching my face. "No. It's not like that at all. I caught her cheating on me with my best friend. I walked in on them. It was the worst moment of my life, but things had been different between us for a long time. We stayed together more out of habit than anything else, and I was ready to move on. Do you understand?"

"I guess so."

His answer should have satisfied me, but it didn't. I felt unsettled and irritated. It must have been pretty obvious.

"But you're still angry," he said.

"It isn't about Brittany, Scott."

"So what is it?"

I let out a long breath. "The granola muffins comment."

He let out an exasperated breath. "You're seriously mad about *that?* It was a joke. Lighten up."

I wrapped my mom's pashmina shawl more tightly around my shoulders. "No. I'm tired of the way you constantly devalue what I do."

He frowned, his brows drawing together, like he couldn't understand my logic. "The cookie baking? Is that seriously your life plan? I thought you had actual goals, Fiona. Are you getting your MBA so you can *bake*?"

The more his temper flared, the more mine rose to meet it. "First of all, I'm a good baker. Some people even call me an artist."

He snorted. "One of your mother's many friends, I assume. So typical."

I glared at him. My heart pounded in my chest, and my cheeks felt burning hot. Even my breathing accelerated. I'd gone from mildly irritated to full-on furious in seconds. When I spoke, the words I said surprised Scott as much as they surprised me, but I couldn't help it. They just came out.

"I think we should take a break."

Scott seemed clearly confused. "What?"

I let out a heavy sigh. "I need time to figure things out."

He tilted his head to one side, forcing me to look at his face. "What kind of things?"

I heard the hint of tears in his voice, and it freaked me out a little. "You and me. This just isn't working."

"But it was working. Perfectly. I don't understand what changed. All of a sudden, you're so *different*."

I couldn't explain it either. I kept thinking about the curse of the Campbell women. Even though I knew it had to be a bunch of nonsense, it still made me nervous. My mom and Aunt Francesca both made mistakes that nearly ruined their lives. Was I on the same path? I hoped not, but I couldn't be certain. I just knew this was the right thing to do.

I folded my arms across my chest and tried to explain it to him as gently as I could. "Look, it's not your fault, but I can't do this right now. With Moses getting hurt and Anderson breathing down our necks . . ."

All the anger went out of him in an instant. He shoved his hands deep into his pockets and leaned against his car, his expression solemn. "I understand. Work has been crazy lately for me, too, but that's no excuse. You've been under a lot of stress, and I should have been here for you. I'm sorry, Fi."

"Thank you."

He touched my cheek. "I'm not happy about it, but I'll give you as much time as you need to get your head on straight. I know, eventually, you'll see the truth.'

"The truth?"

"We're perfect for each other, and we were meant to be together."

"Scott, I don't know . . ."

"I do, and you'll figure it out too. But until then, I need to ask you a favor. Can we still be friends? It would mean a lot to me."

He held out his hand. I stared at it a moment before clasping it with my own.

"Of course," I said.

He pulled me close to give me a hug. He smelled delicious. Part of me wanted to tell him I'd changed my mind, but I knew I wasn't prepared to talk about rings and houses in the country and jobs at a meatpacking plant, and I wasn't prepared to make any promises I couldn't keep.

CHAPTER 10

MODERATION IS DEFINITELY THE ANSWER,
BUT WHAT WAS THE QUESTION? -AUNT
FRANCESCA

It rained all day Friday, the perfect atmosphere for Madame Lucinda's tarot card reading. Although she wasn't a witch, she certainly liked to dress the part. Tonight she had on bat earrings and a broomstick brooch. She dyed her hair brilliant red, and sometimes for special occasions, she even wore a pointy witch's hat.

I'd known Madame Lucinda my entire life. Usually I dreaded her readings, but tonight I wanted to ask her if she'd heard anything more about what happened to Moses.

As soon as I sat down, she started reading the cards. "I see a tall, dark, handsome stranger."

"You told me the same thing last time," I said, giving her a dirty look.

The wind howled outside as she continued to work with the cards. "No. I said a stranger was *coming*. Guess what? Now he's here."

Lightning shot across the sky, brightening the dark shop and making me gasp. The fact Madame Lucinda insisted we illuminate only with candles added to the creepy, other-worldly effect.

She turned over another card, and an ornately painted red heart glowed up at us. "Oh. Love," she said. "You're going to fall in love, Fiona. How nice."

"You said *that* last time too. Is this a rerun, or can we see a new episode eventually?"

She ignored me and turned over the next card. It showed two naked people entwined in a romantic embrace. "Desire." She gave me a saucy wink. "And that was definitely not in the cards before."

Kate peeked over my shoulder and inhaled sharply. "Gosh. It's true. Are you hot for someone?" The question died on her lips when she caught me glaring at her.

"Of course I'm hot for someone. Scott. Duh."

I still thought he was hot, so technically this couldn't be classified as lying. Yes, I'd broken up with him, but I saw no need to broadcast it. I'd tell Kate later when we were alone.

"Then why didn't it show up before?" Kate asked, her brow furrowing in confusion.

I didn't answer, mostly because Madame Lucinda had just revealed the next card, and it sent a chill up my spine. "A man with two faces?" I asked.

Madame Lucinda's green eyes met mine over the table. "Yes. Deceit."

"Oh, great. Well, thanks, Madame Lucinda. Delightful, as always. We have a few minutes before the people who signed up for a reading show up. Do you mind if I ask you some questions?"

She looked surprised. "About the cards?"

I shook my head. "About Moses. Have you heard anything regarding what happened?"

"Nothing. Except . . ."

"What?"

She leaned forward. "Whoever did this to him was inside the café. They may have even attacked him right here."

"Why do you say that? Please don't tell me the cards told you, because if you do, I'm never going to sit for another tarot card torture session with you again."

"Not the cards, silly. It's common sense." She gave me a steady look. "Where did your mom keep the scrub brush?"

I thought about the long black streaks on the kitchen floor. The bag of crushed cookies. Realization hit as a sick wave of nausea passed over me. "In her office, behind the door."

Not only had someone hurt Moses in the café, but they'd dragged him to the door and thrown him outside like a pile of garbage. The idea horrified me, but now I also had other things to worry about. I gripped Madame Lucinda's hand. "Things are bad enough here right now with Anderson and everything else. If people find out someone was attacked *inside* the café . . ."

"I won't say a word." She pretended to zip her lips and then sent a worried glance to the door leading to the alleyway. "We should have a séance, though. That might help."

I blinked and let go of her hand. "A what?"

"To pick up the energies of what happened. It might give us a clue who is behind it. Bad events leave behind a residue, like scum in the bathtub."

I shook my head in disbelief as I stood to go back to the kitchen. "I shouldn't have even brought this up. I never learn."

She stopped me, her dark eyes serious. I saw something else on her face as well. Fear. "You need to be careful. Don't ignore the warning, Fiona. I sense something dark and dangerous in the cards tonight."

"Got it." I didn't put a lot of stock in Madame Lucinda's readings, but this week she'd frightened me more than I cared to admit.

Kate gave me a quick kiss on the cheek. "I've got to go. Mrs. Porter is waiting for me, and storms make her nervous."

Mrs. Porter, Kate's elderly roommate, was mentally alert but physically frail. Her daughters lived in the suburbs and hired Kate to stay with her, mostly for their own peace of mind. Although they wanted her to move in with them, she refused to leave her beautiful, stately home.

It worked out well for Kate. She lived rent-free in a giant house that was more like a mansion in what had once been the ritzy section of the South Side, and Mrs. Porter was able to feel independent for what remained of her life.

We served dessert and coffee for the tarot readings. I put out a tray of cookies and sliced up Mrs. Yoder's lovely pies. My mom handled the rest, so I went upstairs to read a book and relax. The storm raged outside, but a sizable crowd had assembled for the reading. I turned on the light next to my bed and pulled a book off the shelf.

After about two minutes, I slammed the book shut. I couldn't stop thinking about the stupid tarot cards, and Madame Lucinda's words about Moses haunted me. I wanted to tell Matthew about it but had no way to contact him. My phone rang, and I grabbed it from my nightstand, hoping for a split second it was Matthew. It wasn't. It was Scott, and the noises in the background told me he was in a bar. Again.

"Sweet Fiona. Lovely, lovely girl. I'm sorry I made you mad. Are we still taking a break?"

"Yes, we are, Scott." I rolled my eyes. A drunk dial. Great. "Where are you?"

"At Zookie's with Harrison. We're celebrating. We got some good news at work today." Someone yelled, and Scott laughed. "I've got to go. Harrison is making an ass of himself."

"How unusual," I muttered, but Scott didn't hear me.

"I'll be in meetings all day tomorrow, but I think we need to talk."

"We've pretty much covered it, Scott . . ."

He interrupted me, slurring his words slightly. "I know my parents can be a little intimidating, but you're always so beautiful. I love that about you."

"Gee, thanks. What does that have to do with anything?"

"I wanted you to know. Consider what I said, okay? I think I figured out the problem, and you've got it all wrong. You're uncomfortable because my parents have money, but they aren't snobs. You don't have to be embarrassed."

He hung up the phone, and I stared at it. Embarrassed?

Lightning struck again, and the room got dark. Thankfully, because of the candles filling the shop tonight, the people downstairs would be fine. I grabbed a candle from my nightstand and lit it. As soon as I did, the lights flickered back on, but I worried they could go out again. I carried the candle into the bathroom and ran a bath in our clawfoot tub.

I poured some fragrant bubble bath and slipped into the water. The candle smelled like vanilla. The bubble bath was lavender. Aromatherapy heaven, but I still couldn't relax.

"Embarrassed?"

I let out a huff, getting even angrier the more I thought about it. Scott came from money and was proud it. But why should I be embarrassed? Mom was an independent business-woman. She'd made a life for both of us from her little shop. I had no reason to feel ashamed.

I soaked in the tub until my fingers and toes pickled, but I still felt tense. I decided to slip downstairs and have a glass of wine, which would put me straight to sleep. I pulled on my pink robe and fluffy slippers, tucked my hair into a messy bun, and snuck down the back staircase into the kitchen, my cheeks still rosy from the bath.

One of the windows in the kitchen was open a crack, and

the night air made me shiver. The storm had passed, but an occasional streak of lightning flashed in the distance.

I pulled my robe tightly around my body. The tarot reading continued, so no one would come into the kitchen anytime soon. I planned to pour myself a glass of red and scurry right back up to my bedroom.

Mom left a small light on over the stove. I walked over to the wine rack in the back corner of the kitchen and chose a nice pinot noir, humming "Red, Red Wine" as I checked the label.

A voice made me jump. "Drinking alone is the first sign of a problem."

Matthew sat at the kitchen island, eating a whoopie pie. I clutched the robe closer to my chest. "What are you doing here?"

"Do you realize you ask me that a lot?"

"Answer my question, please."

He grinned. "You're so cute when you're angry. Like a crazed . . . kitten or something."

I tapped my foot on the linoleum floor, and he held up his hands in defeat. "Madame Lucinda asked me to come for a reading."

I uncorked the wine and grabbed two glasses. "Did she tell you about a handsome stranger? Her usual line?"

"No," said Matthew. He lifted his glass. "Cheers."

I lifted mine and took a sip, sighing. "This is nice."

Matthew looked at the label. "And expensive."

"Mom has excellent taste in wine. And she gets a discount. She's friends with the owner of the wine shop down the street."

Matthew raised his glass again. "A good friend to have, indeed."

I took another sip. "You were going to tell me what Madame Lucinda predicted for you."

"No, I wasn't." Matthew's eyes twinkled as he took another sip of wine.

I scowled at him. "No fun at all."

He grinned. "Your mom told me there were some whoopie pies left and said I should grab one. So I did." He handed me one.

"Mrs. Yoder is some kind of Amish whoopie pie genius," I said, taking a bite.

He nodded. "Yes, she is. But these don't compare to your cookies, Fiona."

I shrugged. "Cookies are easy. Anyone can do it."

He put his hand on mine. "Don't sell yourself short. You're an amazing baker. A genius."

When Moses said I had magic at my fingertips, it was one thing. He was an old and dear friend. When Matthew complimented me so sincerely, it was something else entirely. My cheeks flushed with pride as I pulled my hand away.

"Thanks, Matthew. But these whoopie pies pair very nicely with a good pinot noir."

We sat at the island, chatting, drinking, and sharing the rest of the whoopie pies. I told him about the scrub brush and the black streaks on the floor, and he agreed with my conclusions.

"Did she know anything else?"

I shook my head. "No, and it surprises me. She has her finger on the pulse of this place. People tell her things. Secrets. If there were any rumors circulating, she would have been the first to know. I'm worried we might never find out the truth."

Matthew covered my hand again with his, and this time I didn't pull away. "But we'll keep asking anyway," he said.

"We will," I said softly, not sure if there was any point. I understood why the police had such a resigned attitude toward cases like this. It would be a miracle if we uncovered anything.

It didn't take long for me to feel a little buzzed. I'd only had a few glasses, but tonight it seemed to go straight to my head. I reached for the bottle, nearly slipping off the stool, when Mom walked in.

"Fiona. I thought you went to bed."

"I did. Or at least I tried to. But I couldn't. I was restless. And irritated. Very irritated."

"Are you *drunk?*" she asked with a little laugh.

Matthew looked at me in surprise. "You only had two glasses."

"Big glasses. Full glasses. And wine affects me more than any other alcohol. I don't know why. What can I say? I'm a cheap date." I frowned. "Was our lunch at Wicked Wienies a date? I told Kate it wasn't, but now I'm not sure."

Mom rolled her eyes. "She hasn't been herself lately. She's upset about Moses." She lowered her voice like I wouldn't hear her from two feet away.

"Um, I can hear you," I said in a stage whisper. "I'm not upset. Not anymore at least. Nurse Brenda said he's doing better, and I'm feeling very not upset at all at the moment. About anything."

I reached for the bottle, this time without falling off the stool, but Matthew took it from my hands and corked it. I frowned. "You're mean, Matthew."

Mom rolled her eyes. "Matthew, I have to take care of our customers. Would you mind escorting Fiona up to her room? I'm afraid she'll fall down the stairs in this condition."

Matthew stood up. "Should I make her drink some coffee first?"

"She needs to sleep. She hasn't been getting enough the last few days." She patted his arm. "Thank you, dear."

He helped me off the stool and offered his arm. "Shall I escort you?"

"Oh, escorting. So formal," I said with a little giggle as Matthew hooked his arm in mine.

"Lead on, m'lady." His words made me laugh so hard I barely made it up the narrow staircase to my room.

"I love this staircase. It's so twisty and winding and fun," I said as Matthew half pushed me up.

"Yes. Lots of fun. Although they put these in originally for servants so they could run up and down without using the formal rooms in the front."

I came to a dead stop and stared at him. "You're *smart*."

He laughed. "And you're *drunk*."

We finally made it to the door of my bedroom. I swayed slightly, and Matthew put his hands on my arms to steady me.

"Two glasses of wine. Hard to believe."

"I know. The good news is I never get hungover."

He raised a dark eyebrow at my comment. "You don't drink enough to get hungover."

I touched his eyebrow with my finger. "How do you do that? I can't." I tried to lift one eyebrow and failed miserably. "It makes you look even more like a sexy French pirate."

"A sexy French pirate?" Matthew bit his lip.

Suddenly, I couldn't tear my gaze away. His lips were beautiful. "I thought so since the first time I saw you." I reached up to touch his face. "A very sexy, very naughty French pirate."

Matthew took my hand and put it back down by my side. "Fiona . . ." he said, but I interrupted him by falling forward. I'm not sure if I did it on purpose or by accident, but it had the desired effect. He wrapped his arms around me, and I nuzzled his neck.

I sighed. "You even smell like a French pirate, like spices and soap and whoopie pies."

"I don't think French pirates bathed. They wouldn't have

smelled nice. You, on the other hand, smell heavenly. Like lavender." He put his nose in my hair and inhaled. I snuggled closer, wrapping my arms around his waist.

"Heavenly," I said, murmuring the words against his skin.

Matthew pushed me away, gently but firmly. "You've had too much to drink."

I held up one finger and tried unsuccessfully to focus on it. "I only had one glass. Or maybe two."

"One too many."

I stuck out my lip in a pout. "Mean, mean Matthew."

"Yes, I'm mean." He led me to my bed, pulled down the covers, and helped me crawl inside. "And you're drunk. If you were sober, I'd climb into bed with you."

My eyes were half-closed, but I forced them open. "Would you? Truly?"

Matthew brushed a lock of hair off my face and gave me a lingering kiss on my forehead. "Yes, Fiona, I would," he said softly.

"What a nice thing to say." I squeezed his hand.

"You only think so because you're three sheets to the wind at the moment. Any other time, you would yell at me."

"Not true, and I'm not *that* drunk," I said with a yawn.

Matthew chuckled and blew out the candle next to my bed. "Goodnight, Fiona. Sweet dreams."

"Mean, mean Matthew," I mumbled and closed my eyes.

CHAPTER 11

NOTHING STARTS THE DAY OFF BETTER THAN
A LEISURELY BREAKFAST WITH A SPECIAL
FRIEND. -AUNT FRANCESCA

The next morning, I woke up and made cream puffs, always a huge hit with the tea ladies, but my mind was not in its usual peaceful baking state. It churned, in fact. I'd embarrassed myself by getting tipsy at the tarot card reading and didn't want to see Matthew tonight at acoustic night. I was unhappy with how things had gone with Scott, and part of me wished we could have a redo. Moses still hadn't woken up, and I couldn't get Simon the chocolate-loving Belgian out of my head. My father now had a name and a face and a dimple in his cheek. A lot to handle. Adding to that was the approaching deadline for the council meeting, looming like a dark, ominous cloud on the horizon. The fate of our café was in the hands of a bunch of strangers, and I was helpless to stop it, change it, or prevent it. It made me want to scream in frustration, but screaming wouldn't help anything either.

I blew out a sigh, hoping to find something to distract me. It was still cool outside; the normal hot summer weather was supposed to resume tomorrow. Kneading a few loaves of bread would make me feel much better.

Mom had already made coffee and worked outside in the garden. Kate came in, a vision in tight black capris and a sheer-red silk blouse with a black lace bra underneath. Kate was always sexy and voluptuous, but she was not a morning person. She went straight for the coffee and sipped it while I started on the bread.

Mom, on the other hand, *was* a morning person. She blew into the kitchen, her arms full of fresh flowers. She put some in vases and arranged others in bouquets to sell.

"I never had the chance to ask you. How did thing go with Scott's parents the other night?" she asked as she worked on the flowers. Kate, beginning to wake up, moved closer to help her.

I shrugged. "Okay."

They exchanged a look. "What happened?" asked Kate.

Mom put a hand on my arm. "Were they mean to you?"

I shook my head. "They were nice and very, very . . . normal."

Until I'd met the Lipmanns, Mom's ability to cook, garden, and select the perfect wine for every meal didn't seem like anything special. I'd been so used to it I'd never noticed or appreciated it before. Suddenly I saw her in a different light.

"What do you mean exactly?" Kate lifted her cat's-eye sunglasses on to her forehead and stared at me. The Betty Boop tattoo on her chest, near the curve of her ample bosom, seemed to stare at me too.

I sighed, and the words came out in a rush. "Oh gosh. They were so *boring*. And I realized something that night. I'm a total snob."

I told them about the awful wine and the weird food. I joked about Mr. Lipmann's football obsession and Mrs. Lipmann's obsession with Scott. My mom started to giggle, and it was contagious. Before long, we were all laughing.

Kate wiped away a tear. "As I have always told you, normal is overrated."

"You were right, Kate."

Kate was still giggling, but she'd given me something to think about as I kneaded my dough. Maybe normal wasn't all it was cracked up to be.

"Tell me more about them," said Mom as she arranged flowers, another thing she did amazingly well.

"Mrs. Lipmann had only artificial flowers, most of them in colors never found in nature," I said as I pounded the dough. "And Mr. Lipmann has a prostate problem. I got to hear all about it over dessert."

Mom seemed very interested in her arrangement all of a sudden, probably to avoid looking at Kate. Kate stared at her nails, most likely to avoid making eye contact with Mom. It didn't work. What started as a soft rumble of laughter between the three of us transformed quickly into huge, almost painful gasps. Soon, we laughed so hard Kate snorted, which made it even worse.

At that moment, Matthew walked in. I had flour on my cheeks, and tears poured down my face. I couldn't stand up straight. I was bent over at this point, and my sides ached.

"Have you been drinking again?" he asked.

There was no hope for us after that. I ended up on the floor, curled in a ball, with my back against the island. Mom and Kate joined me. Matthew laughed, too, even though he no idea what was going on, and sat next to us on the floor. He had flour on his dark jeans and shirt, but he still looked incredibly hot. It took a while, but the laughing fit finally ended with a few final residual giggles. Kate had the hiccups.

"I needed that," said Mom with a sigh. "Laughter truly is the best medicine."

She helped Kate get up, and together they put the bouquets in buckets outside and in vases for the shop. I smiled at Matthew, and he wiped a bit of flour off my face. I'd thought things would be awkward between us, but they were fine.

He got to his feet and helped me up. "What are you making now, goddess?"

I blinked in surprise, and he pointed to my apron. It said "Domestic Goddess" in pink, glittery letters.

"I never check to see what these say. We had twenty-five in the sample box. I just grab the first clean one and use it."

"Well, I'm glad the kitchen bitch isn't here today. She scared me."

I laughed. "She was pretty scary." I narrowed my eyes. "Why are you here?"

"Again with the same question." He shook his head. "You told me about the pancake place on the corner. I wanted to try it, but I'm sick of eating alone. Feel like some breakfast?"

I bit my lip. "I don't know . . ."

Matthew lifted his hands. "Not a date. Friends can eat pancakes together. Right?"

I stared at him for a long moment. "I *am* pretty hungry."

He smiled. "It doesn't surprise me. I've seen you eat."

I wrinkled my nose at him. "On one condition. I get to pay this time."

I ran upstairs to change my clothes, whipping off my normal baking gear of shorts and a cami and putting on a miniskirt and a pretty, sleeveless blouse. I took my hair out of its bun and brushed it until it shone and fell over my shoulders like a blonde waterfall. I also washed the flour off my face and put on a little lipstick and some of the expensive perfume Auntie Mags gave me for Christmas. I slipped on a pair of sandals when my phone rang. It was Scott. I blew out a long breath and answered it.

"I'm sorry about last night. I shouldn't have called you from a bar."

"It's okay," I said.

"And I'm sorry about our argument. Not how I intended things to go."

I hadn't thought about Scott once since Matthew walked through the door, which probably made me a bad person. It also made me even more certain about what I'd done.

"I'm sorry, too, but I still think we're making the right decision."

He paused for a moment. "I'm going to my parents' for the weekend. I won't be back until late on Sunday. Can I stop by sometime to chat?"

I winced, not certain it was a good idea but unable to come up with a valid reason for my hesitation. "Sure."

"Thanks, Fi. I'd come sooner, but my parents need me. They're having some issues with the plant, and I want to sort things out for them."

"You're a good son, Scott."

"To those whom much is given, much is expected. Talk to you later."

I hung up the phone, shaking my head as I thought about his last comment. Scott's parents owned a meatpacking plant. They were not the Kennedys. Scott had occasional delusions of grandeur, but I kind of blamed his parents. He was their spoiled, cosseted little boy and more than a bit self-centered, although I hadn't noticed until recently.

Very recently.

Like as soon as Auntie Mags opened my blocked chakras.

I knew it was a coincidence, but it still made me wonder. Had she actually changed something inside me? I shook my head as I ran down the narrow steps to meet Matthew. It couldn't be. My feelings had changed for Scott simply because they'd changed. It had nothing to do with Auntie Mags, and it also had nothing to do with the man I was eating breakfast with this morning. I was sure of that too. Sort of.

Pamela's had a funky fifties vibe of checkerboard patterns and silver chairs with pastel vinyl cushions. Photographs of old movie stars lined the walls, some of them autographed. Only a few doors down from the café, the diner had been around forever. It would be gone soon, however, if Mr. McAlister sold the building. We got a table by the window and looked through the menus.

"What do you recommend?" asked Matthew.

"Everything."

He laughed. "Can you narrow that down?"

I shook my head. "It's all wonderful, but you should have the pancakes since it's your first time."

Matthew got blueberry pancakes, and I ordered banana walnut. As soon as he took a bite, he sighed with pleasure. "Incredible."

I got some of the banana walnut on my fork and put it into his mouth. He groaned again. "Even better. Trade me."

I shook my head, giggling, as we chatted like old friends. I told him the news about my father, and he reacted appropriately. "How crazy. Are you okay?"

My mouth was full of pancakes, making it difficult to answer. "It's nice knowing they loved each other."

Matthew leaned forward, his face serious. "It doesn't make sense. There must have been some kind of misunderstanding. Something happened to stop him from meeting her."

"Like what?"

His eyes met mine, and the temperature in the room went up by about ten degrees. "I don't know, but if I loved someone the way your father loved your mom, I'd *never* let her go."

Rosie, our waitress, came over to fill our coffee cups, breaking the spell. "Any news about Moses?" she asked.

"Not much. He's getting better, but he has a long way to go."

She shook her head sadly. "It's so awful. We've all been talking about it, but no one has any idea who would do such a thing."

"If you hear anything, even something small, would you let us know?"

"Sure, sweetie. Is this the boyfriend I've heard so much about?"

I froze, and Matthew watched me closely. "Uh, no. This is Matthew. He's hosting acoustic night until Frankie comes back."

Rosie smiled. "Nice to meet you," she said, turning to me. "I have something important to ask you, Fiona. How would you feel about speaking for us at the council meeting?"

I almost choked on my pancake. "What do you mean?"

Rosie was my mom's age, and she treated me like one of her own. Having six kids made her awfully good at mothering. She had faded red hair and bright blue eyes and wore a pink T-shirt that read "Pamela's Diner" in sparkly silver letters. She wrote out our bill and laid it on the table.

"We've been talking, and we think you should be in charge."

The banana-walnut pancakes suddenly felt like a dead weight in the pit of my stomach. "Who's been talking?"

Rosie slid into the chair next to mine. "Everyone on the block. You're cute as a bug, good with numbers, and can think on your feet. Also, you know this place better than anyone. We thought about asking your mom, but you know how she is."

Yep. I did. Mom would get emotional and cry in the middle of her speech. It had happened before.

I fiddled with my napkin. "I don't know if it should be me, Rosie. It's a lot of responsibility . . ."

She patted my hand. "If we didn't think you could handle it, we wouldn't ask."

"Oh. Great. Thanks."

She winked at me. "Thank *you*. Goodness knows we need you, girlie. It looks pretty bleak at the moment."

I'd never actually agreed to do it, but Rosie considered it a done deal. She got up and went back to work. Matthew watched me as he finished his pancakes. I dipped a bite of pancake in syrup but wasn't hungry anymore.

"What are you going to do?"

"I guess I'll have to help. So many people will lose their jobs if we fail. Rosie has six kids and has worked here since she was in high school. What would she do if this place closed? And Sally at the secondhand shop is transgender. Do you think Macy's will hire her if she has to close her shop? Probably not. She doesn't quite fit the Macy's mold, or any other mold, to be honest. And my mom . . ."

Matthew interrupted. "I was asking about your pancakes, but I agree with what you said." I laughed, unable to stop myself, and he grinned back at me.

"Here. Take them," I said. I pushed my plate over to his side of the table, and he immediately dug in. His plate had already been wiped clean.

"Thanks," he said, his mouth full of banana-walnut goodness.

I grabbed my napkin and wiped a bit off his chin. "You have no shame."

He smiled at me, looking like a naughty child. "None at all. These pancakes are fantastic."

"Did you know Julia Child visited Pamela's years ago?"

"So cool," he said, his mouth crammed with pancakes.

"It's more than cool. She loved it, and that woman knew her stuff. She was a culinary rock star." I looked around the restaurant. "I love this place, too, but Scott won't eat here."

Matthew's eyes narrowed. "Why not?"

"He says it's old and dirty." My voice was a whisper. I didn't want Rosie to hear. "It's not true. I mean, the building is old, of course, but Scott doesn't understand it has character."

Matthew studied the high ceiling and the eclectic interior of the shop. "This place is a treasure." He gave me an irate look.

I put down my napkin. "I agree. Why are you mad?"

"Why aren't *you* mad? And why are you with him? Is it because you actually like him, or do you just like the suit and all it represents?" He leaned forward until his face was close to mine. "That would make you awfully shallow. And spineless too."

I blinked, feeling verbally slapped. I picked up the bill and pushed back my chair. "It's none of your concern, is it?"

I got up to leave, and Matthew grabbed my hand. "I'm sorry. I didn't mean it."

I pulled my hand away from his. "Yes, you did. Let me go please."

He *had* meant it. And the sad truth was he might have been right.

CHAPTER 12

I thought about what Matthew said while punching down the bread dough and kneading it. I thought about it some more as I made the shells for cream puffs. I also whipped up vanilla pudding as a filling and covered it in plastic so it wouldn't get a skin. I decided biscotti with dried cranberries would be a good idea and made several different kinds of scones, both savory and sweet. When I finally finished, covered in a layer of flour and sugar and with aching arms, I realized it hadn't helped. I still thought about Matthew and what he'd said.

Kate came into the kitchen and looked around. "What happened in here?"

I stared around at the chaos I'd created in the kitchen. "I broke up with Scott."

Her jaw dropped. "No way. What did your mom say?"

I grimaced. "I haven't told her yet. It's kind of new."

She pulled herself up onto one of the stools and rested her elbows on the island. "It's weird you haven't told her, don't you think?"

I shrugged, but Kate was right. I just wasn't prepared to

deal with it yet. After the lecture on making good choices, an immature and irrational part of me didn't want my mom to think I'd broken up with him based on her advice. She might not say anything, but I knew she'd think it, and that irritated me. And she and I had been a bit awkward with each other ever since she told me about my father.

"Speaking of my mother, she dropped a bit of a bomb on me the other day." I told her about my father, and Kate listened, wide-eyed.

"And your mom never heard from him again?"

"Nope." I handed her a biscotti dipped in white chocolate.

"That's horrible," she said, taking a bite of the biscotti and groaning with pleasure. "But this biscotti is the opposite of horrible. It's fantastic. I love it when you're upset, Fiona. Your tension baking is delicious."

I put pots and pans into the sink, banging them loudly. Kate came up behind me, still munching on the biscotti. "Is something *else* bothering you, my biscotti-making friend?"

I stuck my hands in the sudsy water. "Am I too focused on appearances . . . and money?"

She pondered this like she was trying to figure out the correct answer. It spoke volumes. "Um, what do you mean?"

"Matthew told me I'm shallow."

"You aren't shallow, Fi. Not at all. If you're a little fixated on financial success, it's because that's always been a struggle for you. You've managed things here since you were in diapers. I know you. You don't want money for status. You want it for safety. There's a big difference there."

I stared at her. "Wow. You've thought about this, haven't you?"

She shrugged. "I'm a poet. I ponder."

"Matthew Monroe also insinuated I went along with whatever Scott wanted, implying I don't think for myself."

Kate opened her mouth and then paused. She'd obviously pondered this too. "Well. You *are* easygoing."

My eyes widened. "You think I'm a pushover?"

She shook her head. "You want to make the whole world happy."

"Then why can't *I* ever be happy?" The words were out of my mouth before I could stop them. I stared at Kate in surprise. "Did I say that out loud?"

She nodded. "Progress, I think."

I stared at her as a horrifying realization sunk in. "Scott didn't make me happy. He should have been the perfect man for me, but he wasn't."

"I'm glad you finally see it. We all figured it out a long time ago."

I narrowed my eyes at her. "Are *you* happy, Kate?"

"This isn't about me."

"I'm making it about you. Answer my question."

She wrinkled her nose at me. "Is this the new Fiona? If so, I don't like her. She's pushy. Make her go away."

After putting the pans up to dry and grabbing two cups of coffee, I forced Kate to sit down with me at the island. "Tell me about Chad. Distract me from my problems."

Kate stared at me, wide-eyed. "Pushy, nosy, and confrontational. Who are you?"

"Shut up and talk."

Kate frowned. "Not possible. I can't both shut up *and* talk."

"You know what I mean. You and Chad have both been acting weird lately. What's up?"

She thought about it a minute. "I'll answer your question if you agree to answer mine. Deal?"

I wanted to refuse but knew she wouldn't talk otherwise. "Fine."

She stirred her coffee. "Chad and I hooked up a few weeks ago."

"I suspected as much. Go on."

"He wants to make it official. He wants to *date*." Kate shivered as she said the last word.

"What's wrong with that?"

"Other than the fact we work together and are utterly unsuitable for each other, nothing at all. Oh, wait. There's another minor detail. I live with Mrs. Porter and have to take care of her at night. It would never work. I slept with him once, and Chad acts like it was some big deal. He wants me to meet his family."

"Again, what's wrong with that?"

Kate gave me a steady look. "Chad's father is a *minister*. How well do you think this would go over?" Kate held out her arms to better display the tattoos, the sheer blouse, and the black bra.

"A minister?"

Kate nodded. "Chad is getting his master's in philosophy but plans to enter into some theological seminary next. He wants to be a minister too."

I winced. "It might work, I guess. I never even knew Chad was religious."

Kate's shoulders slumped. "He's a good person. He doesn't broadcast it. He volunteers at soup kitchens and helps homeless people. I usually go for guys who are edgy and kind of dark. Chad is as edgy as a marshmallow."

"So why did you hook up with him?"

"I don't know," Kate whined. "I couldn't stop myself. The sad thing is I don't even regret it. The sex was *that* good. I would do it again in a heartbeat if only Chad would be casual about it."

"Wow. What a terrible person. Refusing to use you for sex."

Kate scowled at me. "Now it's your turn. What are you going to do about Matthew?"

My mouth opened and closed again. I looked like a fish out of water. "What are you talking about?"

Kate took a sip of coffee. "I answered you honestly. Now it's your turn."

I groaned and put my face in my hands. "Is it obvious?"

She snorted. "Uh yes."

I sat up straighter and folded my hands on my lap. "The attraction I feel for Matthew is a random thing. It's irrelevant and meaningless."

Kate paused as she lifted the mug to her mouth. "Is it?"

I swallowed hard. "Isn't it?"

Mom breezed into the kitchen carrying a box of teapots. "Nothing is random. Everything is determined by fate. There is no chaos. It all happens for a reason."

She left the box on the island and breezed back out. Kate and I both laughed. "How does she do that?" asked Kate.

"I don't know," I said, getting worried. "Is she right?"

"I do believe she is." She covered her mouth as a residual giggle popped out. "Holy crap. I still can't believe you broke up with the Ken doll."

I covered my face with my hands. "He brought up subjects like buying rings and having a house in the country next to his meatpacking parents, and I sort of freaked out. I think I led him on, but it's not what I want. At all. Am I a bad person?"

She pulled me into a hug. "Of course not. You're one of the nicest people I know. You rank right up there with Chad. If you were a dude, I would totally do you too."

"Wow. Thanks."

Kate got up and brushed biscotti crumbs off her ample bosom. "Your mom has a point. Everything does happen for a reason. It's a good thing you met Matthew before you and Scott got too serious."

I stood up and carried the mugs over to the sink. "It might not even matter. I have no idea if he even reciprocates those feelings."

"Yeah. Whatever." Kate laughed. "Have you seen the way he looks at you? And have you noticed he's here almost every single day now? He's got it for you bad, Fiona."

"I don't know . . ."

Kate held up a hand to quiet me. "I'm not telling you to sleep with him, although that man is a walking, talking sexual fantasy." She fanned herself to make her point. "But you should spend a little more time with him, get to know him better. Or get him drunk and kiss him. A kiss will tell you what you need to know."

"This conversation was supposed to be about you and Chad," I said with a little stamp of my foot.

"Was it?" Kate grinned at me and went back into the shop.

Between Mom telling me about my father and how she'd felt for him and Kate's revelations about her passion for Chad, it was a lot to think about. My feelings for Scott hadn't been anything wild and crazy, but they had been safe and warm and cozy and . . . boring. The more I thought about it, though, the more I knew Mom and Kate were right. Something vital had been missing from my relationship with Scott. I'd been so sure about him, but once the seeds of doubt were planted in my mind, they'd taken root. I didn't see him in the same way I once did, and it scared me. What if I messed up again?

Before Matthew even showed up for acoustic night, my stomach had tied itself in knots, and I felt jittery and flushed. I realized with disgust I was excited to see him and worried because we'd fought at Pamela's. I was a mess.

We left the windows open so a breeze could blow through, and it felt lusciously cool on my hot skin. I changed my clothes three times before deciding on an outfit, a black miniskirt with a shimmery gray sleeveless blouse. Sexy without being too obvious. By the time I finally dressed, I was extremely irritated and running late. I pulled my hair back into a low ponytail and flew down the steps.

Turning the corner into the kitchen, I ran right into Matthew. He wore a pair of faded jeans that hung low on his hips and a white T-shirt. His hair, silky and loose, brushed against his shoulders. He carried a bag in his hands, and I almost squished it.

"I'm sorry," we both blurted it out at once and then laughed.

He took my hand in his, and my heart did a little flip-flop in my chest. It was ridiculous how much he affected me.

"I was a jerk," he said. "You aren't shallow or spineless. You're one of the strongest, nicest, and most amazing people I know."

My cheeks burned. "You were kind of a jerk, but I got mad because I knew what you said was possibly, partially, somewhat right."

Matthew's lips curved into a smile. "You're admitting I was right?"

"Partially. Somewhat."

"But right?"

"Yes. Scott was wrong about Pamela's, and I should have stood up to him."

Realizing he still held my hand in his, I pulled it slowly away. Matthew stared at me like I was a puzzle he couldn't figure out. "This might be a personal question, but why are you with him anyway?"

"Well, I'm not, actually. Not anymore at least." The words

came out in a rush. I glanced up to gauge Matthew's reaction, but I couldn't read him. His face showed no emotion.

"What do you mean?" he asked.

"I broke up with him. A few days ago."

"Why?"

"Good question." I tucked a lock of hair behind my head. "I thought he was perfect for me. I dated him because he was what I thought I wanted, but I was . . . wrong."

"Is that twice now? Or three times?"

I looked at him in confusion. "What do you mean?"

"You were wrong about me, wrong about the tattoo, and wrong, it seems, about your boyfriend."

I narrowed my eyes at him. "The jury's still out on the first one."

"Well, I think we're making progress. I haven't seen the kitchen bitch in . . . well . . . days."

I tried to look stern, although it was hard not to smile at the impish gleam in his eyes. "You're going to make me mad again. You do realize that, don't you?"

Matthew grinned. "Making you mad is half the fun."

I tried to shoo him out of the kitchen, but he took the bag he carried and handed it to me. "For you."

Looking inside, I grinned. "Hot dogs? No way. You definitely know the way to my heart." I had no idea why those words came out of my mouth. I wanted to kick myself.

There was an awkward silence, and his cheeks got even pinker than mine. "Well, I'd better go and set up . . . "

"You brought four. Come and help me eat these."

I poured him a big glass of iced tea, and we chatted as we ate like we'd never fought. Matthew didn't carry a grudge, yet another thing different about him. Scott was a world-class pouter.

Silently, I chastised myself for even thinking that way. I

needed to stop comparing them. It wasn't fair to either of them, especially Scott, who wasn't around to defend himself.

I spent the evening listening to Matthew play and helping Chad with the smoothies. Mom worked the register and acted as hostess. We kept the office locked and our eyes out for strangers, but all went well. Several people showed up with guitars on their backs, and some were good, but no one compared to Matthew. We had an even bigger crowd than last week, and many of the women stared at Matthew with wide-eyed admiration. It made me ill. I wanted to spit in their smoothies but held myself back.

I didn't want to analyze my feelings for Matthew but couldn't help listing the pros and cons in my head. Scott came out the winner on paper every single time, but when Matthew was around, what looked right logically didn't seem to matter anymore. It was confusing.

Chad kept staring into space and sighing forlornly. Once the rush for smoothies died, I handed him a shot of rum. "Drink up. You need it, buddy."

"Thanks," he said, "but alcohol isn't the answer." He drank the shot anyway. One of the most admirable things about Chad was the way he never listened to his own advice.

"I spoke with Kate today," I said, and Chad looked at me in surprise. "I know, I know. It isn't my policy to interfere, but can I give you my opinion?"

"Yes. Please," he said, his brown eyes huge in his face. "I have no idea what to do. What did she tell you?"

I needed a shot of rum as well. I took it and slammed my shot glass on the counter. "She has feelings for you but is scared about getting too serious."

Chad poured himself another shot. We made two kinds of daiquiri smoothies tonight, banana and strawberry, so we had plenty of rum on hand. A good thing.

"But I *want* to get serious. I want to do this the right way."

I blew out a sigh. "Just sleep with her for now. She'll come around, eventually."

Chad's eyes grew huge in his face. "You think I should?"

"Yes. Tell her you'll take her any way you can get her."

Chad looked uncomfortable. I wasn't exactly thrilled with this conversation myself. "I guess I should call her."

"Do it."

He went into the tearoom, and I realized Matthew stood in the doorway. He'd heard every word I'd said.

"You're giving relationship advice?" he asked.

I winced. "Was I wrong? I don't want to mess things up for him."

"It sounded like good advice to me," he said with a wink before heading back to the main room.

Chad returned to the kitchen with a huge grin on his face. "Kate wants me to come over. *Immediately*. Do you mind cleaning up?"

I shook my head. "Go quickly—before she changes her mind."

Chad flew out of the café. I had a smile on my face as I tidied the kitchen and wiped it down. My efforts had turned out better than expected.

I made strawberry-daiquiri smoothies for Mom, Matthew, and myself and carried them out on a tray. Matthew's eyes twinkled when he saw my apron. I looked down and read it, feeling a blush coming on. "Kiss the Cook." Just my luck. Mom would have said I broadcasted my inner desires with subliminal choices. Maybe she was right.

"Do you want to sit in the garden?" he asked.

I nodded. I'd lost the ability to speak.

The crowd cleared out quickly, and soon we were alone on

the bench next to the fountain. I'd taken off my apron and sat sipping my smoothie. I had no idea what to do next.

"Your mom says this fountain is magical."

I rolled my eyes, relieved to have something to talk about. "Sadly, I think she actually believes it."

"Tell me about it. Please."

Matthew leaned back, his arm resting on the bench behind me. It felt cozy. It also felt wrong. I'd barely broken up with Scott. Even the twinkle lights seemed to mock me from the trees. I scooted away from Matthew and took another sip of my smoothie.

"Mom insists the fountain is linked to an ancient Mayan prophecy about a place with three rivers meeting at one point."

"Like right here. The three rivers meet downtown."

"Exactly. The Mayans said beneath such a place was another river, a secret one, with magical powers. She thinks this fountain is fed by that mystical, hidden river."

"And what are the magical properties?" Matthew's eyes looked very dark in the dim light of the garden.

I let out a nervous laugh. "No idea. It's a bunch of nonsense."

"Let's test it. We'll each take a sip of the water, close our eyes, and make a wish." Matthew got up from the bench, pulling me to my feet.

I tried to yank my hand away. "No. Unless your wish is for intestinal parasites, I strongly suggest you don't drink it either. I'm sure it's teeming with bacteria."

Matthew held fast and led me closer to the fountain. "You're secretly afraid it might be magical, and your mom might be right. It bothers that lovely, logical brain of yours."

I scowled at him. "Not it at all."

He cupped his hands, gathering some of the water as it gurgled out of the fountain. "Prove it. Take a chance, Fiona."

"Famous last words," I muttered as he lifted his hands to my lips. I closed my eyes and took a long sip. Cool and refreshing, it didn't taste contaminated at all.

"Yum," I said.

Matthew took a drink and looked at me in surprise. "It *is* good. I thought it would taste like rusted pipes and sludge." I swatted his arm, and he rubbed it, pretending I'd hurt him. "Ow. Stop beating me up and make your wish before the time runs out."

"What time?"

He sighed. "Magic doesn't last forever. Don't you know anything? Close your eyes and make a wish."

As I made my wish, squeezing my eyes shut tight, Matthew pulled me into his arms. He felt so warm and strong, and somehow, we fit together perfectly. Like the last two missing parts of a large, complicated puzzle.

I lifted my chin, my eyes still tightly shut, as his lips met mine. In some ways it seemed familiar, liked we'd kissed a million times before. In others, it felt new, strange, and sort of magical. But this was real magic. Not a made-up story like the fountain, or a scam like the tarot cards, or something invisible and unreliable like the golden orb in my chest. This felt as solid and as tangible as the stones beneath our feet.

Matthew was hesitant at first, gentle. But when I responded with a soft moan, wrapping my arms around his neck, his kiss changed into something deeper. I tangled my fingers into his hair and pressed my body against his, filled with an urgent need to be as close to him as possible. Soon our kiss became something wild and hungry and a little out of control. My entire body ignited with some sort of internal fire, and I felt ready to combust. I wasn't myself anymore. I was a stranger. And I'd never experienced anything like it in my whole entire life.

It felt right. Predestined. Special. Not random at all. As

our tongues engaged in a wicked dance, he groaned against my lips, his mouth sweet and hot. I ran my hands over his broad shoulders and his arms, desperately wanting to touch him. He did the same, and we acted like two starving people offered a full-course meal.

The sound of distant laughter from the alley behind the garden jolted me back to reality. I jumped away like I'd been stung, putting my fingers to my lips as tears filled my eyes.

He took a step toward me but stopped at the look on my face. "I'm sorry, Fiona," he said softly, his breathing still a bit unsteady. "But the fountain is magic. That kiss was exactly what I wished for."

He looked like he wanted to kiss me again, and I was afraid I wouldn't stop him if he tried. I turned and ran back into the kitchen and straight up to my room. When I peeked out my window, Matthew stood in the garden, his face tilted up to the night sky. He looked so lost and all alone, I wanted to go back out to him, but I knew exactly where it would lead. Instead, I let the curtain fall and crawled into bed fully dressed. Hours later, I finally fell asleep, but all I could dream about was Matthew's kiss.

It was what I'd wished for, too, which made everything so much worse. Falling for a guy like Matthew Monroe was not what I wanted and not what I'd planned, but I couldn't seem to stop myself, and it terrified me.

CHAPTER 13

MUSIC IS THE FOOD OF LOVE. -AUNT FRANCESCA

The next morning, I awoke before dawn. When Mom got up, I'd already made coffee and put together her breakfast. A spinach quiche. I didn't feel like eating, though. I only wanted to cook. I was sticking the quiche into the oven when she walked into the kitchen.

"Fiona, are you all right?" Her hand went to my head to check for a temperature.

"Couldn't sleep."

"Poor baby." She patted my cheek. "You have dark circles. Do you want to do yoga with me outside? It might make you feel better."

I shook my head. "I'll get to work in here. I made a quiche for you. It'll be ready by the time you're done."

"Thank you, dearest." Her sweet face wrinkled into a worried frown. "What happened?"

Part of me wanted to cry on her shoulder about Matthew, but I didn't. I had to face this on my own.

"Is it about the shop?"

I'd forgotten all about Anderson Solutions and the problems with the shop when Matthew gave me the kiss that shook me to my core. Pretending might make it easier, though, so I nodded. "Rosie said people want me to speak at the meeting. I don't know what to say."

She patted my arm. "You'll figure it out. Speak from your heart. It's where the answers lie."

She went outside to do her sun salutation, and I stayed in the kitchen, focusing on the cream puffs and the party preparations to make myself feel better. The morning raced by, and soon it was almost time for the tea ladies to arrive. I ran upstairs to put on a pale-pink dress from Second Hand Sally's. Sleeveless and snug through the bodice, it flared into an elegant skirt. Sally had given me a crinoline to wear under it because she said it improved the line of the dress. The weather was still cool enough that the crinoline wouldn't be too itchy. I slipped on a pair of silver sandals, put a narrow silver belt around my waist, and pulled my hair into a French twist.

I ran down the steps to the kitchen and skidded to a halt at the sight of Matthew at the island eating quiche. He wore jeans and a charcoal-gray shirt, which hugged the muscles of his chest and arms. I knew exactly how muscular his chest and arms were. I'd had my hands all over them last night.

Our eyes met, and we both froze. I looked away first. Mom watched us with interest but had the courtesy not to say anything in front of Matthew. "Fiona, you look lovely. A vision in pink."

She was a vision herself. She'd pulled her hair into a thick bun at the nape of her neck and wore a pale-green A-line dress and low-heeled pumps. Her earrings, made by African tribal women, were long and dangled to her shoulders, but the rest of her outfit looked extremely conservative and normal.

"You look pretty too," I said.

She glanced down at her dress. "I sewed it myself from an old pair of drapes, like Scarlett O'Hara. Isn't it a riot?"

Matthew laughed, and she gave him a little hug. "Matthew agreed to come and play for the ladies again. He's such a doll."

I pursed my lips. "How . . . wonderful." Matthew raised one dark eyebrow at me but didn't say anything. I brushed past him to walk out the door. "I'd better get the tables set up."

"There's no need. Matthew already did it. Isn't he a dream?"

I glared at her and mouthed the words "*Stop it*" over Matthew's head. She frowned.

"I think you're overly tired, Fiona. After all, you woke up at the crack of dawn. Matthew looks exhausted too. Why don't you rest in here while I organize the linens, and then we can carry out the food together?"

She didn't wait for an answer. She strolled right out of the room, leaving me alone with Matthew. I stood in the middle of the kitchen, not sure what to do.

Matthew got up and walked toward me. He was so close I smelled the scent of soap on his skin. I wanted to lean into him, but instead I took a step back.

"Are you upset about last night, Fiona?"

"Yes, I'm upset. I shouldn't have . . . we shouldn't have . . ." I wrung my hands.

Matthew reached for them and held them in his big warm ones. "We didn't do anything wrong."

I looked at him in shock and pulled my hands away. "Yes, we did," I hissed. "I barely know you, and I dallied with you in the dark."

Matthew bit his lip to keep from smiling. "We dallied?"

"It isn't funny. I don't normally do this sort of thing, especially with people like you."

"People like me?"

"Musicians. Artists. Ne'er-do-wells."

"Ne'er-do-wells? First, we dallied and now I'm a ne'er-do-well?"

He found this way too amusing. I scowled at him. "Stop teasing me. I realize you're charming and handsome and extremely adorable, but I'm not dating someone like you. I refuse. I have no time for that in my life. Are we clear?"

Matthew took a step back, his face suddenly shuttered and cold. "Crystal."

"Good." I grabbed an apron, the one with "Kitchen Bitch" on it. Matthew snorted as I tossed it back and picked up another. This one said "Desperate Housewife." Ignoring the snarky look on Matthew's face, I put it on.

Kate and Chad came into the kitchen hand in hand. They both came to a halt when they saw the expressions on our faces.

"Who peed in your granola?" asked Kate.

The rest of the morning was a blur. We had the largest number of reservations ever for our tea party, and Mom had wisely asked both Chad and Kate to come in and help. I worked in the kitchen. Chad and Kate carried the food and tea outside. We would serve our normal Earl Grey and English Breakfast, but my mom had added a Vanilla Rooibos and her own mix called Love is in the Air. A nice blend with a hint of lemon and citrus. She insisted we all try it, although I was less than enthusiastic.

"There's nothing in here, right?" I asked.

She gave me a look of total innocence. "Whatever are you talking about, Fiona darling?"

I narrowed my eyes at her. "If you are giving aphrodisiacs to a bunch of senior citizens and one of them has a heart attack, we could be in some big trouble."

She batted her eyelashes at me. "But what a way to go . . ."

I threw up my hands and went back to the kitchen, feeling Matthew's gaze on me. It was terrible. I was the bad person in this situation. He just proved to be an extremely kissable innocent bystander. I wondered if all the reiki and magic fountain nonsense had finally gotten to me. I wasn't thinking straight anymore.

My phone rang. It was Scott. Just seeing his name on my caller ID made my heart sink. I needed to be kind but firm, and I didn't want to give him any hint to how frazzled I felt at the moment. He might pick up on it and read it the wrong way.

I took a deep breath and let it out slowly before answering his call. "Hey, Scott. What's up?"

"Nothing. I just wanted to check on you. I got back from my parents' a few minutes ago."

"How are they?"

Kind but firm. So far so good. I'd been making out in the garden while Scott took care of his parents, but he didn't have to know. No one had to know. Ever. I truly was a terrible person.

Scott snorted. "They're a pain, but they're my parents. What can I say?"

"I can relate." I relaxed a bit. We were having a normal conversation. Maybe we could end up being friends someday. I decided to treat him like a friend and complain to him about my life. "My mom is driving me crazy."

"What's it about this time?"

"We have a big crowd today, and I'm worried about what my mom may have put in the tea." I sniffed the Love is in the Air. It seemed fine, but you never knew with Mom. "She's mixing funky things together for the old ladies. I'm afraid she might be slipping them something to enhance their libidos."

Scott laughed. "Aphrodisiacs?"

"Stop. It isn't funny. If one of them should have a blood

pressure problem or something, we could be in a lot of trouble. Mom doesn't always make the best decisions." I shook my head at my understatement.

"It's a good thing she has you around to help. I have to go out of town for a few days for work. Maybe I'll stop by when I get back. Okay?"

"Sure, Scott," I said, feeling guilty, confused, and kind of manipulated, although it wasn't Scott's fault. I needed to work more of the *firm* part of my *kind but firm* mantra.

As soon as I hung up my phone, Matthew began to play. The music drifted in through the kitchen window, and without making a conscious decision, I moved outside to watch his elegant fingers move over the strings of his guitar. His dark head was bent, his hair brushing his shoulders, and his arms were strong and muscular. Not the kind of muscles a person got in a gym. Matthew, it seemed, had earned his by doing something. He likely hiked and kayaked and skied and enjoyed the kind of outdoorsy stuff I'd never been any good at, and he looked naturally athletic too.

He caught me staring at him, but I couldn't tear my gaze away. He played a new song. "I call this one 'Girl in the Garden.' I finished writing it last night."

My heart constricted in my chest as he played. It sounded like our fountain, sad and soft and sweet and full of longing and hope. It was complete now, not just a few refrains, and I stood there like a statue and listened to the entire beautiful, heartbreaking melody. When he finished, I clapped along with the old ladies, but inside I wanted to weep.

I don't know how I managed to carry on for the rest of the day. I worked in the shop and sold the ladies tea and phalluses and bongs and jewelry, but inside I was numb. Mom, Kate, and Chad eyed me with concern, but I couldn't talk about it. I couldn't lie to myself either. I had feelings for two different men. Knowing the truth didn't make my heart hurt any less.

Matthew didn't say goodbye, which was for the best. His song had been more of a farewell than I deserved.

After the tea ladies left, I went outside in my pretty pink dress. Mom sat on the bench, drinking a cup of tea. I curled up next to her, put my head on her lap, and cried. She stroked my hair, said soft soothing words, and waited patiently for the storm to pass.

"I didn't know it would be this hard," I said with a little catch in my voice.

"I know, baby. Love is never easy."

I sat up, wiping my eyes. "Scott should be the perfect guy for me."

She nodded. "Yes."

"But I have feelings for Matthew."

She nodded again. "He's completely lovable."

"What should I do?"

Mom laughed. "I can't answer your question, dearest. You need to listen to your heart."

"I don't know if listening to my heart would work. I always use my head." I thought about my heart chakra and how Auntie Mags said it was blocked. "Is there something wrong with me?"

She sighed. "Sweet girl, you are a logical, wise person, but sometimes the most important things can't be seen on a spreadsheet or worked out like an equation. Sometimes the best things don't add up."

"I broke up with Scott."

Saying it out loud made me feel a bit ill. I'd imagined being with someone like him my whole entire life. Giving up on that dream would not be easy.

"When?"

"After the dinner at his parents' house, it all felt so wrong

. . ." I chewed on my lip. "Do you ever wonder if you made the wrong decision? About your fiancé?"

She gave me a sad smile. "I don't regret ending my relationship with William, but I will always regret not being more honest with your father. It was the worst mistake of my whole life."

I sat up and gave her a hug. "I'm sorry, Mom."

She patted my back. "I'm content, but I want more for you. Contentment can sometimes be a curse. Even more than the curse on the Campbell women." She gave me a wink. "I want you to have more than contentment. I want you to have passion and romance and most of all, true love."

I didn't believe in true love any more than I did in chakras, but I couldn't bring myself to say it. "How will I know?"

"The kiss. The magic is either there or it isn't."

I winced. "I kissed Matthew. Last night."

She brushed a strand of hair behind my ear. "And I guess it was pretty remarkable, or you wouldn't be so upset right now."

My lips quivered again. "Remarkable doesn't even come close."

She sighed. "I was afraid of this, my poor Fiona."

"What do you mean?"

"Your head still wants Scott, but your heart wants Matthew. You're split right in half. No wonder your chakra is blocked. We should call Auntie Mags."

I groaned and flopped back onto her lap. "Oh, great. Another reiki session with Auntie Mags. Do you think it will help?"

She laughed at the expression on my face. "It couldn't hurt. But I know one thing that will make you feel better."

I looked at her in confusion. "What?"

She grinned. "I stashed some cream puffs in the fridge for us. Let's go and eat away our sorrows."

As she pulled me into the kitchen, the sun was setting through the trees. Out of the corner of my eye, I swore I saw something sparkling in the fountain, but when I turned my head, it was gone.

CHAPTER 14

KEEP CALM AND PUT THE KETTLE ON. -AUNT
FRANCESCA

The next morning, the summer heat came back with a vengeance, but it was cool and comfortable in my air-conditioned room. "Thank goodness for Marty," I mumbled to myself, and then a strange and unexpected noise broke the delightful silence as someone pounded on the front door of our shop.

Sitting straight up in my bed, I heard words that instilled fear into my heart. "Department of health. Open the door."

I tossed on my robe and ran down the steps two at a time. Wafts of incense pierced my nose as I got closer to the main floor. "Please no naked yoga, please no naked yoga," I whispered to myself. When I reached the bottom, Mom was already opening the front door. The room was filled with people on yoga mats, all of them completely dressed. I sagged against the doorjamb in relief, but it didn't last long. The men from the department of health were serious types with clipboards. One had a nametag saying "Mike" and the other "Ron," but they otherwise seemed completely indistinguishable.

"What's this about?" asked Mom.

"We had a complaint you were conducting . . . uh . . . naked yoga classes. We were called in to check it out."

She looked around, bemused. "We're all wearing clothing, sir, and there is nothing illegal about a yoga class."

Most of the people in the room, senior citizens, let out nervous chuckles at the very idea of naked yoga. I wanted to laugh myself since I'd seen their saggy, bare bottoms here only last week. This could have been a total disaster. The last thing we needed right now was a fine from the department of health.

I'd thrown my robe over my nightie but felt a little exposed. "I'd better get dressed."

Mom smiled. "I'll take these nice gentlemen in the kitchen to have a cup of coffee and a bite to eat."

Mike seemed uncertain. "We've also had a complaint about your teas, ma'am."

She froze. "My teas?"

He nodded. "We'll have to inspect the other rooms, too, I'm afraid."

She didn't hesitate. "Come on back. Do you mind if my friends continue with their yoga class?"

Mike and Ron looked at each other and nodded. I high-tailed it up to my room and dressed faster than I ever had in my life. But by the time I made it downstairs, Mike and Ron were already putty in my mother's hands. They sat at the island, drinking coffee, eating cream puffs, and chatting like old friends. Mom had charmed the uncharmable once again.

They took a few samples of the different teas, had a quick look around the kitchen, and thanked my mom for the best cup of coffee they'd had in a long time.

"And fine work on those cream puffs, miss," said Mike with a smile.

My mom gave them each a bag of cookies to take home to

their children and a hug when they left. She was the hippie version of Mother Teresa.

After they were gone and all the yoga people left, I grabbed her arm. "Was there anything in those teas? Should I be worried?"

She laughed and shook her head. "Of course not, darling. The magic isn't in the tea, although all are a fine mix of the best ingredients possible. The magic is in the *water*."

I froze, hoping she wasn't talking about what I thought she was talking about. "The water?"

She pointed to the fountain in our garden. I groaned, put my head down on the island, and tapped it several times against the cool marble surface. It took a few minutes before I could lift my head and face her.

"Are you making tea using water from the fountain outside that's more than one hundred years old?"

"Closer to two hundred, but who's counting?" I inhaled through my nose and exhaled slowly. Mom watched me. "I'm happy to see you using your yoga breaths, but I cannot understand what has you so upset."

I stopped midbreath. "The water from the fountain might not be clean. It could be contaminated with hundreds of itty-bitty microorganisms. You could make our customers sick."

She had the audacity to roll her eyes at me. "It's from an underground *spring*. The freshest, healthiest water you could possibly drink, and you aren't even considering the fact that it's *boiled* before it's served to anyone. This is exactly why I never told you. I knew you'd overreact."

I no longer did yoga breathing. I'd started to hyperventilate. "You hid this from me on purpose? You're so unbelievably sneaky and dishonest. Can't you be an adult for once in your life?"

I turned away from the shattered expression on her face and stomped up to my room. I had cookies to bake and the books for the week to go over, but I felt too angry to do anything right now. I wanted to hit someone.

I flopped back on my bed and stared at the ceiling as a horrible thought occurred to me. Worse than when I suspected Mom gave aphrodisiacs to old people. Worse than knowing she used unclean, unsanitary river water for her tea. This thought almost caused me physical pain.

Mike and Ron said they'd had a complaint about the naked yoga. None of the people doing yoga would have called to complain. And although I'd told Scott about it, I trusted him. He had no reason to call the department of health on us. What would be the point?

There was only one possible conclusion, and the culprit was the person who'd walked in and seen the naked yoga class just minutes after I did. "Matthew."

His name came out of my mouth in a whisper. As much as I didn't want to believe it, it had to be true. He'd witnessed the yoga, and he must have overheard me asking about the teas as well. He'd hovered around me a lot, eavesdropping on my conversation with Old Blue Hair and acting all charming and perfect and gorgeous. It was all a ruse. He may have even eavesdropped on my conversation with my mother that day as well, the slime bucket.

Another strike against him? He'd shown up right as we were in danger of losing the shop, offering his services to us at no charge. I found it odd that such a talented musician would happen to have every single Saturday night free in an area packed with bars and nightclubs for an entire summer. Something felt wrong about this whole situation, and the fact he kept showing up at the shop on days when we weren't expecting him was very bad another sign. It made me sick to think about it, but my first instinct had been right, and I suspected Mr. Matthew Monroe was not at all what he claimed to be.

There was no point at all in telling Mom. She'd never believe me. I had to figure this out for myself. She thought Matthew walked on water, but he must have blabbed to someone. I had no proof, only a deep gut instinct. After being silent for so long, my gut had started saying a lot lately. This time I decided to listen.

He made me suspicious from the start, but he'd used his charm, his sexy French-pirate looks, and even his kisses to lull me into complacency. He was so freaking kissable. Time for me to wake up and take action.

Mom had gone out into the garden to work, upset about what I'd said. We'd sort it out later. Right now was the perfect opportunity for gathering information.

I opened the door to her tearoom and slipped inside. A desk sat in the corner, piled high with books. It was dark and cool inside and smelled like jasmine, lemon, and rich, exotic spices. I snuck a glance out to the kitchen, pulled open the drawer of her desk, and took out her address book.

She had the address of nearly everyone who'd ever stepped foot in this shop, and she sent out hundreds of hand-made Christmas cards out every year. Sort of an addiction with her. I found Matthew's address almost immediately and jotted it down. He lived only a few blocks away. I shoved the address into my pocket and grabbed my accounting book from the shelf above Mom's desk. As I walked back into the kitchen, she came in from the garden.

"I'm sorry, Fiona," she said softly, her eyes red from crying.

I gave her a hug. "Me too."

She pulled back and looked at my face. "I should have been honest with you. I realize you're right now. I've been irresponsible and impulsive. It must be torture for you to work here."

"No. I love working in this shop."

Surprisingly, I meant it. I loved the baking and the books and seeing all the funky people stroll in and out. I also loved the garden and all our wonderful friends. I'd grown up here but never realized before how nice it was.

She didn't look convinced. "You deserve more. With Moses being hurt and that horrible company trying to knock down our block, it may have been the wrong time to tell you about your father and pressure you about Scott. You're right. I need to be the adult, but you have such an old soul. I forget how young you are sometimes. Forgive me." She got teary again.

I gave her a gentle squeeze. "There is nothing to forgive. We'll pretend it never happened."

She smiled like sunshine peeking through rain clouds. "I'll try to be more honest, darling."

I narrowed my eyes at her. "Will you stop using the water from the fountain?"

Her smile faltered. "In the interest of being more honest, I have to say no." I groaned, and she held up a hand to stop me. "But I will get it tested by the local water authority to make sure it's safe."

"Thank you."

She kissed my cheek. "Although really there is no point. You've been drinking the water for years, and you're fine."

Her eyes went to the cup of coffee I just poured, and my mouth dropped open in surprise. "You put in in the coffee too?"

She grinned as she washed her hands in the sink. "It's why my coffee is the best in town."

Praying Ron and Mike from the department of health did not end up with diarrhea today, I finished the cookies in record time and went out into the garden with a steaming mug of coffee to work on the books. I sat at a table near the fountain, staring at it for a long moment. It seemed perfectly normal today. Not shooting water at anyone. Not making me kiss people. An innocent, gurgling fountain with a crumbling stone basin.

"This had better not make me sick," I muttered under my breath, taking a sip of the coffee. It was delicious, as always, and even knowing where the water came from didn't make it taste bad. I opened my books and tried to relax.

Nothing soothed me as much as accounting. It wasn't as fun when Mom overspent on something ridiculous like stone phalluses, but today I enjoyed it. We were doing well. As long as nothing big or unexpected came up, we'd be fine for the rest of the month.

The columns of debits and credits recorded in my tidy handwriting made me think about Matthew's yin and yang necklace. Accounting was like yin and yang. For every out, there had to be an in, or chaos reigned.

Matthew insinuated if I were less responsible Mom would become more responsible, which sounded like complete nonsense. I wasn't an enabler. I was more like a caretaker. If I became less responsible and my mom didn't step up to the plate, we'd be ruined.

Mom came out to the garden with a huge smile on her face. "Look who's here," she said. Auntie Mags followed closely behind her, making me roll my eyes. This wasn't a casual visit. It felt like an intervention.

She grinned at my reaction. I stood up and gave her a peck on the cheek. "Hi, Auntie Mags."

Mom went back to the kitchen under the premise of getting coffee. In actuality, she left us alone so we could talk privately.

Auntie Mags sat down on the bench next to me and got right to the point. "What's going on, Fi?"

I played with the pencil in my hand. "I think you're right about my heart."

She nodded. "Do you want me to try to help you with it?"

I wanted this pain and confusion to end but wasn't sure about energy fields or chakras or blocked hearts. "I'm not sure you can."

Auntie Mags patted my knee. "I know you don't believe, Fiona. You've always been our little skeptic. It's part of your charm. But it wouldn't hurt to let me try, would it?"

Remembering how it had felt when all those hands hovered over me last time made me shiver. I was fairly certain it had been an anxiety attack and not a chakra blockage but couldn't be entirely sure. "It kind of hurt before."

She sighed. "It won't happen again. It's just you and me this time, kiddo."

I took a deep breath. "Should we go inside?"

"It's beautiful out here. You can lie on the bench if you want."

The bench had long fluffy cushions that tied under the sides. I stretched out, closed my eyes, and tried to relax. The summer sunshine peeked through the leaves of the big oak tree above my head. The wind whispered gently through the leaves, and the smell of roses and lavender and all the other flowers in my mom's garden wafted to my nose. The fountain gurgled softly, reminding me of Matthew's song.

"You're tensing up," said Auntie Mags. "Try to relax again."

Inhaling slowly through my nose and exhaling through my lips made me so relaxed I was almost asleep, like floating on a warm summer breeze. A strange vibration filled the air as Auntie Mags's hands hovered over my body, but it didn't frighten me this time. She started at my head and traveled to my toes, but she went back to my chest several times. At first it was a little uncomfortable, but gradually the achy feeling eased and then left altogether.

"Thank you, Auntie Mags," I murmured, my eyes still closed.

She kissed my forehead and covered me with a light blanket as I drifted off. "Sleep, sweet child, and dream of happy things."

For the first time in a long time, I felt like I could. I snuggled into the blanket and sighed as the sound of the fountain played like Matthew's song in my ears.

CHAPTER 15

GOOD SEX SHOULD BE AS DECADENT AND
DELICIOUS AS GOOD CHOCOLATE. -AUNT
FRANCESCA

I woke up a few hours later, refreshed and ready to go. Mom was in the kitchen making dinner. Pasta primavera, my favorite. I smiled and gave her a hug.

"I feel so much better."

"A little rest, a lot of love, and some help from Auntie Mags's healing hands. It works every time." She filled a bowl of pasta for me, and we sat down at the island to eat. "I stopped by the hospital while you were sleeping. Moses opened his eyes. He went back to sleep right away, but the nurse said it's a good sign. And Sally called. She asked if you could stop by. She has something special for you."

I grinned. When Sally had something special, it was always a lovely find. I finished my dinner and headed right to her shop. On the way, I noticed posted signs in several windows. "Coming Soon: Parking Solutions from Anderson Solutions. Meeting the Needs of Your Community." Many were posted on shops closed ages ago, but some were more recent. I sensed the stranglehold Anderson had over local businesspeople getting stronger. Time was ticking. If we didn't figure out something soon, our café would have a sign in the window too. The idea made a cold wave of fear wash over me. The council meeting was only weeks away, and the signs in the windows made it seem more real. Anderson's "solutions" were tearing our little community apart, and I'd never felt so powerless.

Sally greeted me with her usual enthusiasm. She squealed, hugged me, and gave me air kisses on my cheeks. "Wait until you see what I have for you, pretty girl." She grabbed my hand and pulled me to the back of the shop.

Sally had flaming red hair, ruby lips, and way too much blue eyeshadow and mascara, but it complemented the blue vintage dress she wore. She was beautiful and kind, and she'd been like an extra doting aunt to me my whole life. She also had a brilliant eye for fashion.

She led me into the back room of the shop, and when I saw what hung on a hook in her office, I gasped. "It's Chanel. Vintage Chanel. Amazing, Sally. And it looks brand new."

Sally clapped her hands together in excitement. "Isn't it lovely?"

I reached out to stroke the fabric, pale-blue tweed lighter than air with silver piping and silver buttons. The jacket had four small pockets, two on each side. It was exquisite and also way out of my price range. "It's gorgeous, but I don't think I can . . ."

She hushed me with a wave of her perfectly manicured hand. "It's a gift. You're going to speak for all of us at the meeting. I want to thank you and help you look your best."

I had to blink back tears. So many people trusted and believed in me. I couldn't let them down. "Thank you, Sally."

She pulled me into a big, warm hug. When she pushed me gently away, she had tears in her eyes too. "Stop it. You're going to make me cry, and my makeup will be ruined. Go and try it on, you silly goose."

Sally waited outside the door. The suit fit as if made for me. At least sixty years old, it looked like it had never been worn. I stepped out, and Sally almost cried again. She waved her hands in front of her eyes to make it stop. "Oh, baby girl. You're so beautiful. If only I could have given you a few inches of my height. You might have been a model. You're perfect. Like a little perfect doll."

No one could spend five minutes with Sally and not feel better. She loved everyone, and her praise was effusive and genuine.

"Thanks, Sally."

I went into the room to change back into my clothes as Sally chatted with me from behind the door. "Have you been to see Moses?" she asked. "Your mom said he opened his eyes today."

Almost closing time, the store was nearly empty. I cracked the door a tiny bit and peeked out, deciding to pump Sally for information. "She told me, but I didn't have a chance to go and see him today. Have you heard anything more about what happened?"

"No," she said, shaking her head. "Poor man. And do you know what I find odd?"

"What?"

"No one in the entire South Side seems to have a clue about who did it or why. And people around here are so nosy. Remember when Lizzie Carson went into labor? There were ten casseroles on her doorstep before her cervix had even dilated."

"You're right." I winced just thinking about Lizzie Carson's poor cervix. "We have no secrets here."

"It's almost like . . ." She shook her head. "I don't even want to say it."

"What?"

"This is a stretch, but could it be a hate crime? Because of his race."

"Or it may have been something random. Wrong place, wrong time."

She gave me a sad little smile. "Let's hope. The alternative is almost too much to bear, isn't it?"

I swallowed hard. She was right, and I knew for sure Sally had encountered more than her fair share of hate. Strangely, it hadn't made her bitter or angry. If anything, it made her more tolerant and forgiving.

I slipped back into my T-shirt and shorts and gently put the suit back onto a hanger, stroking the fabric with my fingertips. I let out a sigh. My world might be in chaos, but the suit was perfect. Thank goodness for small miracles.

Sally stood outside the door, humming along to the music playing in the shop. "Oh. I almost forgot. I saw your boyfriend the other night."

I stuck my head out the door again. "What? When?"

Sally wrinkled her forehead as she thought about it. "Saturday. I went to the piano bar you recommended on Station Street with my beau. Oh, what fun. Those piano guys are so naughty."

I blinked. Scott had been at home with his parents until Sunday. He'd been clear on that one. He'd told me several times, in fact. Why would he lie? "On Saturday?"

Sally nodded as she put the Chanel suit into a garment bag for me. "Dueling piano night. We had a blast."

I swallowed hard. What if he'd stopped by at the café? If he had, he might have seen me kissing Matthew, and he would have been devastated. But of course he hadn't, because apparently he'd been at dueling piano night.

"Did you say hello?" I tried to keep my voice nonchalant.

She paused. "It was a bit strange. I waved when I saw him,

and he didn't respond. I thought he maybe didn't recognize me. But he approached me when I came out of the ladies' room. He seemed terribly uncomfortable, poor thing, and kind of drunk too. I was surprised he even wanted to chat. After all, we only met that one time, when you brought him here weeks ago."

I'd dragged Scott into Sally's shop to see some vintage neckties. He hadn't been impressed with the ties, and he'd stared at Sally like she was an alien. We had a spat about it afterward. He called her my "freaky friend," and I lost it. I knew he had to remember her. I also knew it would have been hard to miss her, even in a crowded bar. She stood over six feet tall, sported the shoulders of a linebacker, and usually had on more pastel than an Easter egg.

"What did he say?"

"It was the oddest thing. He wanted to talk about my shop."

"Your shop?"

"Yes." She paused as if hesitating about what to say next, an odd thing with Sally. "And he wanted to talk about your shop too. He said, well, I hate to mention this, but he told me you and your mom were on the verge of selling. Is that true?"

I shook my head and patted Sally's hand because she looked so concerned, but this made me ten shades of furious at Scott. "No. It's not."

She let out a sigh of relief, but a little frown formed between her expertly plucked brows. "Maybe I misunderstood. He asked if I planned to sell, too, and he even gave me his card in case I needed advice. It was quite sweet of him, but I told him my little place made no difference at all. Mr. McAlister owns the shops on either side of me. If he doesn't sell, why would Anderson even want my shop?"

"You're right. Did he say anything else?"

She gave me a little wink. "Well, it was kind of adorable, actually. He hinted around about an engagement in the very near future. I know it's supposed to be a secret, but he seemed over the moon about it. Congratulations, my dear. He's . . . lovely. So good-looking and a great dresser. I wish both of you the best."

I tried to keep my composure. It would devastate Sally if she knew how much her words upset me. "Thank you, Sally, but I'm too busy to even think about getting engaged at the moment."

Sally made a sympathetic tsking sound. "You have school and the shop and so much baking. It's a lot of work. You'll have plenty of time to settle down with Scott later. By the way, Ralph and I plan to come to acoustic night sometime in the next few weeks. I already promised Matthew we would."

"You know Matthew?"

Sally nodded. "Sweet boy. He stops by all the time to chat, and he bought the beautiful leather jacket in the window. It looked fantastic on him."

I remembered the jacket, buttery soft and extremely expensive. I wondered how a guy who played for free at acoustic night and appeared to have no other means of employment could afford it, but that worry was small compared to my other concerns.

"Did you hear about Yonky's?" I asked.

"Yes," she said. "It breaks my heart. And the nut shop closed too. I will miss those nuts."

She sounded so dramatic it almost made me giggle, but a thought occurred to me. "Were they pressured by Anderson too?"

"I'm sure they were. Anderson has been relentless. And they're acting like they own the block already. It makes me wonder what tricks they might have up their sleeve. I don't know why your boyfriend misunderstood, but it's a good thing your mom is standing firm."

"What do you mean?"

She zipped the Chanel suit into a garment bag and handed me the hanger. "Have you seen their blueprints for the proposed garage? The Enchanted Garden is key. If they can't convince your mom to sell, there won't be a project at all."

I kissed Sally, thanked her again, and walked slowly back to the café with my beautiful suit over my shoulder. I pulled my phone out of my pocket and called Scott. Better to deal with him now than to let it stew.

He answered on the second ring. "I'm in a meeting," he hissed. "Hold on." I heard a door open and close, and it sounded like he'd gone outside. "What is it?"

I never called Scott at work, but this happened to be important. "You went to the piano bar on Saturday. You weren't with your parents."

There was a long pause. "What are you talking about?"

"My friend saw you there."

His voice was an angry whisper. "I *was* with my parents. Your freaky friend is a total liar."

I stopped right in the middle of the sidewalk. "I never said who it was, and don't you dare call Sally a freak ever again. I mean it, Scott."

Scott let out an exasperated breath, his tone flippant and annoyed. "Some of us have to work for a living. We all can't hang out all day making cookies and picking flowers like you and your mom, Fiona. I'm in the middle of something very important. I don't have time for this right now."

His comments made my blood boil. "I don't have time for this *ever*."

"What do you mean?" I heard the worry creep through the anger in his voice.

Suddenly, it was so clear. Scott was . . . a total jerk. I don't know why I'd never seen it before. Maybe Aunt Mags's chakra unblocking actually worked.

My words came out in a rush, my heart pounding. "You're nothing but a liar. A fake."

"Because your friend imagined seeing me at a bar? You're being ridiculous."

"She didn't imagine anything. You told her my mom was thinking about selling the café. That's a total lie. And why would you tell her we might get engaged? We're not even dating anymore."

There was a long pause. "We're just taking a break. This isn't a permanent thing."

I let out a laugh, but there was no humor in it at all. Scott had seemed so perfect, so attractive. Now I couldn't even remember what drew me to him in the first place. At this point, I found him almost repulsive.

"Yes, it is. It's very permanent."

"You can't do this to me," he said. I heard a strange note in his voice. Was he crying, or was it something else? I didn't care. I'd moved a step or two beyond ticked off and had just hit my red zone.

"It's not up to you. We're done. It's over. Adios, Scotty."

He let out a frustrated noise. "Look, I can't talk right now. I'll stop by the café when I get back, and we'll sort this out."

"Nope. Don't waste your time or mine."

I hung up the phone. People walked by me on either side as I stood there, my phone in my hand, staring at it blankly. What had just happened?

"Wow," I said softly. "That was . . . weird."

There'd been no lists of pros and cons. No hours spent dwelling on all possible outcomes. I acted instinctively. Impulsively. And I did the right thing. So why did I feel so thrown off?

He tried to call back, and I ignored it, shoving my phone back into my pocket. As I did, I felt the crumpled paper with Matthew's address written on it and knew exactly what I had to do. I walked home with a determined set to my shoulders, hung the beautiful suit on the back of my bedroom door, left a note for my mom, and set off immediately for Matthew's house.

Luckily, I brought a hoodie along. After only a few blocks, the wind picked up, and the sky grew ominously dark. I sped up my pace, hoping I'd make it to Matthew's before it poured but knew it would be close.

Scott called me over and over again. I turned off my phone, not wanting to deal with him. I could only handle one problem at a time, and I wanted to deal with Matthew first. I had to ask him about the naked yoga, or the doubt would eat me up inside. I needed to know the truth, to hear it from his lips.

Halfway there, thunder sounded in the sky, and it started to rain. By the time I got to Matthew's house, I was soaked to the skin. Even with my hoodie on, the rain managed to seep through my clothing all the way down to my undies.

He lived in one of the elegant Victorian rowhouses lining the river. They had recently been renovated and made into high-end condos, and I remembered reading something about the architect in charge of the project winning an award. They sat on the edge of the South Side where the funky hippie shops changed into designer boutiques and fancy restaurants.

I walked up the stone steps and rang the doorbell. No one answered. I banged on the door, but still no one answered. I never considered Matthew might not be at home and willing to listen to my tirade. I sat down on the stone steps in front of his door and wept as rain continued to pour down on me and the sky had turned black. I could hardly see and now had to walk all the way home in the dark.

"Fiona?" Matthew stood directly in front of me, a bag from Wu's Chinese restaurant in his hand and his jacket over his head. "What are you doing here?"

I hiccupped and stood up. "Did you tell anyone about the naked yoga class?" I almost had to shout to be heard about the sound of the rain.

"What?" Matthew stared at me, stunned. Obviously, he had no idea what I was talking about, but I still wanted to hear him say the words.

"Someone reported us to the department of health. I need to know the truth. Have you spoken with anyone at all about it? Even a friend? Please tell me it wasn't you."

Matthew's dark eyes stared steadily into mine. "It wasn't. I swear it. Do you believe me?"

I nodded, rain streaming down my cheeks, because I saw the truth in his eyes. "Yes, I do."

He gave me a little crooked smile. "Can we go inside? My noodles are getting soggy."

I followed him into the house, feeling guilty for dripping on the beautiful wooden floors. Matthew put down his food, grabbed a fluffy white towel from the bathroom, and wrapped me in it, rubbing his hands up and down my arms to dry me off.

"When I saw you outside, I thought you were here to yell at me about kissing you and demand an apology, but I won't do it. I can't. In fact, I *refuse* to apologize for it."

I stared at him, understanding for the first time exactly why I'd come. I put my cold hand on his cheek. "I don't want an apology."

"You don't?"

I shook my head. "No. I want you to kiss me again."

He stared at me, his eyes scanning my face, before he groaned and brushed his mouth softly against mine. It felt like it had in the garden. Perfect. Magical. I wrapped my arms around his waist, wanting him closer. He was almost as wet as me but still delightfully warm. He murmured my name against my lips as his fingers tangled in my hair.

At first, he was gentle and sweet, but soon his kisses grew into something stronger. Deeper. His tongue touched mine, demanding a response, and I answered him. My heart pounded in my chest, and I squashed any niggling feelings of doubt immediately. I knew the truth. I wanted him more than I'd ever wanted anything.

Lightning flashed through the windows, and thunder crashed as the storm outside grew in intensity along with our kiss. I shoved Matthew's jacket down over his shoulders. He pulled off my soggy hoodie. My hands went under his shirt, caressing the firm muscles of his chest and back, touching the smooth expanse of his naked skin. I lifted his T-shirt over his head and threw that on the floor as well.

He pulled back from me, his breathing unsteady, his face illuminated by the flashes of lightning. "Are you sure?"

The do-or-die moment, but I'd already made my decision. "Yes." I whispered the words against his lips. "But this is about tonight. I can't promise you anything else."

Matthew's lips twitched. "Are you using me for sex, Miss Campbell? Am I a one-night stand?"

I shook my head, my voice soft. "I didn't mean it like that."

He laced his fingers in mine and brought my hand up to his mouth so he could kiss it, echoing the words he'd heard me tell Chad in the kitchen. "It doesn't matter. I'll take you any way I can get you."

He gave me a naughty smile that made my heart flutter. When he took my hand and pulled me upstairs, I experienced a moment of alarm. His big bed in the middle of the room made this seem more real somehow, and sort of scary, but soon Matthew kissed me again and I forgot about everything but him.

He pulled my shirt over my head and tossed it onto the floor before unbuttoning my shorts and sliding them down my legs. My hands went to his jeans. I struggled with the button, but I was determined and finally got it opened after uttering a muffled curse.

He laughed as he pushed his jeans to the floor. "Success," he said.

His boxers soon followed, and I froze for a moment, staring at him in all his naked glory, but then he kissed me again, and all my trepidations evaporated like morning mist. He unhooked my bra, and we stood against each other, skin to skin, the most beautiful thing I'd ever felt. When Matthew leaned forward to take my breast in his mouth, I tangled my fingers in his hair and gasped, arching my back. I pressed against him, aching for him.

He pulled off my panties and led me slowly to the bed. He kissed and caressed me, building my need to a fever pitch. When he slid a finger inside me, we both groaned.

He grabbed a condom from his bedside table and moved on top of me. My thighs cradled him, his legs warm and hairy against my smooth ones. His body was all hard planes and angles. I was soft and small. But we fit perfectly together.

I felt him at my entrance and he paused, hovering above me. "Are you sure, Fiona?"

"Don't stop, Matthew. Please."

I wanted him inside me so badly. I lifted my hips, and the sharp rush of pleasure I felt as he entered me made me gasp.

He slid out of me ever so slightly and then back in. He was being cautious, gentle, but I didn't want him to be careful. I wanted everything Matthew had and wanted to give him everything I had too. I wanted to lose myself in him, if only for one night. My mouth found his earlobe, and I bit it.

"Fiona." My name came out as a moan from his lips as he thrust faster and harder and gave me my wish. I lost myself in him. Nothing else existed. I inhaled sharply and felt myself shatter into a million pieces. I held on to him tightly. I'd had sex before, but this was different. What he made me feel was huge and unknown. When he gasped and shuddered against me, I knew. For the first time in my life, I was not in control. This was real magic, and I was powerless against it.

CHAPTER 16

ALWAYS LISTEN TO YOUR CONSCIENCE
UNLESS IT'S TELLING YOU TO SKIP DESSERT.
-AUNT FRANCESCA

I should have been plagued by guilt, but I couldn't take back what I'd done, and even if I could, I wouldn't have changed a thing. Curled up in Matthew's arms, I felt utterly content. He touched me, stroking my arms and back, murmuring softly in my ear. He ran his fingers up my neck and placed little kisses on my forehead. His hands trembled as he pushed my hair out of my face and looked deeply into my eyes.

"Fiona," he said, swallowing hard. "You are . . ." He shook his head, emotional and adorable. "Thank you."

I grinned. "I should thank you. That was . . . quite enjoyable."

I put my face in his neck and kissed him there. He smelled nice, like soap and spice and something singularly his own scent.

He chuckled, and I felt the rumble of his laughter against my lips. "High praise indeed. 'Quite enjoyable.' Like a visit with your grandparents or something."

I swatted his arm. "You understood what I meant. It was perfect. Incredible. Fantastic. Are you satisfied now?"

Matthew's face grew serious. "I didn't mean to rush you into anything. I know you just broke up with Scott . . ."

My cheeks got pink. "There is something you should know. Something I haven't told anyone." I let out a breath. "I never slept with Scott. We dated, but . . ."

My voice trailed off. I couldn't finish. What could I say? That karma had intervened and kept me from making the biggest mistake of my life? Nope. I was not about to go there.

Matthew stared at me so intently I felt exposed. "Why me, Fiona? You didn't even like me at first."

"I guess you grew on me." I kissed the tip of his nose with a smile, not ready for a serious discussion. "You're kind of cute. A decent guitar player. And pretty smart too."

"Wait a second. I'm a *decent* guitar player?" He looked so appalled I giggled.

"And you're honest." I reached out and touched his cheek. "It boils down to trust. I don't know much about you, but I know you'd never lie to me, Matthew. It means something to me . . . something important."

A shadow fluttered across Matthew's eyes. "I know you don't want to hear it, but I wanted this. I wanted *you*. So badly. Part of me still wonders if this is real or if it's some kind of crazy dream."

Panic rose like a wave in my chest, the same way it had when Scott discussed our future together. "I . . . I don't know what to tell you . . ."

Matthew must have heard the fear in my voice. He pulled me even closer. "It's okay, Fiona. I needed to say it, but I don't expect anything in return. You were honest with me when you came here, and I get it. This is a one-time thing. I won't pressure you for anything you aren't ready and willing to give me."

I kissed his shoulder, wanting to change the subject. This was making me too emotional and conflicted, and I hated feeling emotional and conflicted. My eyes went to the skylight above his bed. The storm had passed, and the stars were popping out. On one wall was a giant window with a view of the river. The building retained its Victorian charm but had plenty of modern touches.

"This place is beautiful," I said, frowning, as a disturbing thought occurred to me. "It must be expensive to live here. How do you manage it?"

Matthew stroked my hair. I felt his heart beating against my cheek and found it soothing. "It belongs to a . . . friend. I'm using it for the summer."

"Nice friend," I said, lifting my head to see his face. "Is it a girl friend or a guy friend?"

"Guy. Would you have been jealous if it had been a girl?"

"No," I said with a scowl, and he laughed.

"Are you hungry? I have noodles."

We went downstairs. I wrapped myself in a sheet, and Matthew wore his boxers. He opened the bag he'd been carrying when I saw him outside and reheated the food. After he tossed our wet clothes into the dryer, we sat on stools in the kitchen and talked, feeding each other with chopsticks. Matthew did a better job since half of the noodles I tried to feed him slapped him on the face. We turned it into a game, and we had to lick the sauce off if the noodle missed its target. It started out as something silly, but when I dripped some sauce on Matthew's stomach and licked it off, it turned into something else completely. Soon the sheet and the boxers were gone, and after a delightful experience involving licking sauce off various surfaces, we were back in Matthew's bed.

I'd never realized sex could be so much fun. Matthew made me laugh, and he awoke a passion and hunger inside of me I didn't know existed. I couldn't stop touching him. He intoxicated me, making me feel wild, uninhibited, and just a little irresponsible.

I sent a quick text to my mom telling her I'd met up with friends and would stay the night. She wouldn't care; she trusted me. I'd never given her a reason not to before. Suddenly, I had secrets. It felt a little strange.

The next morning, I woke naked in Matthew's arms, kissing him, still half-asleep. He pushed me onto my back, held my hands above my head, and entered me without saying a word. My body immediately responded, arching against his in seconds.

Afterward, he rested on top of me, staying inside me as long as he could. He gave me slow, deliberate kisses, his eyes taking in every detail of my face as he said goodbye with his lips and his hands. I'd told him this was for one night only, but the look in his eyes nearly crushed me.

"Have I done a terrible thing to you, Matthew?"

He shook his head. "Last night was the best thing that ever happened to me."

"I'm a bad person." The tears slid out the corners of my eyes and down the sides of my face. "I should have taken your feelings into account, but I've been a mess lately. I haven't been thinking straight. I had a huge fight with Scott yesterday."

Matthew pulled away. He turned and sat on the edge of the bed, his back to me. "Wait a second. Was last night about revenge?"

"No." I reached for him, but he pulled on his boxers and walked across the room. He stood by the window, his back to me, staring out at the river.

I got up and slid my arms around his waist, putting my face on his back. "Last night had nothing to do with Scott. It was about you and me. I've wanted this since the first day I met you, although I refused to acknowledge it at the time."

"You're sure?"

"Yes."

Matthew took one of my hands off his stomach and kissed my fingers one by one. "Then why does this have to be a one-night thing?"

"I have feelings for you, Matthew, but I need to get my head straight first." I took a deep breath. "And you have to understand; growing up around my mom and all her friends makes me cautious. I won't be the only adult in yet another relationship. I refuse to do it."

Matthew turned to me, his dark eyes hurt. "Is that what you think will happen?"

"I don't know, and it's what scares me." To my great shock, I burst into tears. I was not normally a crier, but I seemed to weep at the drop of a hat lately.

Matthew pulled me gently into his arms and held me, making soothing noises as he stroked my back. When the storm finally passed and I got myself back under control, I stared at him.

"I'm the awful person in this situation, and yet you're comforting me."

He gave me a little smile. "I'm nice like that."

I put my hand on his cheek. "You are."

He leaned forward and kissed me gently on the lips, like I was the most fragile porcelain and he was afraid I might break. "You aren't an awful person. You're a confused person. And I'm going to give you some space."

I stuck my lip out in a pout. "Right now?"

He gave me a sexy, lazy grin. "Maybe not right now . . ."

Later, we showered, and I dressed in my clothes. Matthew had taken them from the dryer at some point while I slept and placed them carefully near the bed. I felt fresh and clean and more like myself, but also different. I wasn't the same person as yesterday. Last night had changed me.

I looked in his mirror, trying to see the difference. My eyes were a little red from crying, and my skin glowed pink from the hours of loving and the warm shower, but externally I was still me. A strange feeling to look at my old familiar face with new eyes.

Matthew wanted to drive me home, but I needed time to pull my thoughts together. Showing up at the shop with Matthew would cause a lot of questions I wasn't ready to answer.

We held each other quietly as I prepared to leave. He kissed me until my knees wobbled and then rested his forehead against mine, his hands cupping my face. "No matter what you decide, no matter what happens in the future, what happened between us was perfect. Remember that." His voice held a hard edge to it, which almost frightened me. It felt final.

I nodded, my eyes filling with tears once again. "Goodbye, Matthew." I put my hand on the doorknob and opened it, although the temptation to grab him and kiss him again was strong.

As I began the long, slow walk home, I felt Matthew's eyes on my back but didn't turn around. I was afraid I wouldn't be strong enough to go if I did.

I texted my mom to let her know I was on my way. She said it was slow in the shop and told me to take my time. I had tons of messages and missed calls from Scott but ignored them. I decided a trip to the farmers' market would clear my mind.

I strolled around the market, buying fresh veggies and fruits, chatting with friends, and enjoying the sunshine on a summer day. Even though I wasn't sure what to do about Matthew, I couldn't seem to stop sighing as I thought about what happened last night. He was right. It *had* been perfect.

Every bit of it. Well, except for the part when I had to say goodbye.

Sally waved to me, and I went over to speak with her. She'd bought fresh flowers and put one behind my ear. "You're *glowing,* Fiona. I guess that's what happens when you're in love."

I nodded, my cheeks getting pink. "Right. Love."

"Yes, love," gushed Sally. "The best thing in the whole wide world. It makes you feel like you're floating on air, doesn't it?"

"Uh, sure."

She put her hands on my upper arms. "I almost forgot to tell you the most fantastic news. Our Moses woke up this morning."

"He did?" Tears of relief filled my eyes. Maybe he was going to be okay after all. It was actually more than I'd dared hope for. "Really? What happened?

"He asked for a drink and went back to sleep. Not much but a start."

I grinned. "That's wonderful."

A short, balding man with a dark moustache waiting in line to buy a pie from Mr. Yoder kept looking over at Sally. When I caught her giving him a smile and a flirtatious little wink, I grabbed her sleeve.

"Is that him?"

Sally nodded, putting her hand over her heart rather dramatically. "Ralph. My dream man. Isn't he gorgeous?"

Ralph wasn't exactly a male model. He did have warm brown eyes and a kind smile, and he obviously was madly in love with Sally. "He's glowing too. Every time he looks at you, Sally."

Her eyes filled with tears. "Aren't you the sweetest little thing? Come here, I want you to meet him."

Ralph was lovely. Soft-spoken and sweet, he treated Sally

like a priceless gem. There was something subtly beautiful about them in the way they touched and the look in their eyes. I would have missed it before, but now I understood.

I said goodbye and walked home, a worrisome thought forming in my mind. If I could tell in a second Sally and Ralph were in love, it would be pretty obvious I had feelings for Matthew, because I did have feelings for him. Big ones.

I'd never been able to disguise my emotions. Auntie Mags had tried to teach me poker and failed miserably. She said I showed my thoughts as clear as day on my face and should play gin rummy instead.

I walked in through the side of the garden, sat down on a chair, and stared into space. I hadn't slept with Matthew to satisfy a physical urge, although he'd done the job. He was wrong for me in every possible way, but I had to admit he was special to me. And if anyone saw me with him, they'd know it immediately. I'd jumped into the deep end without my floaties on, and now I wasn't sure if I could swim.

Had Aunt Francesca felt like this with her steel baron? Had my mom felt like this with my father? Could this be what my mom had been trying to explain to me?

Suddenly, it felt a little hard for me to breathe, and my heart pounded erratically, like something was stuck deep in the middle of my chest. I had to put my head between my knees. It was the strangest thing I'd ever felt, and for a moment, I thought I might be dying. I could almost hear the story on the evening news.

Otherwise healthy, if slightly unstable, twenty-five-year-old woman dies unexpectedly of a heart attack in the back garden of her mother's café after having a mind-blowing sexual encounter with a virtual stranger. Story at eleven.

People filed out of the shop and into the garden. The reiki class was over, and I got some curious glances. I sat up slowly, trying to breathe normally. It took a few minutes, but eventually I got it under control.

My chest hurt. My heart center must have reblocked itself and now caused me actual physical pain. I hoped Auntie Mags was still inside. Either I'd finally become as crazy as all the other people in the South Side, or this ridiculous stuff was real. I wasn't sure which idea frightened me more.

CHAPTER 17

WHEN IN DOUBT, BAKE COOKIES. -AUNT
FRANCESCA

I gathered my purchases and ran into the shop. "Auntie Mags, are you still here?"

She was in the kitchen, sipping tea with Mom. "Fiona, what's wrong?"

I sat down next to her, still rubbing the spot in my chest. "I think my heart chakra is blocked again. Help."

Auntie Mags put a hand on my cheek. "I told you the problem was emotional, sweetie. Have you tried to find your heart center?"

Mom got up to give us a little privacy. I closed my eyes and tried to relax and feel the glowing light in my chest. It didn't work.

"I can't do it. It's gone." My eyes flew open, and panic crept into my voice.

Auntie Mags leaned forward and looked me straight in the eye. "Stop it, Fiona. You're letting other things get in the way. We need to go somewhere quiet. Peaceful." She led me back out to the garden. The reiki people were gone, and we were all alone. She made me lie down on a bench near the fountain.

It was warm from the sun and covered in soft cushions. "Close your eyes and calm down."

I followed her instructions but not well enough. "Relax your face. You look like you sucked on a lemon. And your shoulders are almost up to your ears. Goodness me. You're a tense little thing today, aren't you?" I opened my eyes, about to snap at her, but she pointed her finger at me. "Shut your eyes and relax. For real this time."

I scowled but followed her instructions. Soon I felt calm and limp, my breaths coming slowly in and out of my nose.

"Good girl," said Auntie Mags. "Now picture what you love most in the world. The person or thing or even a place to bring you joy."

I inhaled slowly through my nose, picturing the man I'd always thought I'd be with. Someone with a suit and a job and a savings account, who also looked an awful lot like Scott. I imagined having a family and building a beautiful, normal life together. I felt the stirrings of my heart center but couldn't quite connect with it. I decided to try again.

This time I pictured Matthew. The way he kissed me. The look on his face when he'd been inside my body. The way his hair fell into his eyes when he played guitar. I breathed in and breathed out, using slow, steady breaths, and then I felt it. The glowing orb in the center of my being.

My eyes flew open. "No."

A life with Matthew also meant dealing with someone a lot like my mom. The only thing that could be possibly worse than falling for a guitarist was falling for a drummer. Or a bass player, but no one ever truly fell for bass players.

Was this really what my mom had meant when she talked about the Campbell women being cursed? Falling for the wrong men at exactly the wrong time and never learning from our mistakes? Well, if so, I planned to break with tradition. This was not going to happen to me.

"No, no, *no*," I said, shaking my head firmly.

Auntie Mags looked at me in surprise. "What happened, Fiona? You were so peaceful."

I stood up, dusting off my shorts. The fountain gurgled behind me, mocking me. "Ever since you unblocked my heart chakra, things have been . . . confusing."

She clicked her tongue. "Oh dear. I should have warned you, dearie. Sometimes the mind does not want to accept what the heart tells it."

I narrowed my eyes at her. "And sometimes the heart is wrong."

Auntie Mags shrugged. "That's something you have to figure out for yourself, but in my opinion, the heart always tells the truth. Often, however, we don't want to hear it."

I stomped back into the kitchen, muttering something about "superstitious mumbo jumbo" under my breath. When the lunch crowd streamed in, it took my mind off everything else. Later as I cleaned up, my thoughts went back to the events of the night before. I remembered Matthew's hands on my body and the way he kissed me and made me feel so precious and important. I washed the same pot three times before realizing what I'd done. Unfortunately, I wasn't alone. Kate witnessed the whole thing.

"What are you doing, Fiona?" she asked with a giggle. She wore a black cami with hot-pink skulls made from glitter, black capri leggings, and a hot-pink tutu. She looked like an edgy, curvy ballerina.

"Nothing. I got . . . distracted."

Kate walked over to me, took me firmly by the shoulders, and looked deep into my eyes. "You got laid."

"How did you know?" I gasped, my voice a whispered hiss.

"It's in your eyes, cupcake. I could tell right away."

"Oh man. I hope my mom doesn't figure it out."

"Like she would mind," she snickered. "I guess you and Scott made up?"

My hands froze on the plate I washed, and I swallowed hard. Kate stared at me, her face pensive. "Unless Scott isn't the one you slept with," she said softly.

My lower lip quivered. "I need to talk to someone."

Kate took my hand and pulled me up to my bedroom. I plopped down on my bed, and she closed the door behind her. I put my hands over my face and wailed. "I'm a terrible person."

Kate pried my hands away from my eyes and gave me a stern look over her glasses. "You're one of the nicest people I know."

"No, I'm not. One minute I was fine and happy with Scott. The next minute, I broke up with him and jumped into bed with another man."

"Well, that's understandable. Matthew is . . . well . . . hot doesn't cover it. He's magnificent. It *was* Matthew, right?"

I flopped down and groaned into one of my pillows. Kate patted my back. "There, there now. It can't have been bad."

I let out a shaky little breath. "It wasn't."

"So what's the problem?"

I looked down at my hands clenched in my lap. "I always thought I'd end up with someone like Scott. He fits neatly into my life plan."

Kate brushed a strand of hair out of my eyes. "Love isn't so simple, Fiona."

"I wish it were."

"What are you going to do?"

I winced. "I tried to be nice to Scott. Kind but firm. My new mantra."

She snorted. "Oh God. You have a mantra now?"

I glared at her. "Shut up. Please. You're supposed to be helping."

"Sorry. You're right."

"I may have been a little lacking in the firm part, though." I blew out a sigh. "He wasn't getting it. I'm not sure if he gets it even now. He still wants to talk things out."

"Well, what about Matthew?"

"He told me it was the best night of his whole life, and he said he'd never regret what happened between us."

Kate clutched her hands to her chest. "Aww. What did you say?"

I blushed again. "Nothing. I'm not good at romantic banter."

Kate gave me a stern look over her glasses. "You're seriously messed up in the head."

"I know. It's the whole 'love' thing."

Kate rolled her eyes. "You've explained it to me before. If you can't see it, touch it, or calculate it, you want no part of it. So why were you in Matthew's bed?"

My shoulders slumped. "Auntie Mags unblocked my heart chakra, and I felt all confused. Then my mom told me the fountain water was magic, and Matthew and I both drank it. She's using the same water for her teas, by the way. If we don't all get dysentery, it'll be a miracle."

Kate swallowed hard. "She uses the fountain water for tea?"

"And coffee too. She thinks it has magical properties. Another thing to worry about."

Kate cleared her throat. "Not to add to your list, but your mom is planning a surprise party for you. I think it was originally intended to be a way to 'welcome Scott into our South Side family and make him feel loved and included.' Her words, not mine. But when you broke up with him, the theme changed."

"To what?"

"I'm not exactly sure. I think it has something to do with 'one last chance to party before Anderson destroys us all'?"

"Oh no. When?"

"Next Friday. I don't want to ruin her surprise, but in light of the circumstances . . ." Kate looked worried. I gave her a little hug.

"You were right to tell me. Thanks." I sighed. "What should I do about Matthew?"

Kate stood up. She had to get back to work. "I can't answer your question, but I do know one thing. I have a feeling your 'kind but firm' mantra isn't working with Scott. You're going to have to get harsh with him, and it has to be soon."

"I was pretty harsh to him last time," I sniffed. "But you're right. I know."

It was getting hot, even with the air-conditioning on, so I took off my hoodie. It smelled like Matthew's detergent and fabric softener. It smelled like him. I put it up to my face and cried again. I felt something in the pocket and took it out. A note from Matthew.

I'm sitting here in the darkness, watching you sleep. The only light is from the moon, and I swear I've never felt this way about anyone before. You're so utterly radiant and sweet and wonderful. In the light of day, when you're gone, this might seem stupid and sentimental of me, but I had to say it. I fell for you the first moment I saw you standing in your mom's shop. All you had to do was scowl at me, and I was lost. Completely and hopelessly yours. For always.

The last few words of Matthew's neat and elegant handwriting were a blur. I was full-out weeping now, holding the note against my chest and crying in huge, silent sobs until I felt like it would be physically impossible to cry any more. I folded his note carefully and put it in the treasure box on my dresser. Mom had given me the box years ago to hold all my special things. Shells and rocks and other small trinkets filled it. I tucked Matthew's note inside too.

I went to the bathroom to wash my face. My eyes looked puffy and red, making it obvious I'd been crying, and I felt exhausted, both mentally and physically. I called down to my mom in the kitchen, "Do you mind if I take a little nap?"

She shouted up, "Sure, honey. Kate is helping me. You must have stayed up late last night. I bet you had fun."

I was glad I couldn't see the expression on Kate's face at the moment. "Yeah, I guess so. Thanks, Mom."

I curled up on my bed, the hoodie smelling like Matthew clutched in my arms. My body was sore in odd places from the thorough loving I'd received. I thought about the way it felt, the way my body caught on fire each and every single time he kissed me. Kate was right; he was magnificent, and his note made me feel even more confused than before, but I fell immediately into a deep and peaceful sleep. Hours later I woke with a start, disoriented and thinking I was still in Matthew's bed because I smelled him on my hoodie and on my skin. I let out a small, muffled sob. I had no idea what to do to make my life okay again, so I decided to bake.

My mom didn't say a word when she found me in the kitchen kneading bread and covered in flour. I had two pies in the oven, and I'd mixed up sugar-cookie dough as well. I felt like decorating as many intricate cookies as possible. She made both of us a cup of herbal tea and sat down at the island to watch me. I wore an apron that read "Make Cupcakes, Not War." It seemed appropriate.

"Have I ever told you about the archers I saw once in Japan?" she asked. I shook my head. "They dress like samurai, but they wear these funny woven hats. They can shoot arrows while galloping on a horse. It's pretty amazing. When they train, they're told not to think about hitting the target. If they practice and relax and become one with the bow, eventually they will hit the target automatically."

"That seems backward. Isn't hitting the target sort of the point of archery?"

She took a sip of her tea. "Yes and no. Archery has almost a religious significance to them. They consider their training a form of meditation. You know about Zen Buddhism. Remember the adorable meditation teacher who used to come and give classes? What was her name?"

"Helen, but she changed it to Lotus Blossom."

She smiled fondly at the memory. "Lotus Blossom. Whatever happened to her? She was lovely. I should send her a Christmas card."

I bit my lip to keep from laughing. "She married a hedge fund manager and moved to New York."

Mom cringed. "Oh, right. I guess I blocked it from my memory. He was a nice hedge fund manager, though, and he loved our Lotus Blossom. Sometimes opposites attract."

I punched the dough down and kneaded it again. Mom took another sip of tea, watching me as I attacked the poor lump of bread dough. "I think cooking is your meditation," she said. "It's so Zen and beautiful. Your hands are busy, and it helps your mind reach enlightenment. The purest and simplest path to Nirvana."

I looked up at her from my pile of mutilated dough. "I'm nowhere near enlightenment."

She laughed. "You're like the archers in Japan. You're focusing on the process instead of the target."

I brushed some of the flour off my hands and picked up my cup of tea. "I don't have a target."

My mom kissed my cheek. "My point exactly. You're a Zen master, and you don't even realize it."

"I don't want to be a Zen master. I want to be a CPA." In a flash, I remembered something, and my eyes flew to the calendar. "I was supposed to take the books to Mr. Jenkins today and forgot. I'd better call him."

She patted my shoulder. "Don't worry. I took them over."

I frowned at her. "You remembered?"

She nodded. "Of course, darling."

When she left the room, I shook my head. Sometimes my mom hovered in the atmosphere, floating in a slightly different dimension than other people, and sometimes she surprised me. She never remembered to take care of the books. Mr. Jenkins always had to call her and harass her to bring them in until I took over. But she was right about one thing. Maybe baking was my meditation.

I stayed up late, cutting out cookies and decorating them with royal sugar icing. I made ornate little teacup cookies for my tea party ladies, tarot card cookies for Madame Lucinda's group, and even some pagan symbols for the Wiccans who met at the café once a month on the night of the full moon. By the time I was done, I was tired and my arms were sore, but I'd avoided crying or thinking about Matthew or Scott for hours. I considered it an accomplishment.

Afterward, I went out into the garden and sat by the fountain. The night air cooled my hot skin, making me sigh with pleasure. I'd been inside next to a warm oven for hours. The sweet chill of the night air was refreshing.

The moon was almost full, and the Wiccans were scheduled to come on Thursday. Tomorrow, Madame Lucinda would read her tarot cards and tell me all about a handsome stranger. I frowned, remembering her reading last week. She knew someone was lying to me. I was kind of curious and kind of terrified about what she might say tomorrow.

A breeze ruffled the leaves in the trees above me, and the moonlight sparkled on the water in the fountain. I thought I saw a glimmer of silver again, but when I got up and looked at it more closely, I realized I was mistaken. It was a trick of the light.

My shoulders slumped as I remembered how Matthew had kissed me for the first time in this very spot. I heard a bell chime in the distance, the old clock by the church. I dipped my fingers into the fountain as the bell chimed over and over again. Midnight.

I cupped my hands, filled them with water, and drank as the clock chimed twelve. I let the cold, sweet water slide down my throat, and closed my eyes.

"I wish I could know what I really want."

As soon as I said the words, a gust of wind came and blew my hair around my face, making the wind chimes my mom hung all over the garden play an eerie melody. It lasted only a few seconds, and just as I started to feel a little frightened, the wind died and everything went quiet. The only noise was the gurgle of the fountain and the furious beating of my own heart.

CHAPTER 18

THE BEST RECIPES CALL FOR A BIT OF SPICE.
-AUNT FRANCESCA

Madame Lucinda's tarot card reading was scheduled to commence promptly at seven. Prior to that, I had the rest of the day free. I spent most of it at the hospital with Moses, telling him all about Matthew and Scott and my mess of a life. He never opened his eyes or gave any indication he heard me, but the bandages were off his head and the swelling down on his face. He looked more like himself every day, but he still wasn't better. I was straightening his blanket when Nurse Brenda came in. She smiled when she saw me.

"Did you hear the news? He asked for a drink yesterday. And he thanked me for it."

"I heard," I said, blinking away a tear. "But I talk and talk and talk to him, and he hasn't opened his eyes once."

Brenda put her hands on my shoulders and gave me a steady look. "He will. Give him time. And I wouldn't be surprised if he heard every word you've said to him."

I cringed. Maybe I shouldn't have gone into so much detail about Matthew. When Brenda left the room, I leaned forward to whisper into Moses's ear.

"Please forget most of what I've told you, especially the private parts. I have a feeling you don't want to know that stuff. But I want to tell you something important. I'm going to find out who did this to you, Moses. I promise."

I thought I saw a slight flicker of his eyelids, but it may have been my imagination. I squeezed his hand one last time, kissed his forehead, and left the room.

When Madame Lucinda showed up, I plopped myself down in the chair in front of her. She folded her hands on the table and raised one well-penciled brow at me.

"You said someone would lie to me, and it happened. You talked about a stranger who just arrived, and that happened too. How did you know?"

She'd also mentioned desire, but I didn't bring that up. She already had a superior look on her face. "It wasn't me, Fiona. The truth is in the cards."

I frowned. Candles flickered all over the shop, making it feel eerie and strange. She shuffled her cards without taking her eyes off me, a knowing little smile on her face. Kate and my mom stood behind my chair, as eager as me to find out what she had to say.

"I don't believe in any of this stuff."

Madame Lucinda shrugged. She wore a brightly colored scarf on her head. It was tied under her curly hair, and the ends of the scarf hung over her shoulder like a waterfall made of rainbows, sparkles, and butterflies. Butterflies must have been the theme for the evening. They fluttered all over her blouse, twinkled on an enamel pin she had clipped to her lapel, and hung on dainty gold chains from her ears and around her neck. It should have been tacky, but on Madame Lucinda, it worked.

"You've told me the same thing before. I think the first time you expressed doubt may have been kindergarten, sweetheart. It doesn't matter. The cards will see the truth and tell it, whether you want to listen or not. Do you want me to read for you?"

"Yes. I mean, I guess so."

"I'm going to do a more in-depth reading. Usually, I can only get you to sit for a card or two. This time will be different."

She spent an awfully long time playing with the cards. Madame Lucinda loved a little suspense. Then she placed the cards one by one on the table. Every time she laid a card down, she made a little "ah" or "oh" noise. It was extremely irritating. I waited impatiently, tapping my foot. It took her a while, but finally she pointed to the first card. The fool.

"Do you know what it means?"

I glared at her. "I can guess. I feel like a fool for sitting here like this."

Madame Lucinda chuckled. We'd always bantered about my lack of belief. "It isn't about being foolish, Fiona. The fool is the first card in the deck. It's all about new beginnings and new ideas. If it pops up first, it tells me you are about to go in a new and exciting direction."

I tried to maintain a neutral expression. If I looked too interested, Madame Lucinda would make this even more painful.

"What about this one?" I pointed to a card with two naked people on either side holding out a hand to each other.

Madame Lucinda winked. "Of course, you would ask about that one, wouldn't you? The lovers. But yours is weak. You have a lack of faith in your own ability to make important decisions."

Kate gasped. If she'd been closer, I would have kicked her.

"Not exactly helpful information," I said.

Madame Lucinda tapped her finger on another card. "Yes, it is, because this is the chariot. It's a vehicle. It means you're in charge. You can choose which direction you want to go.

And this card is strength or lust. It's all about passion, living life . . . and making love."

She looked up at me with a twinkle in her eye. Like Kate, somehow Madame Lucinda knew I'd very recently slept with someone. I wondered if there was some kind of sign posted on my forehead, reading "Fiona just had the most mind-blowing sex of her life."

Madame Lucinda bit her lip to suppress a grin at the expression on my face. "Now here's the good news. This is the tower. Usually, I'd be worried if I saw this. If it were in your past, it would indicate you weren't willing to accept a change. But it's in your future. It tells me soon your views will change on something you thought you were certain about, and you will embrace the change. And the best part of all, this is the star. It means your wishes will come true."

She looked at me triumphantly. Kate pointed to the deck. "Isn't there one more card?"

Madame Lucinda looked down. A card, still facedown, had been pushed off to the side. "How strange."

She turned it over slowly, and we all gasped. The devil.

"Oh dear," she said. "This is unexpected."

"What does it mean?" Even the picture was scary, a demon with horns on a throne made of skulls.

"Someone does not have your best interests at heart. They're motivated by an obsession with their career and money and social standing. This card is about ambition and a need to dominate that's so strong, it overrides any thoughts for the desires and wishes of others."

I swallowed hard. "Who is it?"

The door to the shop opened, letting in a gust of wind, which blew out several candles. We all jumped, including Madame Lucinda. The room was now so dark I couldn't see who had entered. He walked slowly closer to us, and when we finally saw his face, we all let out a mutual sigh of relief.

"Matthew," said my mom. "How good of you to come."

Matthew answered my mom, but his gaze was on me. "I appreciate the invitation."

I hopped out of my seat. My entire body responded to his presence, like just seeing him turned on a switch somewhere deep inside me. "I've got to get back to the kitchen. Thank you for the reading."

I almost knocked over Kate in my haste to get out of the room. Madame Lucinda gave me a knowing look, and I heard her chuckle as I fled to the kitchen. Once there, I took a deep breath, trying to center myself. This was ridiculous.

I wore another vintage dress from Sally's. Cream with little lilac flowers on it, the dress had a tightly fitted bodice, a lilac belt, and a short, puffy skirt. It was cool and comfortable. I tossed on a pink apron over it, which read "Keep Calm and Have a Cookie," and with shaking hands, put my beautiful tarot card cookies on a serving dish. I giggled about the words on the apron, a crazy-sounding giggle. I was on the verge of losing it and needed to pull myself together. I heard the bell on the door ring as people arrived for the event. We never knew exactly how many people would show up each week, but it seemed like a big crowd tonight. I took a deep breath and tried to get my head in the game.

Picking up a cookie with a carefully detailed devil on it, I paused. Odd that Matthew had walked in just as the devil card was turned. I shivered involuntarily and frowned. Matthew was the least likely person to be obsessed with work. He didn't even have a job.

An image of Scott in his business suit fluttered through my mind, but I refused to dwell on it, not believing in this tarot card nonsense. I was putting coffee mugs and water glasses on a tray when Mom and Kate walked in. They looked serious. Sensing another intervention, I scowled at both of them.

"What?"

"Are you okay, honey?" Mom wasn't exactly wringing her hands, but close.

"I'm fine. Why do you ask?"

Kate and my mom both exchanged a long look. I hated when they did that. Then Kate got pink. With Kate's pale complexion, she blushed in a full-body sort of way. It usually started at her chest and went right up to her hairline.

"You seemed upset about the reading . . . and other things," said Mom.

I gave Kate a steady look, but she couldn't meet my eyes. I slammed a spoon onto the counter. "You told."

Kate looked close to tears. "She knew. I didn't say anything, I swear."

I was about to go on a rant when the door to the kitchen opened, and Matthew strolled in. I rolled my eyes. "Now what?" I asked.

Matthew's lips twitched as he tried not to laugh. He spoke to my mom. "Madame Lucinda is ready to start. She asked me to let you know."

Mom and Kate grabbed the trays. I made a move to help them, but Mom shook her head. "Kate and I can handle this. You stay here and chat."

They nearly sprinted out of the kitchen, a feat considering they carried trays full of food and coffee. Matthew watched their exit with a crooked little smile. "Subtle."

I groaned and took off my apron. "We need to talk."

Grabbing his arm, I pulled him into Mom's tearoom. It was dark inside. The only light shone from a small lamp on Mom's desk. I locked the door and leaned against it. Matthew watched me, his eyes dark in the dimly lit room.

He was glorious. His hair hung to his shoulders like silk. He wore a loose black shirt with the sleeves rolled up and faded blue jeans. The yin and yang necklace rested against his chest. I gazed at him, swallowing hard, unable to speak.

He came closer, a predatory sort of gleam in his eyes. "You wanted to talk?"

I nodded but forgot what I meant to say. Instead, I stared at his mouth. I hadn't realized the impact his closeness would have on me. I caught one whiff of his scent, and immediately my panties felt damp. Embarrassing.

Matthew licked his lips, all the incentive needed for me to grab his head and pull it down for a kiss. He moaned and gathered my body against his the moment his mouth touched mine.

I kissed him like a crazed, starving beast, and he kissed me back with equal abandon. He sucked on my lower lip and kissed his way down my neck. I nibbled on his ear, my hands still knotted in his hair, and he groaned. His hands caressed my breasts through the thin fabric of my dress, and when they moved lower to cup my bottom, I nearly lost it. I wanted him so desperately it was almost physically painful.

He seemed to understand. His dark eyes were hungry as his hands slid up my naked thighs and found my panties. The bit of white lace was gone in seconds, and when I tried to unzip his pants with my clumsy, shaking hands, he gently pushed them away and did it himself. In seconds, he lifted me off the ground and thrust inside me. My legs were wrapped around his waist, and my back rested against the door as he slid slowly in and out, creating the most exquisite torture as he kissed me, his sweet tongue tangling with mine.

My hands clung to his shoulders, and he held my bottom as his movements became faster and more intense. In moments, I gasped as we came together in a sudden and powerful rush. Feeling him shudder against me as I climaxed almost drove me over the edge a second time.

Afterward, he held me and stared into my eyes. My dress

was still hitched up around my waist. I should have been upset we'd done this nearly fully clothed in my mom's tearoom while there was a party going on in the next room but didn't care. I sighed and closed my eyes, resting my head on his shoulder.

"Are you okay?" His voice was deep and soft.

I'd been getting that question a lot lately. "Yes."

Matthew released my legs and put me gently on my feet. He zipped up his pants and scooped my panties off the floor. I slipped them on, my cheeks getting hot. When I stood up, Matthew straightened my dress and brushed a strand of hair behind my ear. His face was serious.

"I didn't expect this to happen again." He swallowed hard, and a muscle worked in his jaw. "I thought it was a one-time thing."

"I thought so too." I let out a deep breath. "I got your beautiful note. Then you came here, and I saw you, and I didn't realize . . ."

"You didn't realize what?"

I took a deep breath. "How I'd feel. How I'd react to seeing you. I couldn't stop myself."

Matthew grinned and kissed my forehead. "I'm so glad you couldn't." His lips brushed my ear. "I'm crazy about you. You know that, don't you?"

I twined my arms around his neck and lifted myself up to my tiptoes to kiss his cheek. "Thank you."

It seemed like every time I was with him, the bond between us grew more and more powerful. There was nothing logical or rational about how I felt or the way I acted. Madame Lucinda had been wrong. I wasn't driving this chariot. It careened out of control.

I heard the door to the kitchen open, and Scott called out my name. "Fiona? Where are you?"

I covered Matthew's lips with my fingers as my heart sank

to my toes. Scott was about to catch me with Matthew the same way he'd caught Brittany with his best friend. That could get ugly, and as much as Scott annoyed me, I didn't want to cause him any additional pain. If he caught me with Matthew, it would be like stomping on his heart.

A few minutes later, we heard the door open and close again. Scott must have gone out to the garden. I heaved a sigh of relief and slumped against the door. "Close one."

Matthew nodded, his face grim. "Sorry if I didn't time it perfectly. I had no idea I was here for a booty call."

I blinked at him in surprise. "What's that supposed to mean?"

"It means I need to stay as far away from you as possible. I'm not comfortable sneaking around like this and don't think it would be possible for me to hide the way I feel from your mom or your friends or anyone else. I'm not that kind of man, Fiona. I'm not as cold and reasonable and logical as you are. You wanted honesty from me, but maybe the person you need to be honest with is yourself."

Matthew reached around me to unlock the door, and left. I smoothed down my dress, lifted my chin, and took a deep breath. Counting to ten, I tried hard to compose myself and failed. I needed to exit the office, sneak up the back stairway to my room, and cry my eyes out. Unfortunately, as soon as I walked into the kitchen, I noticed Scott had left a giant bouquet of pink roses on the kitchen island. I stared at them, willing myself not to cry. He was trying to win me back. I knew it, but it felt like a knife in my heart.

I glanced out the window and saw Scott leaving through the side door of the garden. His shoulders slumped, and he seemed upset, but he still looked gorgeous and perfect and well groomed. A Ken doll. But I was no Barbie, unless Barbie turned secretly slutty and slept with a doll that looked like he belonged in a boy band. I couldn't say because I'd never been allowed to have a Barbie growing up since Mom thought they were a monument to warped and manipulative ideas about feminine beauty.

Madame Lucinda came in and saw the roses. She took a whiff of their sweet scent. "How lovely. I saw your boyfriend carry them in. He's a handsome devil, isn't he?"

She winked at me, grabbed another plate of cookies, and strolled back to the front room. I stared after her in shock, wondering what she meant to convey with that comment. One thing was certain. When Auntie Mags messed around with my chakras, she did something to my brain as well. I didn't know what to do or who to trust anymore. I had to wonder if the devil card wasn't about Matthew or about Scott. Maybe it was about me.

I walked out into the garden and sat by the fountain. There was no magic, no sparkle, and no music. My whole life had been perfectly planned. Now I'd become a woman who'd slept with a man she barely knew. Several times. And he probably hated me.

"It's your fault," I whispered to the fountain. "You made me kiss him."

I brushed a leaf off my skirt and stood up. I didn't like the person I'd become, but there was no going back to who I'd been. Fiona with the lists of pros and cons, dos and don'ts. Fiona with the timeline in her head, her whole life mapped out and organized. Fiona with the definite ideas about who she wanted in her life and why. That girl didn't exist anymore. It was time to grow up.

CHAPTER 19

A BONFIRE MAKES EVERY EVENT MORE
EXCITING. -AUNT FRANCESCA

The Wiccans were a fun bunch. They came once a month for a midnight party on the night of the full moon. Tonight would be no ordinary full moon party, however. It was the summer solstice and a big deal for Wiccans. They called it Midsummer or Litha, and it always turned into a huge event.

Mom and I started working early. It was a beautiful, cloudless day and would be the perfect night for a Midsummer celebration. We had an area in the back of the garden we could use as a fire pit for a bonfire. Although there were restrictions on burning things in the city, we had a special permit because of the religious nature of the ceremony. The leader of the Wiccan coven, Eliza Dragonsong, made sure she renewed the permit every year.

Eliza, a lawyer who wore designer clothing and had her blonde hair perfectly highlighted and cut in a bob, didn't look like a Wiccan priestess. She had on a dark blue suit and an expensive pair of pumps and carried a briefcase imported from Italy. In legal circles, they called her the "dragon lady." Beautiful, professional, and all I aspired to be someday except for the little part about her being a witch and embracing her inner goddess.

Her face lit up when she saw the flower-covered arch we'd made for the ceremony. "Beautiful, ladies. You never fail to get it right." She waved a piece of paper in the air. "Here's the permit. Sorry I'm late. They gave me a little trouble over it this year."

Mom sighed. "I'm sure it has to do with Anderson Solutions and their legal team. Their goal is to make everything as difficult as possible for all of us."

Eliza frowned. A divorce lawyer, she couldn't handle our case, but she had recommended a friend, Janet Kilpatrick, and we'd hired her on the spot. Janet worked for a big firm in town. She was also a South Side girl we'd known for years, and she'd been happy to take the case. She never expected a small zoning issue to take up so much of her time. She gave us a serious discount, but Anderson Solutions had a lot of time, money, and resources invested in this case, and they pulled out some big guns on our little café.

"The city council meeting is coming up soon, isn't it?" Eliza's office, located only a few blocks away, put her in the center of the South Side and made her aware of what had been happening.

Mom nodded. "Fiona will speak for us. We took a vote and decided she's the best person for the job."

I blushed, and Eliza smiled. "No one could handle it better than you, Fiona. I hear Mr. McAlister is sending someone to attend for him. He's too sick to come himself."

"Has he made a decision yet?" I asked.

She shook her head. "I doubt it. Anderson Solutions wouldn't be so jumpy about little things like bonfire permits if he had. They've been putting pressure on the other businesses to convince Mr. McAlister to sell. They stand to lose a lot of money if this deal doesn't go through."

"And we have a lot to lose if it does," Mom said quietly, staring at the garden with its beautiful crumbling walls and flowers. Her life's work. A thing of beauty lost forever if Anderson got their way. I changed the subject.

"Tell me more about the Midsummer celebration."

Eliza smiled. "Our beliefs are tied to the moon and its cycles. The summer solstice is a shift of power. Each day has been building up to the longest day of the year, but when it finally happens, we almost mourn it. It's a paradox, a time of change. The full moon triggers natural rhythms and breeding cycles. It inflames passions and makes even sane people act a little wild. The summer solstice brings all of the crazy to a whole new level."

I listened to her, my eyes widening. Maybe this explained a great deal. "How do you make it stop?"

Eliza laughed, a deep, throaty sound. "You can't make it stop, Fiona. It's ageless. The moon is yin to the earth's yang. It brings life and holds mysteries and affects us in ways we can barely comprehend."

Her cell phone rang. She spoke for a few minutes and then hung up. "Got to go. One of my clients is going through a nasty divorce. Her husband's full moon was seen in someone else's bedroom, and he's going to pay for it dearly," she said with a wink. "Fiona, please join in our celebration this evening. Your mom always comes, and it would be an honor to have you as well. I think you'll enjoy releasing your inner goddess. Also, we can put a blessing on you for the meeting. What do you think?"

I wasn't feeling up for a Wiccan festival but couldn't offend Eliza when her offer was so genuine and kind. "I'd love to come."

She grinned. "Great. I'll see you next by the light of the moon, Fiona Campbell."

"Yippee," I said softly as she left the garden.

Mom giggled. "You're in for a real treat."

The party preparations took all day, and the Wiccans arrived at ten. The bonfire burned, and we'd set up tables piled high with good things to eat. Another table had paper and pens requested by the Wiccans and sheets of beeswax to make candles. Not sure what to wear to a Wiccan Litha festival, I chose a long white sundress that hung loose and light down to my toes. Mom and I spent the afternoon braiding flowers and leaves into wreaths for the Wiccans to wear on their heads. My hair hung down, and I put a wreath on my own head as well. I got a shock when I saw my reflection. I looked more like a flower child than my mom ever did.

Mom dressed a lot like me, and many of the Wiccans wore similar clothing. There were a few men wearing flowing white shirts, but most were women in long dresses. Eliza grinned when she saw me. She wore a full-length white lace dress with spaghetti straps and a tightly fitted bodice. It screamed Paris in the lace, color, and style and in every stitch of the fabric.

"Your dress is beautiful," I told her.

She spun around. "It's nice to have the chance to wear something that isn't a suit. I've found the more feminine I dress, the easier it is to connect with my goddess."

"Yeah. Me too." I looked at Mom, trying hard not to laugh.

"Come out to the garden, Eliza. I want to make sure we did what you wanted." Mom led Eliza out as Kate strolled in, dressed like a curvy, sexy goddess herself in a white dress with a short skirt. Her breasts nearly exploded out of the corset top, and her tattoos provided a sharp blast of color on her pale skin.

I gave her a hug. "What are you doing here?"

"Your mom told me to come. Mrs. Porter's daughter offered to stay with her so I could have a night off."

"I'm so glad." I grabbed a wreath from the table and put it on her head. "Have you done this before?"

Kate shook her head. A woman walked past dressed as a fairy, and Kate snorted. "This is going to be a hoot."

We went out to the garden where the guests gathered. Madame Lucinda was already there. She smiled and waved. The moon glowed in the sky, bright and beautiful. Other than some candles and the twinkle lights in the trees, it provided all the light we needed. Kate and I nibbled on pagan-symbol sugar cookies and waited for the party to start.

"How did things go with Matthew last night?" she asked, and I choked on my cookie. I grabbed a glass of water, but a few minutes passed before I could speak.

"It started out well, but . . ."

Kate grew still. "You did him *again*, didn't you?"

I nodded and whispered in her ear, "In my mom's tearoom. Standing up."

We spoke quietly, but Kate gasped so loudly several people glanced our way. I shushed her and pulled her away from the dessert table. "I think I'm a nymphomaniac."

Kate laughed. "Until a few days ago, you seemed like a bit of a prude. No offense."

"None taken, but Matthew unleashed something. I'm sex crazed. It's out of control."

Kate rolled her eyes. "It might be that way with Matthew, but it isn't like you're sleeping around. Can you even *imagine* doing it with someone else?"

I stared at her. Kate munched on a cookie, oblivious to the fact she'd shifted my nicely planned and organized life right off its axis. "I can't. Oh, *crap*." I winced. "This is a disaster. I'm just like my mom and Aunt Francesca. I think Matthew has ruined me for other men. I don't want anyone else. I want him."

Kate thought about it. "What are you going to do?"

"I have no idea. For tonight, I'm going to release my inner goddess and hope she doesn't jump some unsuspecting man."

Kate's eyes danced with mischief. "This is going to be fun. I've always wanted to see you let go for once, get a little wild and irresponsible."

"Matthew said if I acted more irresponsibly, Mom would become more responsible." I frowned, thinking about how well she'd organized things lately, even bringing the books to Mr. Jenkins. Maybe Matthew had a point.

"Well, there is only one way to test his theory." She pointed at the punch bowl set up by the food. "Is that mulled wine?"

I nodded, and she poured each of us a glass. We lifted our cups into the air. "Cheers," I said as we touched our glasses together.

"To irresponsible behavior," said Kate.

I took a sip of the sweet and spicy wine. Immediately, my belly felt warm, and I was a little bit happier.

"Yum," said Kate. "What did you put in this stuff?"

Mom came up to Kate and kissed her cheek. "Magic and moonlight and a touch of mulling spice," she said. "It's the only way to make punch worthy of a Litha celebration."

She grabbed a plate of cookies and brought them to some Wiccans admiring our fountain. Kate looked at me and giggled. "How does she always do that? She comes up when we are in midconversation and says something profound and yet a little . . . well . . ."

"Off? I know. I've lived with it my whole life. It looks like they're ready. Let's go to the bonfire."

Eliza called the quarters. We faced east, and she said, "From the east come the winds, cool and clear. Be part of our circle now."

The Wiccans all responded, "Hail and welcome."

We turned to the south, and Eliza spoke again. "The sun

is the light of fire on the land, the sea, and the heavens. Be part of our circle now."

"Hail and welcome."

Eliza turned to the west. "From the west come rain and fog and life-giving water. Be part of our circle now."

"Hail and welcome."

At last, she turned to the north and said, "The earth is below my feet with soil rich and fertile. Be part of our circle now."

"Hail and welcome."

A cauldron provided by Eliza hung over the bonfire. Eliza placed herbs in the water of the cauldron, and soon the air grew rich with the scents of rosemary, thyme, bay leaf, and several other things I couldn't pick out. We burned cedar wood for the bonfire, also supplied by Eliza, and it smelled rich and soothing.

One of the Wiccans gave us each a piece of paper and a pen. We all stood around the fire, cheeks rosy both from the warmth of the flames and the wine. Eliza addressed us with a small smile playing on her lips.

"You are part of the divine. You are one with the universe. Open your hearts and your minds. Use this paper to write down your greatest desire, your special wish, or your secret pain, and then throw it into the fire, releasing it and sending it out into the heavens."

The Wiccans scribbled on the slips of paper. I wasn't sure what to write. I had pain from never knowing my father, dreams of becoming a professional, and way too much desire for a man who wasn't my boyfriend. I decided to keep it simple. *Show me my heart's desire.*

I threw it into the fire and watched as the bright flame ate my piece of paper until it curled up and burned into nothing but ash. As soon as all the wishes were tossed into the fire, several of the Wiccans picked up drums and a few other instruments, and we danced. We held hands and moved in a clockwise direction around the bonfire like an adult game of ring-around-the-rosy.

I'm not sure if it was the mulled wine or if they burned something other than cooking herbs in the fire, but I felt joyful and free. I held on to Kate's hand as we danced. We moved faster and faster as the drums pounded and people swayed. The music reached a fever pitch; then it stopped, and all was quiet. We stood looking at each other in confusion, panting a bit after the exertion of the dancing, and Eliza spoke to us in a loud, strong voice.

"To the fountain."

We walked to the fountain, laughing and excited. I had no idea what was about to happen but didn't care. Living in the moment. The new me.

We stood around the fountain, and Eliza told us to use the sheets of beeswax to make a candle. We filled it with herbs signifying what we needed help with the most. There were bowls of herbs labeled "Health," "Wealth," and "Happiness," and the last was "Love." Kate and I went straight to the love bowl, sprinkled the herbs on our sheets of beeswax, put a long wick through the middle, and rolled it up. The Wiccan with fairy wings gave us little drip guards so the hot wax wouldn't burn our fingers.

We stood in a circle around the fountain. Eliza led the Wiccans in prayers of thankfulness for the longest day of the year and asked for protection as the days grew shorter and the nights grew longer. They put a blessing on me for the council meeting. Very peaceful and normal. Not knowing what to expect from a Midsummer celebration, I'd pictured cackling witches stirring cauldrons full of nasty, smelly, and foul things. These people simply loved nature and were tied to it in ways I hadn't expected.

The Wiccans sang softly in a strange language. The sound,

mournful and yet beautiful, carried into the night. As they sang, they lit the candles one by one. After Eliza lit her candle, she used her it to light the candle of the person next to her. Soon candlelight bathed our faces, and slowly, softly, the song ended.

Eliza's candle had burned down to a nub. She stood directly across the fountain from Kate and me and spoke. "Wells and springs are connections to the otherworld, and right in front of us is a sacred spring, rising up from a secret river far below the land."

I looked at Kate and rolled my eyes. Kate bit her lip to keep from giggling. My candle was nearly gone. I'd polished off my glass of mulled wine quickly and felt more than a little buzzed at the moment.

Eliza continued. "By bathing in the sacred water on this holy day, we ensure the rain will be brought to the crops."

My eyes widened in alarm as some of the Wiccans undressed. The woman in the fairy costume wore nothing but a set of wings by the time she finished. I looked around for Mom and heard a strange noise as the fountain began acting peculiar. The normal gurgling sound it usually made had grown louder and stronger. Suddenly water shot out of the fountain and straight up into the air. It fell on our heads like a gentle rain. In spite of my panic about the naked Wiccans in our garden, it was a beautiful sight. I tilted my head up to the sky and laughed.

The music started again, and the Wiccans danced. A little differently this time, more sensual and erotic. Eliza raised her hands to the sky. The "dragon lady" lawyer was gone. In her place stood a pagan priestess.

"All of the men are naked," whispered Kate. "It figures. Men love to be naked."

Several of the women pulled Kate off to dance in their circle. A naked man tried to dance with me, but I managed to scamper away. I moved to the edge of the group, and that's when I saw him. Matthew stood in the shadows, watching me. He wore a white shirt like the other pagans, but he was so beautiful, he looked like he could have been their god.

Show me my heart's desire. I'd made the wish, and only moments later, he stood right in front of me. This Midsummer wishing method had proved to be extremely effective.

He held out his hand to me, and I took it. His hand was warm and big and his grip strong. He led me to the darkest corner of the garden, as far away as possible from the wild Wiccans and their Midsummer party. He dragged me behind a huge, flowering rhododendron and pulled me into his arms for a passionate, angry kiss. I melted against him, taking in his anger and answering it with soft, sweet nibbles on his lips and gentle, hesitant strokes of my tongue. My hands were on his shoulders, and as soon as I felt his muscles relax and knew he wasn't as angry anymore, I slid my hands up to his hair and pulled him closer.

He pressed me against the back wall of the garden, his hands hot as they moved over my body, greedily covering my breasts and moving to my bottom to grab it firmly and pull me closer to him. I moaned into his mouth, and his hands reached down to pull my dress up to my waist. He yanked off my undies, his movements frantic. I pushed him down to the ground and climbed on top of him. The pagan drums pounded in the background and I'd imbibed enough to feel brave. I straddled his body, my eyes on his face, and gently lowered myself on top of him. He groaned, but the Wiccans were so loud no one heard him. I wouldn't have cared if they had because all that mattered to me at this point was having Matthew inside me.

The drums continued to play. Matthew's hands gripped my hips, helping me find my rhythm. The scent of the cedar from the bonfire mixed with the perfume from the wreath of flowers in my hair. I leaned forward and clung to Matthew, kissing him with everything in my heart and my soul. I felt myself getting closer and closer to a climax, and just before we both came in the most perfect kind of unison, I whispered in his ear, "I love you, Matthew."

CHAPTER 20

S lowly, steadily we both fell back to earth. Matthew
helped me up and straightened my dress. He buttoned
his jeans and stared down at me, his face hidden in
shadows.

"What did you say?"

My cheeks got warm, not because of the wine. "I love you,
Matthew."

He cradled my face gently in his hands, his thumbs
stroking my cheeks. "Are you sure?"

His dark eyes, illuminated by the moonlight, were no
longer sad or angry. They were full of hope.

"I've known for days but was afraid to admit it," I said.

Matthew touched his forehead to mine. "Last night, the
look on your face when that suit showed up . . ."

He sounded like a person in pain. I tilted my chin up to
give him a gentle kiss. "Scott's last girlfriend cheated on him.
He walked in on them. I didn't want it to happen to him
again. It seemed unnecessarily cruel."

Matthew went still. "It wasn't because you still love him?"

"Is that what you thought?" He didn't have to answer. It

showed on his face. I grabbed him by the shirt and pulled him close. "I don't love Scott. I never did. I've never loved anyone but you."

"I love you, too, Fiona. So much." He pulled me close, his face in my hair, and spoke in a whisper. "What are we going to do?"

I played with a button on his shirt. "Well, first I'd better get out of these soggy clothes. My dress is still damp from the fountain water."

"Yes, it is." Matthew brushed the hair out of my eyes. "You're soaked to the skin . . . again."

I reached up to whisper in his ear. "And we did it in a public place . . . again."

He laughed, low and soft. "Yes, we did." He ran his hands up my arms. "I seem to notice a pattern here, but you're getting cold. Do you want to go to your room and change?"

"Only if you come with me," I murmured against his lips.

He gave me a sexy grin. "My pleasure." He paused and muttered an oath as he searched the ground around us.

"What happened?"

"I can't find the condom. I thought I left it right here."

"We used a condom? I lost my panties, too, by the way."

He grinned, a flash of white in the moonlight. "You're taking this whole free spirit thing a little too seriously."

"I'm a changed woman. What can I say? Let's go inside. I'll find everything tomorrow."

Later, after peeling off my soggy clothes and making love one more time, we curled up under the quilt Mom made for me when I was a little girl. I had my back to Matthew, and he held me close, his big, warm body fitting perfectly next to mine.

"What were you doing in the garden, and who were those naked people?"

I giggled. "Wiccans. Summer solstice. They invited me to their party."

"Wow. What was going on with the fountain?"

I turned to see his face. "I have no idea. It suddenly shot water straight into the air. Very strange."

Matthew's lips curved into a smile. He was half-asleep, and he looked completely content and satisfied. I felt exactly the same.

"Why did you come tonight?" I asked. "You were so mad at me."

He kissed me softly on the mouth. "Yes, but I couldn't get you out of my mind. I decided to go for a walk, and my feet led me right here. I don't seem to have the ability to stay away from you, Fiona Campbell. I'm sorry I was a jerk."

I stroked his cheek with my hand. "I'm sorry I was a jerk too. I made a wish to have my heart's desire for Midsummer, and you came. These Wiccans know their stuff."

He gave me a crooked smile. "I smelled smoke and thought the café was on fire. The front door was locked, so I ran around the side. I heard the drums and found you dancing in the moonlight with a bunch of naked people and with flowers in your hair." He yawned and pulled my back tightly next to his stomach again. I loved the way my bottom fit against his body, the way his legs twined with mine. He had his arms wrapped around me, and he laced my fingers in his. "Tell me again."

I sighed, my eyes growing heavy. "I love you, Matthew. Now go to sleep." And like a magic charm, it worked.

Matthew was still asleep the next morning, looking all luscious and tousled, when I slipped out from under his arm and put on my robe. I wanted to grab some coffee and make him breakfast in bed but came to a skidding halt when I saw Mom sitting at the island. She was sipping coffee and waiting for me, a pair of slightly muddy white undies in her lap.

"Good morning." I went straight to the coffeepot, hesitating for only a moment before grabbing two cups. No point in hiding the fact Matthew slept in my bed. I was an adult. He was an adult. Mom, the most free-spirited, sensual, and accepting person in the world, adored Matthew and certainly wouldn't have a problem with any of this.

It turned out I was wrong. On several counts.

She held up my undies with one finger. "I found these behind my rhododendron bush this morning, along with a used condom. At first, I thought they must have belonged to one of our naked pagans, but then I realized they were yours. Care to explain?"

I opened my mouth and closed it again, but no sound came out. Her face froze when she heard the sound of Matthew's feet as he softly padded down the stairs. He wore his slightly crumpled white shirt and jeans, and his feet were bare. His face lit up when he saw me. It took him a second to realize my mom sat at the island with my undies in her lap. His cheeks turned instantly pink.

"Good morning, Claire."

My mom stood up, set the underpants down on the chair, and walked outside. Matthew looked at me in surprise.

I slid my arms around his waist, kissing his neck. "You may have been right about your whole yin and yang theory. As soon as I acted just a little irresponsibly, she suddenly became super responsible. And a little snippy. Let's give her a few minutes. I'll talk to her later."

Matthew's eyebrows narrowed into a worried frown. "I don't want to cause a problem between you and your mom."

I didn't tell him about the condom. I went up on my tiptoes to kiss him softly on the lips. "You aren't. And good morning, by the way."

"Good morning to you too." He gave me a sexy smile as his arms wrapped around me. My body immediately responded. I sighed and pulled away. We'd already done the deed in my mom's garden, in her tearoom, and in my bedroom. It wouldn't improve matters if she caught us in her kitchen.

After a simple breakfast of eggs and toast, we sat together at the island, sipping coffee and talking. "I don't know anything about you," I said. "Where are you from? What are your parents like? Do you have brothers and sisters?"

He grinned. "You are full of questions this morning. I'm from Philly, but I've lived all over the place. My parents died in a car accident when I was small. I don't remember them."

I touched his arm. "Sorry."

He shrugged. "My grandfather raised me, and he's wonderful. I don't have any brothers or sisters, but I have cousins and lots of good friends. Sometimes they feel like family to me."

"I grew up thinking I had tons of aunts and uncles. It wasn't until I got older I realized I wasn't related to any of them. Mom and I are kind of alone in the world."

The sun peeked in through the kitchen window, bringing out the flecks of green and gold in Matthew's eyes. He brushed a lock of hair behind my ear, and his face grew suddenly serious. "There's something I need to tell you."

The bell on the front door rang, and Kate came stomping into the kitchen in search of coffee. She froze in her tracks when she saw Matthew and I cozied up at the island, a huge grin spreading across her face.

"Looks like somebody had fun at summer solstice last night."

I winced. "Sorry, Matthew. She has no filter. Good morning, Kate."

"Good morning, lovers." She poured herself a cup of coffee and wiggled her eyebrows at us. "Don't be embarrassed. You do realize the 'Great Rite' is part of the whole

Midsummer thing, don't you? Eliza will make a good little pagan of you yet."

She went back to the front room, and Matthew looked confused. "Is the 'Great Rite' what I think it is?"

"I believe so. What we were doing behind my mom's rhododendron last night." I glanced out into the garden. "Speaking of my mom . . ."

Matthew stood up and kissed the top of my head. "I'd better go. I have some errands to run. Can I see you later?"

I stood up and pulled him close. "Yes. But give me a real kiss before you go."

Matthew cupped my face in his hands and kissed me until my toes curled. When he let me go, I felt a little dizzy. I looked up at him, blinking as I tried to compose myself. "Wow."

Matthew didn't look altogether steady himself. "I love you."

"I love you too."

I was almost scared to face my mom at first. I found her sweeping up the ashes from the bonfire and putting them into garbage bags. She didn't look up when I approached, but she did speak to me. A good sign.

"The Wiccans gather the ashes from their summer solstice party every year and use them as a charm for protection and also for performing magic spells. I promised Eliza I'd collect the ashes this morning. Do you mind dropping them at the courthouse for me while I make lunch?"

"Sure. Can we talk about what happened in there?"

We sat down on a bench. She wore jeans and an old tie-dyed T-shirt. Ash covered her hands, and she had a spot of ash on her face. I waited quietly for her to collect her thoughts. When she finally spoke, her voice sounded tiny and lost.

"I don't want you to make the same mistakes I did."

I looked at her in surprise. "I'm not."

Her blue eyes filled with tears. "Yes, you are. You had sex in the garden, behind my rhododendron, after getting drunk at a pagan ritual. You were in a public place. What's going on with you? You're turning into me."

I shook my head at her convoluted logic, took a deep breath, and spoke to her calmly. "I wasn't drunk, but the rest is pretty accurate."

She brushed a bit of ash from her jeans. "I know you hate the word, but is there any chance you might love Matthew, Fiona?"

I didn't hesitate. "Yes."

Her eyes grew huge in her face. "Really?"

"I don't know if it was the unblocking of my chakras or the tarot card reading or the magic of that silly old fountain, but something has changed. I love him, Mom. I'm sure."

She smiled. "I like him, Fiona, but I saw the way things were going and was afraid you would end up a mess and alone. Like me."

I put my arms around her and gave her a hug. "You aren't a mess, and you aren't alone. You have me, and you always will."

The ash filled two garbage bags, but it was easy to carry. The courthouse was only a few blocks away, so I slipped into a short dress the color of sunshine and nearly skipped the whole way to deliver the ashes to Eliza. Joy filled me so completely I thought I might burst. I loved Matthew, and he loved me. The upcoming council meeting still hung like a dark cloud on the horizon, but even that couldn't take away my joy. I no longer had to go to my heart center to feel the glowing orb. My whole body hummed with happiness.

Eliza met me in front of the courthouse, looking like a lawyer once again. She grinned when she saw me, and I grinned right back, handing her the bags of ash and kissing her cheek.

"Midsummer has been good to you. You're positively glowing, Fiona."

I ducked my head shyly. "Well, I'm in love."

Eliza squeezed my hand. "An especially lucky omen during Litha. Many of our coven wait for Midsummer to perform their hand-fasting ceremony for that reason and end our celebration with the performance of the 'Great Rite.' Love is in the air during summer solstice."

I was about to leave when her expression changed. A bunch of men in suits approached the courthouse, and Eliza pulled me off to the side. "That's the group from Anderson Solutions. They're meeting today."

I watched the men walk up the steps of the courthouse. My heart stopped, and I nearly sank to my knees in shock. I grabbed onto the stone balustrade on the side of the steps to steady myself.

"Fiona. What's wrong?" asked Eliza as she put an arm around my shoulders.

I couldn't speak. I could only stare as Matthew, *my* Matthew, walked up the steps surrounded by men from Anderson Solutions. He wore a suit and carried a briefcase. Even from a distance, it was obvious his suit was expensive and custom-made. He had a large tube slung over his shoulders like the kind architectural students used to carry blueprints.

After they entered the courthouse, I sat down on one of the cold and dirty steps, not caring about my pretty yellow dress. Not caring about anything.

Eliza looked worried. "Should I call your mom?"

I couldn't tell Mom that Matthew had betrayed us. It was bad enough to deal with it myself. I forced myself to stand. "I'll be fine."

Eliza didn't look convinced. "Your entire aura changed in a second. It went from glowing and golden to . . . dark."

I almost laughed. I didn't believe in auras any more than chakras or tarot cards or magic, but Eliza was correct. Everything went dark the minute I realized Matthew worked for Anderson. The little door to my heart I opened to him now slammed shut and welded closed. I'd never be stupid enough to let anyone in again.

Eliza watched me with a worried frown on her beautiful face. I squared my shoulders and forced myself to smile. "Well, Dragon Lady, maybe a dark aura is a good thing right now. I have a battle to wage. Will you help me?"

She nodded, but there was something sad in her eyes. "Darkness is never good, Fiona."

"Neither is falling in love with a liar."

CHAPTER 21

REVENGE IS A DISH BEST SERVED COLD. SO IS
ICE CREAM. -AUNT FRANCESCA

I spent most of the afternoon in Eliza's office, using her computer to research Mr. Matthew Monroe. He wasn't hard to find. He was the award-winning architect who'd done the renovation project on the row of Victorians down by the river, including the one he lived in. If the photographs of him online had not been enough, the photos of his home would have been. I knew it well. It was where I'd done the horizontal mambo with him only days ago. The vertical mambo, too, if I took into account what we'd done in the kitchen. And in the shower. I'd basically mamboed all over the place in that house.

The pictures of him wearing a tux and attending different galas got me. He wasn't a poor musician. He was glamorous and wealthy and had a different beautiful girl on his arm in every photo.

"Did you find anything to connect him to Anderson Solutions?" asked Eliza.

"It doesn't matter. We saw him with them. He's designing the parking garage."

Eliza frowned. "But it says he's famous for restoration work . . ."

Bitterness rose in my chest. "He goes where the money is and doesn't care who gets hurt in the process." Thoughts of my mom and Rosie at Pamela's Diner and poor, dear Sally almost brought a wave of hot, heavy tears. I quashed those tears with my anger. It was stronger than my hurt right now.

Eliza glanced at her watch. "I have to get going."

I stood up. "I'm so sorry. I've tied you up for hours."

She shook her head. "I keep my schedule open the day after summer solstice. I never know how tired I'll be."

"Thank you, Eliza." As I walked toward the door, Eliza stopped me with a hand on my arm.

"He's innocent until proven guilty, Fiona. Remember that."

I pursed my lips. "The proof was in front of my own eyes."

It was almost dinnertime when I got back to the café. Scott sat outside, waiting for me. He hadn't brought roses this time, a wise decision.

He frowned at the expression on my face and gathered me into a warm hug. "What's wrong?" he asked.

Big and solid, he looked and smelled so nice, but I didn't love him, and I knew I never would. It made me want to scream in frustration. I found the man I'd always wanted and then found a way to mess it up. Maybe I was more like my mother and Aunt Francesca than I realized.

Scott reached into his pocket to hand me one of the handkerchiefs embroidered with his initials, but I wasn't crying. Not anymore. My heart felt like a cold, black rock in my chest.

He shoved his handkerchief back into his pocket, confused. "I stopped by last night, but you were having a private party."

Blushing, I thought about the very private party Matthew and I enjoyed behind the rhododendron. "We need to talk, Scott."

We went into the garden and sat near the fountain in a set of wrought-iron chairs. Mom said the chairs reminded her of spring in Paris. Scott turned his chair to face me. We sat so close our knees touched. He reached for my hand and held it in his. "Do you love me, Fiona? Even a little?"

I took a shaky breath. Part of me wanted to lie to him, but I couldn't. My lower lip trembled. "I *should* love you, Scott. You're perfect for me." The fountain made a strange sound, almost like a hiccup.

Scott didn't seem to notice. "But you don't." He cleared his throat. "So why exactly did you date me?"

"I thought liking you was enough."

"After Brittany, I didn't think I'd ever be able to love someone again, but I do. I love you." His voice shook as he spoke. "Maybe you can learn to love me too."

He leaned closer, about to kiss me, when the fountain made a louder sound. A burping sort of sound. This time it got Scott's attention too. "Did you hear something?"

"Yes," I said. "I think it was the fountain."

He looked concerned. "Is it going to spit at me again?"

I couldn't make any promises at this point. "I'm not sure."

Scott stood up and pulled me to my feet. "I'm going to prove myself to you, Fiona. I'll make you love me."

He kissed me, his lips firm and warm against mine, and he was determined. Very determined. He wanted to elicit some sort of emotional reaction from me but failed. I felt nothing. Nothing at all.

Scott jumped away from me like he'd been stung. "What the . . ."

"I'm sorry," I said. "I tried. I honestly did."

It took me a second to realize he wasn't referring to my

lack of ardor. He stared down at his feet, feet now resting in the middle of what looked like a small stream. The water came from the fountain and covered his shoes. I stood right next to him, but my feet stayed dry.

"There must be a leak," I said. "Which would explain those weird sounds."

Scott stomped away, furious, and sat down on a bench far from the fountain. "It's a menace," he said as he took off first one shoe and then the other, dumping out a significant amount of water. "These are my custom-made Johnson and Murphy's. I lost one pair the night we had dinner with Harrison and Mindy, which is ridiculous. Who loses shoes? I think they were stolen. And now these are ruined. Five-hundred-dollar shoes. Do you realize that?"

I had on a pair of flip-flops I'd gotten for free at a block party last year. It didn't seem fair he'd been the one to suffer the wrath of the fountain.

I shook my head. The wrath of the fountain? The fountain was an inanimate object, a lump of stone and rusted pipes. It did not feel wrath, and it didn't target Scott, although it felt that way, especially to him.

"This whole place is a dump. An accident about to happen. I can't believe your stupid mother won't sell this shack to Anderson and move on. She's a complete and total idiot."

He attempted to dry his $500 shoes with his expensive, embroidered handkerchief. I stared at him, unable to hold myself back any longer. "She isn't an idiot, and this isn't a dump."

He snorted. "I beg to differ. The proof is right in front of you, but you're too blind to see it."

"You're the blind one, Scott."

He frowned, glancing up at me. "What do you mean?"

"My mother is amazing. And this place might be in disrepair, but it's still beautiful."

He looked around the garden and studied the back of the house. "Which part? The dilapidated fountain or the house about to fall down around your ears? You both need to wise up and accept the offer before it's too late."

"Too late for what?"

He froze for a second and then went back to cleaning his shoes. "Before they rescind it. Most of the people on the block have finally woken up, but not you and your mother. Oh no. You have to be difficult and hang onto a place that is literally falling apart."

He wrung out his handkerchief, now dripping with water, and glared at me. Suddenly he didn't look quite as perfect and handsome. He looked more like a spoiled, nasty little boy.

"I didn't want to hurt you, Scott, but you've given me no choice. I tried to be nice. I tried to be gentle. Now you need to listen. Carefully. I don't want you to come here ever again."

He shook his head. "You're angry. You'll come to your senses eventually."

"I already did, and I fell in love with someone else." I didn't bother adding Matthew had broken my heart. Scott didn't need to know that part.

He looked like he'd been slapped. "No."

"It's true. And karma might punish me for saying this because I know I hurt you, but I'm not even sorry about it." I blurted out the words. I couldn't help it.

He pulled on his shoes with quick, angry movements. His socks were soaked, which gave me great pleasure. I hoped he would get a blister.

"This makes things so much easier for me. To think I felt guilty . . ." He shook his head and laughed. Not a pleasant sound. "Goodbye, Fiona, and good riddance."

He turned on his heel and stomped away, although the effect wasn't as dramatic as he'd hoped. His shoes squeaked with every step, and I thought I heard water sloshing. I would have laughed except the whole situation felt so tragic.

I sat outside and stared at the fountain a long time. It had stopped leaking as soon as Scott left. Weird.

The sun was setting when I walked into the shop. I thought I'd reached my low point, but things got worse when I found Mom sitting in the kitchen with Auntie Mags, Sally, and Madame Lucinda. She had a piece of paper clenched in her hands.

"Fiona. You're back."

I looked around, trying to figure out what was going on. No one would meet my eyes, which made me worried. "What happened?"

Mom handed me the paper. I read it twice to make sure I understood. It was a citation for noise pollution and disruptive behavior due to the pagan festival in our garden last night. Our final warning. The café was going to be closed. Permanently. They gave us until the council meeting to tie things up. I stared around the shop in dismay. We had only a few days left and no way to fight back. Anderson had won.

"I'm done." Mom cried softly as Sally put a reassuring arm around her shoulders and handed her a tissue.

I read the paper again, trying to wrap my head around the fact that it was over. "Not to make things even worse, but I have some bad news too." I told them about how Matthew secretly worked for Anderson. Mom stared at me in disbelief. It felt like we were hit from all sides.

"Oh, Fiona. I'm so sorry."

Sally looked a bit shell-shocked. "I can't believe it. Matthew is such a nice boy."

Madame Lucinda agreed. "Nothing in the cards predicted this. Is there any way you could be mistaken?"

"I saw him with the people from Anderson. And there's more." I grabbed my laptop and showed them what I'd found online.

Auntie Mags stared at the photos with a wrinkled frown. "He looks so familiar."

"You probably saw him here. He hung around often enough."

Mom looked at the pictures sadly. "Why would Frankie recommend him to me? How did Matthew even *know* Frankie?"

"I have no idea, but he lied to us, and he lied to me." I closed my laptop and folded my hands on top of it.

"And you loved him," said Auntie Mags. "You opened your heart to him, and he failed you."

"A good lesson. I won't make the same mistake again."

Auntie Mags looked like she was about to say something else when our lawyer, Janet Kilpatrick, rushed into the room. Janet, small with short with dark hair and delicate features, was always a ball of energy, but today she seemed so wound up she nearly vibrated. Eliza had come with her. They both wore their work clothes.

"Where's the citation?" asked Eliza, and I handed it to her. Her gaze skimmed the page, and she handed it to Janet. Janet read it over too.

"Bullshit." Janet might look like a pixie, but she had the language of a longshoreman. She'd grown up on the South Side, like me, and her father owned Paddy's Pub down the street.

"Who told them about the festival last night?" asked Eliza. "The only people here were our fellow Wiccans and Kate."

My eyes met my mom's. "And Matthew," I said.

Eliza sank into a chair. "The one you saw with the Anderson people?"

"He walked in on the naked yoga class too. And he may have overheard me talking to Mom about what was in her tea. I asked him if he had called the department of health on us and he denied it. All lies. He used me to get the dirt on us."

I stood next to Sally, and she pulled me into her arms so I could rest my head on her broad shoulder. She might be a former linebacker dressed in vintage pink Oscar de la Renta and wearing a jaunty little pillbox hat, but Sally was the kindest and most nurturing person I knew. She was currently on a Jackie Kennedy kick and adored clothes from the sixties. Finding them in her size was another matter altogether.

"Poor, poor poppet," said Sally.

Mom shook her head. "He wasn't using you. Even if he does work for Anderson, even if he did lie to you, I know for a fact he loved you, Fiona. I saw it on his face every single time he looked at you."

"I hate to say this, but I never liked Scott," said Sally, and the others murmured in agreement. Sally never said a negative thing about anyone, so this was a big deal. "But I did like Matthew. I don't understand how he could do this to us."

Janet pulled some files out of her briefcase and scanned the contents. Her dark head bent over the pages.

"What are you looking for?" I asked.

She frowned. "This is documentation from Anderson about your many 'infractions.' When you mentioned the yoga class, I remembered a note inside one of these files. It was about who called in the information. The name was something odd. I can't remember what it was, but I don't think it was Monroe."

"Who was it?" I had no false hopes Matthew was innocent but wondered if someone else was involved.

Janet closed the files with a groan. "I got this stuff today, and it's a total mess. This is another trick they play because they know I'm on my own. I need to sort through it. I'll let you know as soon as I find something."

Mom patted her hand. "Thank you, Janet, but I don't know how much more we can afford for you to do . . ."

Janet's cheeks got pink. "I'm not charging you for this, Ms. Campbell. I had to charge you court fees since those were incurred during office hours. I'm doing this on my own."

My mom's eyes filled with tears. "I don't want to take advantage of your kindness or generosity. Are you sure, Janet?"

Janet nodded. "We're in this together."

"All of us," said Eliza.

Sally stood up and raised her glass in the air. "All for one and one for all," she said, chugging what was left in her glass. The other ladies giggled and did the same.

I looked around at our odd little group, a Wiccan priestess, a lawyer, a reiki therapist, a tarot card reader, a transgender shop owner, a former hippie, and me. Suddenly I didn't feel so hopeless or alone anymore. Scott had disappointed me, and Matthew betrayed me, but I still had a lot of people on my side.

Janet pulled me aside. "I heard you're going to speak at the town meeting."

"They asked me to help."

She smiled. "You're the perfect person for it. Once you decide what you want to say, I can look over it for you."

"Wonderful. Thank you."

Janet yawned, exhausted. "It's the least I can do. Do you know once when I was little my dad got sick? Your mom and Auntie Mags and one of their friends, I think her name was Anna, helped out at the pub for months until he got better and could work again. They saved his business. I don't know what we would have done without them, and they expected nothing in return."

Janet gave me a wobbly smile, and I put an arm around her shoulders. I felt like a giant standing next to her. This must be how Sally felt next to everyone.

"I'm sure they were glad to help."

"They were, and they did the same for more people than you can count. If it's okay with you, I'd like to get the word out that your mom is in trouble. If nothing else, I think it'll mean a lot to her to see her friends at the meeting."

"If you think it will help."

"I do. And one last thing, avoid confronting Matthew. I know it is a lot to ask, but it might work to our advantage if they don't realize we're onto them."

I felt a little sick to my stomach. "I can't pretend to feel the same way about him."

"Could you make up another reason for being upset?"

I nodded. I could think of lots of reasons for being upset with him at the moment.

Later, after helping my mom clean up, I sat with her by the fountain, drinking a glass of red. The wine was so good; it had to have been expensive, but I didn't care. The fountain seemed quiet and peaceful, different from how it had been when the Wiccans held their party. Or from how it had acted with Scott only a few hours ago.

"I don't think the fountain likes Scott." I explained to her what had happened. "Do you think it's broken?"

She shook her head. "I think it's an excellent judge of character."

"How did you make the water shoot up into the air during the Wiccan party?"

"Pagan magic." I gave her a steady look, and she giggled. "Okay. I found a lever in the basement years ago. I only do it during summer solstice because it's so old and rusted I'm afraid it might break, and we could end up flooding our garden."

"It didn't flood the garden today, but it flooded Scott's five-hundred-dollar shoes. Thank you, fountain."

She clinked her glass with mine. "Here's to his shoes."

I took a drink. "I hope he gets trench rot from those wet socks. And a blister."

"Shhh, Fiona. Karma."

I rolled my eyes. If karma rewarded me with a blister of my own, it would be worth it if Scott suffered too.

"You never told me about the lever in the basement."

"I have my secrets." She winked at me and took a sip of wine. "And I didn't allow you to attend the Wiccan festivals when you were younger for obvious reasons. They aren't for virgins or skeptics."

"I'll always be a skeptic. Now more than ever."

She let out a sigh. "I'm sorry Matthew hurt you, but would you have traded those moments with him, even if you had known the outcome?"

"I don't know." When things had been good with Matthew, they had been very good. "What about you? With my dad?"

She sipped the last bit of wine from her glass and turned to me. "I would not have traded one moment, not even one second with your father, and the time we spent together wasn't perfect. We argued, and sometimes we hurt each other, but we truly loved each other. A powerful and magnificent thing."

She got up and carried the glasses inside, and I sat by myself a few minutes longer. Matthew hurt me, but if he hadn't shown up, I probably would have married Scott and ended up totally miserable.

I sighed and put my fingers in the cool water. I knew Matthew worked for Anderson, and he'd done something unforgivable by spying on us. I knew I should hate him, but I couldn't. I was a complete fool.

I didn't believe it was magic, but there was one thing I could wish for, and I spoke the words softly into the night wind.

"I wish I could be wrong about him."

CHAPTER 22

IF THE CAKE CRUMBLES, COVER IT IN
CUSTARD AND CALL IT A TRIFLE. -AUNT
FRANCESCA

The next morning, I forgot about Matthew's betrayal for a few minutes before coming fully awake. I dreamed we were both naked and loving each other, our bodies saying what words could not. When I forced myself to open my eyes, my body still ached with desire for him, but my mind cruelly reminded me of the truth. The sad and lonely truth.

Mom left coffee on downstairs and put two fresh chocolate croissants on a plate for me. She must have gotten up early if she had time to make croissants. The tea ladies would be in heaven tomorrow.

Thinking about the tea ladies made me realize Matthew would be here for acoustic night. I groaned as Mom came in from the garden.

"Good morning to you too," she said.

I plopped down into one of the chairs at the island. "Tonight is acoustic night. I don't want to face him. Do you need me here?

She kissed my cheek. "I already asked Kate and Chad to cover for you."

"Thanks." I took a sip of coffee. "Janet asked me not to bring up Anderson Solutions to Matthew. Can you avoid mentioning it tonight?"

She nodded. "Janet is such a sweet girl."

She stood by the window, humming as she trimmed flowers for an arrangement in the kitchen sink. If I hadn't known she was on the edge of losing her business, I would never have suspected she had a care in the world.

"She said you helped her family out years ago."

She shrugged as she put roses in a vase. "It was nothing."

I took a bite of the croissant and moaned. Mom made the most perfect croissants. They were crunchy and buttery and filled with decadent dark chocolate. Some of the chocolate dripped down my chin. I wiped it with my napkin.

"Janet thought it was something. She said you and Auntie Mags and another lady saved their business. Who was she?"

She paused, her hands on the flowers. "Anna. Dear, sweet Anna. The reason I went to India."

"What do you mean?"

Mom poured herself a cup of coffee and sat down next to me. "I'd graduated from college, and my parents put major pressure on me to marry William. They wanted us to set a date, and it drove them crazy I kept putting it off."

"They didn't notice you spent more time abroad than at home during college?"

She laughed. "You're right. A semester in France, a semester in Japan, and a whole year in England. I signed up for every summer program too. Did I ever tell you about the time I spent in Istanbul? It may have been my favorite city ever."

"I remember," I said with a smile. "Tell me about Anna."

Her eyes grew sad. "I knew her since I was small, and Auntie Mags too. They were my dearest friends. Anna and her husband were killed in a terrible accident. Pointless and tragic for two people so young and so in love. They'd just married and started a family. I needed to find a way to make sense of it. Frankie told me about the ashram in India, and I decided to go. I met your father there, and the rest is history."

"Did you learn anything at the ashram to help you?"

She sighed. "I found peace and knew my friend would live on. Buddha said, 'Do not dwell in the past, do not dream of the future, concentrate the mind on the present moment.' Isn't it beautiful? And so freeing. It takes away all your worry and regret if you live in the now."

I nodded, not sure I bought into that philosophy. It was the reason my mom didn't have a 401(k).

The phone rang. She answered it in her office and came back to the kitchen with a huge smile on her face. "The hospital called. Moses is awake. He's sitting up and talking to the nurses."

We got dressed as quickly as we could and nearly ran to the hospital. Ten minutes later, we stood on either side of Moses, holding his hands. Mom cried, of course, and so did I.

"There's no need for tears," he said, giving our hands a gentle squeeze. "I didn't die. I took a little nap."

Officers Miller and Belfiore came in with Nurse Brenda. "Can we ask you a few questions, Mr. Richards?" asked Officer Miller.

"Of course," said Moses.

Officer Belfiore whipped out his notebook. "What can you tell us about the night you were attacked?"

Moses frowned, his brows knitting together. "It's all a bit fuzzy. I remember playing at acoustic night. Does anyone know what happened to my saxophone?"

"I have it," I said. "It's at the café waiting for you."

He gave me a grateful smile. "There is so much goodness

in this world. Thank you, Fiona. I was afraid he might have stolen it."

"Who?"

"The man in your mother's office. I saw him going through the papers on her desk. I told him to get out, and that's all I remember."

"Can you give us a description?" asked Officer Belfiore.

Moses shook his head. "It was dark, and I saw him from behind. Maybe if I saw him again, I might recognize him."

Moses couldn't add much else. The man had on dark clothes in a dark room, and Moses suffered a traumatic head injury. The policemen tried to remain upbeat, but I saw the truth in their eyes. They had little to go on.

"What was on your desk, Mrs. Campbell?" asked Officer Miller. "Was anything missing?"

Mom frowned. "A pile of mail, most of it advertisements. I didn't have a chance to go through it before Moses was attacked, but I don't think anything was taken."

The policemen got a call on their radio and had to leave. They said they would let us know as soon as they had any leads and told us to double-check and make sure nothing had been stolen. Moses promised he would rest, and Nurse Brenda said she'd contact us if he needed anything.

I spent the rest of the day baking cookies and getting ready for the tea party on Sunday. I thought it was a little weird Matthew hadn't stopped by at all, but I came to a sad conclusion. He must have gotten all the info he needed from us and now had no reason to continue the lie. It made me feel dirty and used. I planned to hide in my room during the acoustic show in case he showed up, but Sally called and invited me to go to the piano bar for dinner with her and Ralph. I put on a black dress that suited my mood and hung out at Sally's until it was time to leave, not wanting to see Matthew even by accident. It would be too painful.

Sally wore a sexy red dress and lipstick to match. Ralph showed up in a bow tie, looking adorable. He was a gentleman, too, opening the door for Sally and me and even helping us into his car.

"Ralph treats me like a queen," said Sally. She and Ralph looked at each other and laughed. "Wait. I *am* a queen."

I giggled too. It was impossible not to feel better around Sally.

She smiled at me. "It's nice to hear you laugh, little girl. Nothing cures a broken heart better than having fun with friends. And we have so much to celebrate since Moses is finally awake and feeling better."

I told them about our visit to the hospital. "He didn't remember much about what happened that night. It looks like Officer Miller was right. He said most of these cases go unsolved."

We had a table slightly off to the side of the main stage of the piano bar, where we ate a lovely dinner and shared a wonderful bottle of wine. The piano players were funny and a bit risqué. I was glad they didn't take any jabs at Sally. She would have been an easy target.

Mindy approached our table as we ate dessert. I almost groaned. She was the last person I wanted to see. She wore something hot pink and sparkly, with her boobs barely covered. There was an empty chair at our table. She asked if she could join us for a minute. I couldn't think of a reason fast enough, and Sally, being Sally, encouraged her.

"Oh, please sit down, sweetheart. Any friend of Fiona's is a friend of ours. And aren't you as bright as a hibiscus blossom in your little dress?"

Mindy smiled and slid into the chair. Ralph and Sally were deep in conversation, and Mindy leaned close to me.

"I heard you and Scott broke up."

I nodded, not sure where this would lead. "News travels fast."

She pursed her lips. "I'm glad. You're way too nice for him."

I blinked. Mindy always seemed to like Scott. "Thanks."

"I broke up with Harrison too. He cheated on me."

"I'm sorry, Mindy."

She smiled. "I'm not. I got a job working at the Playboy resort in Cancun. I can't wait."

"Oh." I wasn't sure how to respond to this. "What will you do there?"

Mindy giggled. "I'll be a cocktail waitress and hopefully hook up with someone way hotter than Harrison."

"Be careful. The men who go to those places might not be nice."

She patted my hand. "I'm always careful, and I don't plan to hook up with customers. Ew. I've always had a thing for Mexican men. I'm hoping to live out a few fantasies of mine while I'm down there," she said with a wink.

I nodded seriously. "I hope it works out for you."

Mindy's friends called to her from across the room. Buxom and blonde, they all matched. They even had nearly identical tiny sparkly dresses.

"I've got to go, but there is something I need to give you. Can I stop by your shop tomorrow?"

"Sure," I said. I began to write down the address, but she stopped me.

"I know where it is." She kissed my cheek before she left. "You're a good girl, Fiona. Thanks for always being so nice to me."

As she and her glittering entourage left the building, I thought about what she said and felt kind of sad. I hadn't been nice to her. I'd barely even been polite and couldn't imagine what she wanted to give me.

Sally and Ralph dropped me off in front of the shop. Matthew was still inside, but it looked like he was packing up. I slipped through the back gate and went into the garden to wait for him to leave.

I sank down on the bench beside the fountain. A couple sat at one of the tables, oblivious to me and totally in love. Not in the mood for young lovers at the moment, I glared at them until they got up and left.

"Hi, Fiona."

I hadn't even noticed Matthew's approach. He had his hands shoved into the pockets of his jeans and dark circles under his eyes.

He sat down on the bench next to me, so close I felt his warmth and smelled the scent of his skin. I resisted an urge to reach out and touch him by keeping my hands in my lap and my fingers clenched together.

"Can we talk for a moment?" he asked. Too wound up to answer, I gave him a curt nod. "I saw you yesterday. In front of the shop. With Scott. You looked pretty upset."

"I was."

He kept his eyes straight ahead, unable to look at me. "You worked your problems out, I take it."

"We did."

I could tell by the look on his face he thought Scott and I were back together. At least that explained why he hadn't stopped by sooner, but I saw no reason to correct him. Playing the dejected, despondent lover was all an act, obviously. He didn't deserve the courtesy of hearing the truth, and it was easier this way. With one lie of omission regarding the status of my relationship with Scott, I'd avoid other lies. Bigger lies. Like telling him I didn't love him anymore. That would be the biggest lie of all.

A muscle worked in his jaw, the only outward sign he was

upset. "I thought . . . well, it doesn't matter at this point, but it would have been nice if you'd let me know."

I felt cold and dead inside. "I didn't have a chance. This is the first I've . . . spoken with you." I was going to say "seen you," but that wasn't accurate. I had seen him. With the Anderson people.

"You've been busy, I guess." I heard the bitterness in his voice, and it stung but not as much as what he'd done to me. I may have broken his heart, if he even had one, but Matthew did something far worse. He methodically set out to destroy my mother. And he used me to do it.

I managed to speak over the giant lump of anguish forming in my throat. "I guess it's none of your concern."

"You're right." He shook his head and stood up to leave. "I didn't come here to fight. I already spoke with your mom. Next week will be my last acoustic night."

I nodded, my arms folded tightly across my body. I wanted to tell him the café probably wouldn't even be open after next week, thanks to him, but couldn't. "I imagine you have to get back to work. I'm sure you have lots of other things to do."

"Something like that."

I refused to look at him. "Goodbye, Matthew."

"Goodbye, Fiona."

I waited until he left, until absolutely certain he was gone, and then walked over to the fountain and sank to the ground next to it. I put my cheek against the cold, stone base. The gurgle of the fountain soothed me, like reassuring words from an old friend who knew me well. I stayed there a long time before finally heading up the narrow staircase to my quiet, lonely little room.

The next morning, my eyes were puffy from lack of sleep, and I looked pale, but I dressed in a sleeveless black-and-white gingham dress from the 1950s with a tight bodice, flared skirt, and black embroidered detail on the waist. I pulled my hair into a tight chignon and put enough makeup on to cover the dark circles under my eyes.

Mom was in the kitchen. She took one look at my face and handed me a steaming mug of coffee.

"Thank you," I said, and took a sip, sighing. Nasty fountain water or not, it still was the best coffee in town.

Her worried eyes studied my face. "You spoke with Matthew last night."

"Yes."

She pulled out some eggs and cooked them for me. "What are you going to do?"

"Nothing. He's a liar."

She paused. "But Fiona . . ."

I held up a hand, my eyes filling with tears. "I don't want to talk about this right now."

She looked like she was going to say something else but instead went back to cooking the eggs. She tossed in some feta cheese and fresh herbs from the garden. She knew it was my favorite breakfast, and I needed comfort food right now.

Kate and Chad came in hand in hand. I was glad they were so happy, but it was almost painful for me to see them. Kate took one look at my face and gasped. I must have looked worse than I thought.

"What happened?" she asked.

Mom stepped in and saved me. "We aren't going to talk about it right now. Can you two set up the tables for me in the garden? That would be a great help."

Kate and Chad went out into the garden, and I sighed in relief, not up to facing people or their questions today. I ate my breakfast and later kept busy by arranging my beautiful sugar cookies on a plate. I'd outdone myself this time with my intricate teacups, each one a different design. They were colorful and pretty, and the ladies would love them. I'd also made lemon squares and oatmeal-raisin cookies. With Mom's savory quiches and sandwiches and her decadent little chocolate croissants, it would be wonderful. She had also carved out a watermelon and filled it with fruit. It looked beautiful, with fresh flowers arranged all around it.

Before the party started, Mom told us the teas we would serve and had us taste her special mix to make sure we liked it. It was different from her usual teas, sort of rich and dark with undertones of black cherry and plum and something a little strange and exotic in it.

"This is nice," said Kate. "What's it called?"

She looked at me with a sad little smile on her face. "I called it 'Believe in Love.' I'm glad you like it."

I scowled. The tea was good, but I hated when she did things like that. "I wish you would stick to Earl Grey once in a while."

She wrinkled her nose. "But where's the fun in that?"

As the guests sat in the garden nibbling on finger sandwiches and sipping their tea, Mindy strolled in. She wore a tight white dress, no bra, and a thong. Her ensemble left nothing at all to the imagination. She looked ready for the Playboy resort in Cancun.

She smiled when she saw me. She had expensive sunglasses perched on her head and a designer bag slung over her shoulder. She gave me a little wave and walked over to where I worked at the register. "Hi, Fiona. Are you having a tea party?"

"We have one every Sunday. Would you like a cup of tea?"

I gave her Believe in Love, and Mindy let out a sigh. "This is fabulous. Can I buy some?"

I put some tea in a beautiful little pastel bag. "My gift to you. Have a wonderful time in Mexico. I'm so glad you're getting away from Harrison."

She heard the sincerity in my voice and smiled. She was a

pretty girl, once I looked past the flash and glitter. "And I have a gift for you."

She pulled an envelope out of her purse and handed it to me. Dirty, stained, and addressed to my mom from the National Registry of Historic Places, it had already been opened. I frowned and pulled a letter out of the envelope, looking at her in surprise after I read it. "Where did you get this?"

"I did a sweep of Harrison's apartment before I left, looking for proof he cheated on me. I found it. He had gold earrings in his desk drawer."

"Maybe they were for you."

She shook her head. "I don't wear gold. I made it clear from the beginning of our relationship. And I found naked pictures on his phone from a girl named Kelsey. All the proof I needed."

"How did you find this letter?"

"It was in his desk drawer next to the earrings. I thought it was strange. And it wasn't stealing since it was addressed to your mom in the first place."

I looked down at the official looking piece of paper with a frown. The National Register of Historical Places was part of the National Park Service. My heart thumped in my chest. "The café is registered as a historical building?"

Mindy nodded. "It looks that way."

"Why would Harrison have this?"

She shrugged. "I can't help you there, but I can tell you one thing; Harrison isn't a nice person. You should stay as far away from him as possible."

I touched her arm. "It's a good thing you aren't with him anymore. You deserve so much better."

She gave me a shy little smile. "Which is why I'm going to Mexico. Olé."

A sudden thought occurred to me. "When are you leaving?"

"Not for another two weeks."

"Can I ask you a favor?"

"Sure," she said with a nod.

"Do you still have the key to Harrison's apartment?"

"Yes."

"Do you want to get even with him?"

She grinned. "Of course. As long as it's nothing illegal or super mean. Slightly mean is fine. Just not super mean."

I wrinkled my nose at her. "I think this falls within those parameters. Would you let me into his apartment? I want to see if he has anything else there that doesn't belong to him."

"It would be my pleasure. He and Scott are going out of town. How would tomorrow work for you?"

We decided to meet in the morning. She thanked me for her tea, gave me a kiss on the cheek, and looked around the shop. "This is a nice little store, Fiona. I wish I'd known sooner Harrison had your letter."

"Thank you for doing this, Mindy."

She winked. "Anything I can do to hurt Harrison is my pleasure." She gave me a finger wave and sashayed out of the shop. A man walking past almost ran into a telephone pole when he saw her. She knew how to use her assets.

I pulled Mom aside and showed her the letter. She blinked in surprise. "I applied for this ages ago and completely forgot about it. Where did you find it?"

"Scott's friend Harrison had it."

She looked at me, a puzzled frown on her sweet face. "But how? Why?"

"I have no idea, but I plan to find out."

The rest of the tea party went off without a hitch. It was a beautiful day, and we had a big crowd. We moved a few tables inside because the entire garden was full. I was so busy it took my mind off Matthew, although occasionally one of the old dears would ask where he was, and thinking about him sent me spiraling back down into a pit of despair.

I called Janet to tell her about the letter. She asked me to bring it in the next day so she could take a look at it.

"I'd planned to call you today anyway," she said. "I finally had a chance to dig through the files and find the name of the man who called the health department about the naked yoga. Do you know someone named Sal?"

"No," I said with a frown.

"I haven't heard of him either. He works for one of Anderson's subsidiaries, but it doesn't give me the name of the company, and I have no idea why he would be involved."

Much later, long after we'd washed and dried the china and cleaned all the linens, I finally had time to sit and think about what Janet said. I went out into the garden and sat next to the fountain with a cup of herbal tea. Something tugged at my memory, but I couldn't grasp it. I closed my eyes, leaned back against the soft cushions of the bench, and listened to the sound of the fountain gurgling next to me, like it tried to speak to me. Suddenly the answer came to me, almost as if the fountain had whispered it in my ear, and I realized I knew the identity of the mysterious person named Sal, and it explained exactly how Harrison had gotten the letter.

Sal. SAL. The initials embroidered on his fancy handkerchiefs.

Scott Anthony Lipmann.

CHAPTER 23

BE UNEXPECTED, LIKE WHISKEY IN A TEACUP.
-AUNT FRANCESCA

"I'm glad I hurt his feelings," I said with a scowl as we walked to Janet's office on a bright Monday morning.

Mom hushed me. "Be quiet, Fiona. It's bad karma."

"What about Scott's karma? He's connected to all this. His company, Burgess and Garrett, is a subsidiary of Anderson. I looked it up last night. He supplied them with the information, and I'm sure he had something to do with Harrison getting the letter. No wonder he kept asking me when you were going to sell."

She shrugged. "I never liked him. Did you know that?"

I snorted. "Yes, I did."

"I didn't realize it was so obvious," she said with a frown. "The lesson here is to always listen to your gut."

"I listened to my gut with Matthew, and he lied to us." Since it appeared Scott had been the informant, I didn't understand what role Matthew played in all of this, but he was still part of Anderson Solutions, which made him one of the bad guys.

"I'm not sure about that," murmured Mom as we arrived at Janet's office.

I rolled my eyes. Once my mom liked someone, she did it with all her heart. She refused to see their flaws and imperfections. The fact she still wanted to give Matthew a second chance was proof positive of her generous nature. I was not so kind or forgiving.

Janet sank down into her chair. "Sal is your boyfriend?"

"Ex-boyfriend," I said, wanting to be clear.

"And your new boyfriend is Matthew Monroe?"

"Another ex. Sort of," I said, my cheeks getting warm. I wanted to crawl into a hole and hide. I was officially a slut and a horrible person with the worst possible taste in men.

Janet gave me a sympathetic smile. "Do you have the letter?"

"Yes, I do." I handed it to her, and she read it quickly, sitting up in her seat as a huge smile spread across her face.

"Well, I have to say, this letter is valuable. It's like gold, in fact. It won't keep Mr. McAlister from selling, but it should be enough to sway the council into preserving the café and the garden."

Mom gasped. "The garden too?"

Janet nodded. "It says clearly right here the house and grounds are deemed to have historical worth and significance."

I sat back in my chair, my thoughts racing. "What will happen to the other buildings on the block?"

Janet looked up from the letter. "Mr. McAlister has reportedly made his decision. It will be announced at the meeting. I guess he figured it was better for us all to learn at once. How did you get this certification?"

"I applied for it almost a year ago," said Mom. "I didn't say anything to Fiona. I never thought we'd be approved."

Janet smiled. "Well, this is perfect timing, and it's a good thing Mr. Philips is so messy."

"What are you talking about?" I asked.

She held the envelope out to me. "Look at this. Finger-prints all over it. It'll be easy to prove he had it."

She was right. Smears and dirty, brown fingerprints covered the outside of the envelope. I'd been so worried about the contents, I hadn't noticed.

"The question is, How did he get it?" Janet asked.

"It must have been *Sal*." I didn't even try to disguise the anger in my voice as I spit out his name. "He was at the café often enough. I'm sure he stole it from our mailbox or something and gave it to Harrison."

"It could be." She sealed the envelope in a plastic bag. "I'll want a statement from Mindy. I'm not sure it'll be admissible in an actual court, but it's extremely valuable as far as the council meeting is concerned. Don't tell anyone about the letter. Let's keep it as a lovely surprise for those Anderson bullies. They think Mr. Philips has it and we have no idea it even exists."

"I'll let Mindy know. I'm on my way to meet her now."

I didn't add we planned to do another potentially illegal search and seizure and wrap it up in time for lunch. I left Mom and went to meet Mindy a block away from Harrison's apartment. She had on tight black pants, a black T-shirt, big sunglasses, and a black baseball hat.

"Are you going incognito, or are you a ninja?"

"Both," she said, raising a finger to her lips, giggling. "Shhh."

Feeling nervous, I linked my arm with hers as we walked to Harrison's apartment. He lived in a ritzy renovated loft in the Strip District, the old warehouse area of the city. Located right on the Allegheny River, the apartment complex had once been a cork factory. Now it boasted luxury apartments that brilliantly combined brick walls with exposed pipes and ductwork that made it feel industrial and yet somehow homey.

Matthew, the architect, would have loved this place.

As soon as I had that thought, I pushed it from my brain. Why did I keep thinking about Matthew? I needed to get over it now and focus on the problem at hand.

I gave Mindy a nervous look as we approached the door to the lobby. She whipped a key with a fob out of her pocket and used it to buzz us in. I let out a nervous sigh.

"I don't think this is illegal exactly," I said softly as we passed the lobby decorated with stainless-steel finishes and rich velvet chairs. "I mean, after all, you do have a key. He gave you the key. Having a key makes it a *visit*, not breaking and entering. He, uh, knows you have a key, right?"

She shrugged, completely comfortable with this whole situation. "He may have forgotten. I have a feeling Harrison handed out keys to a lot of girls."

When we got to the door of his apartment, I took the key out of her hand. "I'll take it from here. You're about to leave on your Mexican adventure. If we get caught, I don't want you to get into any trouble for this."

She took off her sunglasses and winked at me. "Fine. I'll stand watch. If anyone comes, I'll make a birdcall."

"Or you could ring the doorbell."

She gave me a thumbs-up. "That works too."

I unlocked the door and stepped into the apartment, closing it softly behind me. Spacious and modern and with a small balcony facing the river, it was also fairly neat and tidy. Harrison most likely spent little to no time here since he traveled so much for work.

I located his office and looked through his desk but found nothing out of the ordinary. I tried to open a locked file cabinet and wasted a lot of time looking for the key before realizing it was right on top. I shook my head at myself in disgust. I was a baker, not a spy. Being here was a huge mistake, but I had to do it.

Leafing through his hanging files, I found one labeled "Anderson." Inside was a manila folder labeled "The Enchanted Garden Café."

"Easy peasy," I whispered to myself. The folder contained papers, notes, and piles of carefully documented information. Like the letter from the registry, this was pure gold. Maybe I didn't make such a bad spy after all.

I couldn't steal it, so I did the next best thing. Harrison's printer sat next to his desk. I put all the papers into the document feeder, made sure the paper tray was full, and copied the contents of the file. It would take a while, so I decided to check out the rest of his apartment as I waited.

I stepped into the kitchen, which barely looked used. The only things in his pantry were bottles of alcohol, a jar of peanut butter, and ramen noodles.

"Are you still in college, Harrison?" I asked softly.

I rifled through all the drawers in the kitchen and those in the coffee table in the living room, and then I went into his bedroom. His large bed, covered in black satin sheets, was unmade. The only messy part of the apartment. I stuck my head into his walk-in closet and peeked through the row of suits and dress shirts still with their dry-cleaning bags on them. I was about to turn off the light and close the door when I noticed something strange in the corner. Something out of place in the otherwise tidy and well-organized closet. A lumpy, dirty garbage bag.

"Please don't be anything gross," I muttered to myself as I picked it up and looked inside. When I saw the contents, I frowned.

"Scott's shoes?"

Inside the garbage bag, stained and filthy, was a pair of expensive men's dress shoes with the name "Scott Anthony Lipmann" stamped in gold script inside. It didn't make sense. Why would Harrison have Scott's shoes? These had to be the ones Scott lost the night we all went out to dinner together. Although dirty and discolored, they were otherwise identical to the ones he'd had on the second time the fountain attacked him.

I giggled at the thought. Instead of an attack dog, we had an attack fountain. We should post warning signs.

I brought the bag to Harrison's office with me, grabbed the copies I'd made, and shoved them into my purse. I put the file back into the cabinet, locking it, and heard a funny noise in the hallway. It sounded a bit like a birdcall. Then the doorbell rang. Frantically. Several times. Before I could respond, the door to the apartment opened with a swish, and an older woman stepped inside, an apron over her clothes and her dark hair pulled into a messy bun. Mindy stood behind her, a panicked expression on her face.

"This is Sue, Harrison's cleaning lady," she said. "We met outside, and I told her we were on our way out. Are you ready to go to lunch?"

I smiled at her, trying to still my pounding heart. "Harrison said you'd be in. I was dropping off his . . . uh . . . dry cleaning."

Sue narrowed her eyes at me. "You're the new girlfriend?"

"Guilty," I said, heaving a huge sigh of relief that she didn't know Mindy. We would have been in serious trouble if she had, but we weren't out of the woods yet.

"What's in the bag?"

"This?" I asked, holding it open for her and letting her catch a brief peek. "Shoes. I don't know what he tramped through, but I'm pretty sure they're ruined. Men. I'll have to see if I can get them cleaned. Well, I'd better run."

Sue nodded, still not convinced. "I didn't catch your name."

"Oh," I said, racking my brain as I tried to remember the name Mindy mentioned of the girl who'd sent Harrison naked photos. Luckily, it came to me just in time. "Kelsey. Nice to meet you."

When we got outside, I almost collapsed in relief. "I'm not cut out for this. I'm going to stick to making cupcakes from now on. That was so awful. Great birdcall, by the way."

Mindy giggled. "I thought it was fun. Let's do it again."

Later, when I had some time alone, I went outside and stared at the fountain. I couldn't believe what I'd done. Surely the cleaning lady would mention it to Harrison. We might be in some very serious trouble.

I pulled out the papers I'd copied and looked through them. Every single complaint that had been made against the café was listed. The notes were detailed. Methodical. Cruel. They'd worked on this together for months.

But as much as I searched and studied the pile of papers in my hands, I found no mention of Matthew. I still couldn't understand what part he'd played in all this, but he didn't seem directly connected to Scott or Harrison.

I dipped my hand in the fountain and thought about our first kiss. I'd jumped to get involved with Scott, someone absolutely wrong for me, and then jumped into the sack with Matthew. I'd lost my inner compass. I had no idea who or what I wanted anymore.

As I got up to go back into the house, I thought I heard the faint strains of the music Matthew played on his guitar in the gurgle of the fountain. I turned around, half expecting to see him sitting there with that sexy smile on his face and the yin and yang necklace resting on his chest. But the garden was silent and empty. I was completely and utterly alone.

CHAPTER 24

NEVER ANNOY A CHEF, ESPECIALLY ONE
HOLDING A BIG KNIFE. -AUNT FRANCESCA

"**Y**ou did *what?*"

Mom didn't respond well to the news that I kind of broke into Harrison's apartment and copied files. I'd woken up early, made her coffee, cooked her some breakfast, and even arranged a little bouquet of flowers for her. I sat and waited for her with the files neatly stacked on the island. Unfortunately, all my efforts to soften her up were for nothing. She seemed disappointed about what I'd done, which ticked me off.

"They've been spying on us the whole time. Even before I dated Scott. This proves it."

She rubbed her temples. "That does not justify breaking into a person's home. Haven't you listened to a single word I've said about karma, Fiona?"

I rolled my eyes. "Karma shwarma. This is concrete evidence. Something we can use for our case. You're being ridiculous. Can't you see that?"

I gathered my files and stomped away, furious at her, mostly because I knew she was right. Breaking into Harrison's apartment had been the wrong thing to do, but the value of information I'd collected assuaged my guilt. We had the upper hand now. Finally. But my mom would never see it.

I sniffed the odor of burning sage coming from the kitchen. It meant my mother was detoxifying our space, getting rid it of the bad vibes I'd just brought in. A typical Claire Campbell reaction to a crisis, stinky herbs and a lot of nonsense, but I was surprised to find Janet, our attorney, wasn't pleased either. When I made copies of the documents and dropped them off at her office, she gave me an odd look.

"And where exactly did you get these, Fiona?"

I lifted my chin, feeling defiant. "In Harrison's apartment. His ex-girlfriend had a key. We didn't break in."

"How does your mom feel about this?"

I nibbled on her lip. "She isn't happy about it. She's worried about karma and stuff, but I think it was worth the risk. It could help our case."

Janet shook her head and put the files back into the envelope. "I won't be able to use this information, Fiona."

"Why not?"

"Because it was stolen."

I swallowed hard. Taking the files from Harrison's office had felt wrong, but what he did felt *more* wrong. Using my mom's karmic scale, his was definitely the bigger crime.

"But you used the letter . . ."

"Which was addressed to your mom. It was her property. And you didn't steal it. It was given to you by a third party."

"Oh." When she explained it that way, I felt even worse.

When I stood up to leave, she walked to the door with me and put a hand on my shoulder. "I understand why you did it, but I have to advise you against this sort of thing in the future. Don't stoop to their level, Fiona. I have to side with your mom on this one. You're better than that."

She was right, and I knew it. As far as I could see, the only good thing that came from stealing those files had been figuring out Matthew didn't seem connected to Harrison or Scott. For that, it may have been worth disappointing both my mother and Janet. I now had the slimmest bit of hope that maybe Matthew wasn't involved. But that hope led me nowhere. He hated me at this point.

I spent the rest of the day in a snit. I was mad at the world. Auntie Mags came in, and in spite of her rather aggressive efforts, I refused to let her even attempt to unblock me. She looked disappointed, but I stood my ground.

"I will not let you anywhere near my chakras ever again. You messed me up last time. You made me connect with my heart center, and before I knew it, I connected with a man I barely knew. In bed."

Kate giggled, and I glared at her. "I'm sorry, Fi," she said. "Your first sex joke. So cute. We need to put this in your baby book."

That earned her another glare, but Auntie Mags continued to try to mess with my energy fields. "Unblocking your heart center led you down the path you were supposed to take."

"The path that made me miserable? Thank you very much."

She held up her hands and advanced on me, but I held up a spatula to stop her. "Don't you dare come any closer. Put those away. Now."

Auntie Mags let out a noise of pure exasperation. "I was showing you that these are only hands. Your heart and your dreams and your desires are all inside of you. The only thing I did was force that logical, beautiful mind of yours to realize your heart has a voice, too, and you need to listen to it."

I was putting together salads for her reiki class. I picked

up a large knife and slammed it down onto the cutting board, neatly slicing a tomato in two.

Her eyes widened in surprise. "There's no need to get violent about it, girly. I'm only telling you the truth."

I turned on the blender to mix the dressing for the salad. Auntie Mags rolled her eyes. "And I guess you don't want to hear it." She raised her voice over the sound of the blender.

I shut it off and gave her a tight little smile. "No, I do not. I've heard enough."

Auntie Mags lifted her hands in defeat. "I won't try to fix your chakra or give you any more advice, but I will tell you one thing. I love you and want the best for you. For a few days, when you were with Matthew, you seemed happier than I've ever seen you. I wish you could be that happy always."

I had to blink away the tears filling my eyes. I seemed to cry at the drop of a hat lately. Totally out of character. "Thanks, Auntie Mags."

She kissed my cheek and went back to her reiki class with a swish of the brightly colored scarf she had wrapped around her neck. Kate stared at me after she left. "She's right, you know."

I feigned extreme interest in the tomato I was chopping. My apron read "I Kiss Even Better Than I Cook." I'd forgotten to wash the other aprons and was down to either this one or one that said "I Licked the Bowl," which might not instill positive feelings in our customers.

"What do you mean by that, Kate?" I moved onto the cucumber. I peeled it in the kitchen sink and diced it on the cutting board.

"Would you please put down the knife first?"

I looked at her in surprise, with the knife paused in midswing. "Are you implying I might be dangerous?"

Kate sighed. "I'm implying you might not like what I have to say."

I put down the knife and gave her a steady look. "Okay. Shoot."

Kate sat up a little straighter in her chair. "You love Matthew. Auntie Mags is right. I never saw you so happy, and I've known you a long time. I know you think he lied to you . . ." I opened my mouth to protest her choice of words, but she held up a hand to stop me. "But maybe he had his reasons."

I stared at her, dumbfounded. "What reasons?"

She shrugged. She wore a sexy off-the-shoulder black blouse that showed her creamy cleavage and tattoos. "I don't know, and you won't know either unless you talk to him."

I stuck out my lower lip. "He's leaving soon."

Kate slid off the stool and sauntered out of the kitchen. "Then you'd better ask him soon."

I frowned. Every time I considered talking with Matthew, my stomach clenched into knots of anger. Perhaps because I loved him, his betrayal hurt me so much worse than Scott's, even though Scott's was much more devious and cruel.

I thought about Scott as I put the salad on plates, trying to figure out what had attracted me to him in the first place. Sure, he was handsome, but other handsome men had asked me out in the past, and I'd never been terribly interested before.

The truth hit me as I put out butter for the rolls, even though most of the reiki people stayed away from butter or anything fatty. Scott had attracted me because he was the exact opposite of my mom. Truthfully, I didn't want to end up like her when it came to money, security, or career and personal choices. The whole "live for today" thing seemed to work for her, but it would drive me nuts. I never understood, however, that I wanted to be like her in all the ways that mattered. She was beautiful and kind and creative and smart and fun. She made every day of my childhood special, even though I may not have appreciated it at the time. Not only a mom, she was also my best friend.

She came into the kitchen with an empty tray. She put it on the island and gave me a smile before loading it up with more salads. "Beautiful job on the salads, sweetie, and your rolls would make a French baker jealous."

I gave her a hug, wrapping my arms tightly around her waist. "Thank you, Mom. I love you so much."

She froze for a second before putting her arms around me. "I love you too, darling."

"I mean it. Everything I am, everything I ever was, is because of you."

She looked confused. "You made those salads all by yourself, dearest."

I laughed. "It isn't about the salads. I was so stupid. I thought I'd be happier being someone different but didn't realize I'm perfectly happy being myself."

"Is this about Scott?"

"Yes. No. Maybe. I'm so glad I didn't stay with that man. And now I'm scared. I almost made a terrible mistake. What if I do it again?"

She squeezed my hand. "I can't promise you'll never make mistakes, but they are well worth it if you learn from them."

I stared at her. "Why do you always have to sound like some kind of inspirational quote with a photo of a sunrise behind it?"

She laughed. "Am I that predictable? I'll have to change it up a little, I guess." She wiped her hands on her apron. "Scott wasn't a mistake, he was a learning experience."

I frowned. "A bad learning experience."

She winced. "Maybe, but it wasn't entirely about the terrible, sneaky, despicable things he did. You were too young to be so serious. I wanted you to have some excitement and adventures before you settled down."

"Maybe I will. I'm free and clear now."

She gave me a long, steady look, the kind she always gave me when trying to see through what I was saying and find the truth of the matter. "Are you?" she asked, smirking at me as she pushed open the kitchen door and went back to work.

CHAPTER 25

IT ISN'T A PARTY WITHOUT CAKE AND KISSES.
-AUNT FRANCESCA

The next few days passed in a blur. Moses got better every single day. Madame Lucinda had a special palm-reading session on Wednesday. She tried to sneak a peek at my palms every time she got near me, but I kept my hands clenched in little fists. I didn't want her to look at my palms and tell me things about my future, good or bad. I didn't want to know.

All my energy went into baking and working on the speech for the meeting. Janet was preparing a legal argument. The police were doing what they could about Moses's attack. I decided to focus on what was important, relieving my stress using a mixture of flour, sugar, and lots and lots of butter. Both Julia Child and Aunt Francesca would have been proud. We now had so many cookies we ran out of freezer space, and Mom finally told me to stop. The speech for the council meeting was finished, but I kept remembering additional things and spent a lot of time practicing it in front of Kate and Mom. They said it was perfect. I wasn't so sure. A lot of people depended on me to speak for them, and I didn't want to screw it up.

I also put a lot of time and effort into researching the café's new historical status. I knew there had to be a way to convince the council the building had significance. I wasn't sure if it would be enough. I went online and read about historical preservation until my brain hurt, but I kept coming up empty.

By the time Friday rolled around, I'd worked myself into a tizzy, counting the hours until acoustic night and going back and forth between excitement and fear at the idea of seeing Matthew again. Mom handed me a list of errands on Friday afternoon and told me to please take my time. My nerves were getting on her nerves, not that I could blame her.

I stopped and talked to every person on the block to make sure I hadn't forgotten to include anything in my speech. Because I'd already asked them several times before, they seemed sick of seeing me. Even Sally shooed me out of her shop and told me to finish my errands.

I thought about visiting Moses but decided I didn't have enough time. He was recovering and would be released from the hospital any day now. I still felt mad at Scott and heartbroken over Matthew, but there was an awful lot for me to be grateful about, especially Moses.

I had to walk all over the South Side to get the things my mom wanted. It took me much longer than expected. I didn't finish until well past dinnertime, and by then I was sweaty and irritated. Fear replaced my irritation as I approached the shop and I realized all the lights were out. It was dark and appeared closed.

I opened the door slowly, scared about what I might find. "Mom?"

As soon as I spoke, the lights went on, and I faced a room full of my friends and neighbors. "Surprise," they shouted.

I stared at them as my heart returned to its normal rhythm. "What's going on?"

Mom came up and grabbed my hand. She wore a fancy dress. "It's a party for you, Fiona."

"But it isn't my birthday . . ." I remembered Kate's warning about the surprise party my mom had been planning. A banner with the words "Welcome, Scotty" hung on the back wall. Someone had crossed off the word "Welcome" with a sharpie and written the words "Good Riddance" instead.

"Was this supposed to be a party for Scott? The one you mentioned ages ago?" I hissed in her ear. "The one I never agreed to?"

She spoke without moving her lips. "It was, and I forgot to cancel it, so now it's a different kind of party. I didn't think you'd mind, and we wanted to do something nice for you since you've been working so hard on that speech. Also, you've been so sad lately. We wanted to cheer you up."

I looked at all the smiling faces. Moses sat front and center in a wheelchair. He opened his arms to me, and I flew into them. "They let you out of the hospital?" I asked. "How are you feeling?"

He chuckled. "I'm as right as rain, and I wouldn't miss your party for anything."

As I gazed around the room, I realized if Scott had been here, he would have thought they were a bunch of freaks. Sally towered over everyone in a sparkling cocktail gown, with Ralph standing proudly next to her. Madame Lucinda wore a brightly colored turban and a matching dress. Auntie Mags had on a Polynesia-inspired muumuu and flowers in her hair. Kate and Chad had brought Mrs. Porter. She wore a red blouse, and I had to assume Kate bought it for her because tiny black skulls decorated it. The entire neighborhood was there, from our accountant, who thankfully had clothes on, to Rosie from the diner with several of her brood of redheaded children. We were the island of misfit toys, or at least that's what Scott would have said, but in front of me were the faces of the people who had loved and cared for me unconditionally, some since the day I was born.

Mom looked at me hopefully, and I smiled. "I'd better get dressed so we can get this party started."

Suddenly, music and laughter filled the air, and I felt a million times better than I had in days. I ran upstairs and took a quick shower before putting on a dress Sally had set aside for me ages ago, sleeveless with black lace over a nude shell. The lace had sequins sewn into it, so it sparkled as I moved. It fit tightly to the waist and flared out, ending below my knees. An elegant little satin bow sat right at the waist in the front. I put on black satin heels and let my hair hang loose. It was still a little damp, and the humidity of the day made it dry in sexy, curly waves.

I went downstairs and beamed as people fussed over my dress. I twirled around and did a little curtsy, feeling beautiful and special and loved.

I spent the evening with the people I cared most about in the world. We danced, sang, and told funny stories. We all drank a bit too much and ate until we thought we might burst, but it was the perfect night. We put our worries aside, and it felt good.

Moses would be staying with Sally until well enough to go home on his own. Mom wanted him to stay with us, but we didn't have a bedroom on the ground floor, and our staircase would have been hard for him to maneuver. Sally couldn't stop fussing over him, and I felt better knowing someone would look after him. I brought him his saxophone case, and his whole face lit up.

"I missed this old girl. Thank you, Fiona."

"I'm so sorry, Moses."

"What reason do you have to be sorry?"

"I should have walked you home that night, but I was preoccupied, and . . ."

His brows drew together in a frown. "Do you honestly blame yourself for what happened to me?"

The tears I tried to hold in slipped down my cheeks. I couldn't speak, so I nodded.

"Well, that is ridiculous." I looked up in surprise, but Moses's eyes were gentle. "Do you think you can control the whole universe? That you can stop every bad thing from happening? You can't. You are only one spoke on a giant cosmic wheel. You're spinning around like the rest of us."

"Then it's all so meaningless."

"Not at all. Every single step you take has meaning, and everything happens for a reason. It isn't always possible to see the why and how of it, but it's true. Good things come even from bad things. Take Matthew for example. We met him as things were falling apart, but he's been such a gift. Coming to the hospital every day. Checking on me. Reading to me."

"He did?"

"Yes. He's an honorable person. I could tell the minute I met him."

"I couldn't. I didn't trust him."

He leaned forward to speak soft enough the others couldn't hear. "From what you told me in the hospital, you figured it out."

I gasped. "You heard what I said?"

He chuckled. "Most of it, I think. Don't worry, it's nothing I haven't heard before."

"What should I do, Moses? I'm so confused."

He reached for my hand. "Have some faith, little girl, and listen to your heart. It won't steer you wrong."

Later, we all sat in the garden, talking quietly and enjoying the beauty of the night. The air was rich with the smell of night and blooming flowers, and I couldn't sit still. I felt restless.

"I might take a little walk," I said to Mom.

She gave me an odd look. "You walked all over the entire South Side today. I made sure of that. It was the only way to get you out of here so we could set up for the party."

I kissed her forehead. "Yes. You were very devious. I'm a little antsy. I'll be back in a few minutes."

I strolled around the block, past the college kids out drinking and the aging hippies out for a night of music in one of the many clubs. A soft breeze blew through my hair, lifting it off my shoulders. I was way too overdressed for a walk around the South Side on a Friday night, but needed to look around and remind myself about what I was fighting for on Sunday. I had other motives as well. Part of me hoped I might randomly run into Matthew.

Nothing is random.

I heard my mom's words whispered on the wind. I decided I was being stupid and turned to walk back to the café. When I reached the corner, I saw Matthew standing in front of the shop with his hands shoved deep into the pockets of his jeans. He stared into the window of the café like a child might stare into a candy shop, his expression wistful. In that moment I knew, without any doubt at all, how much I loved him. I also knew this might be my last chance.

"Matthew."

He ducked his head. "Sorry. I didn't mean to interrupt. I was passing by, and . . . well . . . goodbye."

He turned and walked away, moving so fast he almost ran. I chased after him in my satin heels, not an easy task. When I caught up with him, I pulled on his sleeve.

"Would you please stop for a second?" He stopped and faced me, his eyes haunted. He suffered as much as me, a pleasing realization. It made me bold. "We need to talk."

He raised one dark eyebrow. "Usually when you say that, we end up naked."

I bit my lip, unable to deny it. "Is that necessarily a bad thing?"

He ran an aggravated hand through his hair. "Stop playing games with me. Please. Say what you need to say, and I'll leave. I don't want to keep you away from your party. Or from Scott. "

I wrinkled my nose. "Scott?"

He led me back to the window of the café and pointed to the banner. It sagged in the middle and only the word "Scotty" was visible at this point.

"Oh, that reads 'Good Riddance, Scotty.' Not nice but accurate. Scott and I aren't together."

Matthew looked so adorably confused I could barely keep my hands off him. "You're not with the suit?" he asked.

I shook my head. "Nope. We weren't reconciling that day you saw us in front of the shop. You misunderstood, and I didn't correct you."

Matthew had trouble keeping up. "You don't love him?"

I stepped closer, tilting my chin up so my lips were only a few inches from his. "The only person I've ever loved is *you*, Matthew Monroe. It's always been you. Only you."

He inhaled sharply but didn't kiss me, which I found disappointing. I ached for his kiss at this point.

"So why were mad at me? Why did you let me believe the two of you were back together?" His eyes studied my face, his voice soft and husky. "I can't do this over and over again. We were together but not together, and I hated the way it made me feel. There's a difference between love and lust, Fiona."

In spite of what Janet said, I owed him an explanation. I had to find out a way to do it without compromising the future of the café. I decided to tell him as much as I could. "I thought you were spying on us. For Anderson. It broke my heart. And I was furious. I don't handle betrayal well, it seems."

He blinked. "Anderson?"

"It's not important. I figured out you weren't the one supplying them with information, so I couldn't care less who you work for now. There is one thing that matters to me and one thing I want."

He stared at me. "What is that?"

"You," I breathed. "I love you, Matthew. With all my heart. Even if you do work for Anderson, it doesn't change that. And I'm so sorry I hurt you."

He pulled me into his arms and buried his face in my hair. "I love you too. I can't seem to stop loving you, but there is something you need to know." He gently brushed his lips against mine and cupped my face with his hands. "I don't work for Anderson. I can't understand why you thought I did."

I stared at him. "I saw you the day after the bonfire. You were walking into the courtroom with them."

"That's where this came from?" he asked, shaking his head. "I was there for a meeting, and so were they. We walked in together. It was random."

"Random," I said, my voice a soft whisper. "But who do you work for?"

"A private client." He hesitated. "It's a bit complicated and confidential . . ."

I covered his mouth with my fingers. "You know what? It doesn't matter. As long as you aren't working for the evil Anderson Solutions, I'm okay with it."

He smiled at me. "I'm definitely not working for them, so I guess we're good now."

"We're better than good, Matthew."

I reached up to wrap my arms around his neck and pulled him close. He kissed me until my knees were weak. I was afraid if I let go of him, even for a second, I might fall to the ground. Matthew did that to me. His kisses were a full-body, soul-wrenching experience.

I heard the sound of applause, and it took me a second to realize it came from the café. Matthew didn't hear it at all. When I gently pulled away from him, his eyes were unfocused, and he looked deliciously aroused.

I stood on my toes to whisper in his ear. "We have an audience."

Matthew blinked and turned his head. Mom and her guests watched us from the entrance of the shop, clapping.

Matthew's cheeks turned pink. "Oh, this is terrible," he said softly.

Deciding to embrace it. I held the side of my skirt with one hand and gave a regal curtsy, like greeting the queen. Matthew grinned and took a little bow himself.

Mom smiled at us. "Come inside, you two. Now we have something to celebrate."

CHAPTER 26

THERE IS ALWAYS SOMETHING MAGICAL
ABOUT A GATHERING UNDER THE STARS.
-AUNT FRANCESCA

ax from the wine shop opened a bottle of his best champagne, and we went back to the garden. Everyone seemed to have a funny story about me they felt compelled to share, and Matthew appeared to enjoy each and every one. I sat next to him on the cushioned bench, my shoes off and my feet tucked under me. Matthew had one arm wrapped around my shoulders, and every so often, he brushed his hand against my hair or touched my skin with absentminded strokes of his thumb. I was utterly content. If I'd been a cat, I would have been purring.

As the talking and laughter quieted down, several couples got up to dance. Matthew turned to me with a smile. "Shall we?"

He pulled me off the bench and into his arms, and we swayed in the moonlight, our bodies pressing tightly together. He wrapped his arms around me, and my cheek rested against his shoulder. Sally and Ralph danced near us. Ralph's head barely reached Sally's chest, but he stared up at her adoringly, and every so often, she kissed his bald spot.

Max pulled my mom out for a dance. They were old and dear friends. Kate danced with Chad. He held her close and whispered to her as he softly kissed her cheek. Mrs. Porter snoozed under a blanket nearby with a smile on her face. The perfect night. Even the fountain seemed happy, gurgling a bit louder than usual and not shooting water at anyone.

"Tell me again," Matthew whispered in my ear.

I smiled against his neck. "I love you, Matthew Monroe."

He kissed my forehead. "And I love you, Fiona Campbell. I'm so glad you're not mad at me anymore."

I looked up at his warm brown eyes and his beautiful face. "I would have forgiven you sooner if you had just kissed me. You are the most remarkable kisser."

He raised a dark eyebrow and gave me a sexy grin that was full of promise. "So I'm a 'remarkable kisser,' am I? Perhaps you and I could go back to my place . . ."

"Okay."

He laughed. "That was tough."

I shrugged. "I want to take a closer look at your house now that I know the talented young architect who designed it."

"So you're seducing me because of my architectural skills?" He lifted my hand to his lips and kissed my palm, sending chills of anticipation up my spine. I leaned close to whisper in his ear.

"I'm curious about your skills as an architect, but I'm seducing you because of your skills in a different area alto-gether." I pulled on his earlobe with my teeth and smiled when I heard him inhale sharply.

"Can we leave now?" he asked, his voice husky.

"Definitely."

As we left the garden hand in hand, I waved goodbye to my mom. She smiled and blew me a kiss. Several of the others called out their goodbyes. Sally had the audacity to wink at me, and I winked right back.

When we got to his place, he stood for a moment, staring at me, his hand gently touching my face. "I've never been this happy. You're amazing. Do you know that?"

My cheeks got warm, and I leaned onto his palm. "So are you."

He grabbed my hand and pulled me into his house, eager to show it off. He explained the renovations he'd made and why, and he seemed thrilled to finally share something he was so passionate about with me.

I ran my finger along the marble of the island. The baker in me itched to roll out dough on it. "You aren't only good, Matthew; you're brilliant."

He beamed. "You haven't even seen the best part." Still holding my hand, he pulled me up the steps to his bedroom.

I bit my lip. "Uh, I have seen it. It *is* the best part," I said, shooting a glance at his bed.

His eyebrows almost hit his hairline. "Ms. Campbell, are you talking about what I think you are talking about?"

I nodded seriously. "Yes."

Matthew pointed a finger at me. "We'll discuss that shortly and in great detail. But first, my big surprise."

He led me up to a rooftop terrace with a view of the river and the lights of the city skyline. I spun around, staring up at the stars. My dress flared out and sparkled as I turned.

"It's perfect, Matthew."

He pulled me close. "*You're* perfect."

I wrinkled my nose at him. "Hardly. I was mean to you. And rude. And I took advantage of you sexually. Then tried to push you away because the way I felt for you scared the living daylights out of me. Far from perfect."

He nodded, thinking about it. "You're right. You did take advantage of me sexually. Care to do it again?"

I gave him my hand and let him lead me straight to his bedroom. It was different this time. There was no insecurity or doubt between us. No questions or fears. We were comfortable with each other in ways we hadn't been before. And something else had changed as well. We both knew, without even saying a word, this was the beginning of something important.

Matthew kissed me in the moonlight that shone in through his bedroom window. It was a clear night; the moon reflected off the river, making it look like diamonds sparkled under the surface. He kissed me slowly, softly, gently. As always, as soon as his lips touched mine, my body responded. I wanted him. Badly.

I tangled my fingers in his hair. Our kisses grew more urgent, and soon we were both breathing hard. His tongue sent jolts of pleasure through my body as it danced with mine. I pressed my hips against him and felt his erection through his jeans. I gasped, wanting him to be closer. And naked. Naked would have been good right now.

Matthew pulled back, and I made angry little noises of frustration. I wanted him closer, not farther away. "Patience, Fiona," he said with a little laugh.

"Matthew Monroe," I said, my breath coming out in short little gasps, "I'm all out of patience. I need you right now."

I saw a flash of white as he grinned in the darkness. "Your wish is my command."

He proceeded to show me, with his lips and tongue and his glorious body, exactly how much he cared about me. Each touch a promise. Each caress a vow. Each moment magical.

Afterward, as I lay curled up in his strong arms staring at him as we both caught our breath, I realized for the first time I didn't feel guilty and hadn't held anything back. It was magnificent and so overwhelming it made me cry.

Matthew pushed himself up on an elbow, brushing the hair out of my eyes. "Are you okay?"

I sniffed, placing my hand over his heart. "I'm happy."

Matthew smiled a smile of pure male satisfaction and pulled me back into the warmth of his embrace. He kissed the top of my head. "I am yours, and you are mine. I love you, Fiona."

"And I love you."

I fell asleep in his arms under a canopy of stars that sparkled through the skylight above his bed, and I woke up the next morning to the warmth of his naked body and his sleepy kisses. I stretched, enjoying the way my body felt as it moved against his. I was tired and a little sore but utterly content.

"Tell me again." His voice was husky with sleep.

I smiled, my eyes still barely open. "I love you, Matthew Monroe."

I had to go to the shop to help my mom get ready for the weekend events. Matthew made breakfast while I showered. He was in his boxers and a T-shirt making bacon and eggs when I came into the kitchen. I wrapped my arms around his waist, my face in his back. Even the thought of the meeting the next day didn't dim my happiness.

We sat eating breakfast and watching the boats go up and down the river as we glanced through the newspaper. Matthew poured me another cup of coffee, and I took a sip, watching him over the rim of my cup. He was rumpled and sexy and completely desirable. He caught me looking at him and gave me a wicked grin.

"Are you thinking what I'm thinking?" he asked.

I glanced at the clock and stuck out my lip in a pout. "Yes, but I'd better go. Leaving you is so difficult."

He pulled me into his arms and kissed my neck. "Then don't do it again. Ever."

I took his face in my hands, knowing exactly what he wanted to say. "I'm sorry I hurt you. I was confused and stupid. Do you forgive me?"

He nodded. "Do you forgive *me?*"

I kissed his forehead. "Of course. And no matter what happens at the meeting tomorrow, it won't change anything."

He tugged on a lock of my hair. "This thing with you is so perfect. I'm afraid . . ."

I put my lips against his ear. "I am yours, and you are mine. Don't forget that, okay?"

He smiled, but worry lingered in his eyes. "I won't."

As he got dressed, I looked through his bookshelf. Most of the books were about architecture, with big, gorgeous photos. One particular book caught my interest. It was on historical preservation, published by the National Registry of Historical Places.

"Do you mind if I borrow this?" I asked as he came downstairs.

"Sure," he said. "In the mood for some light reading?"

I laughed. The book was old and the print tiny, but it was possible I might find something I could use in my speech later. "I'm researching. You do this kind of thing every day. Does it ever get boring for you?"

He shook his head. "I love it, and I still have so much to learn. There is a lot that goes into preserving an old place. Certain details require special attention that you could ignore in a more modern structure. And the paperwork involved can be daunting. Do you know how difficult it is to apply for a grant? They teach classes on that stuff because it's so complicated. But it's worth it."

"Why? Is it a lot of money?"

"It can be but not only that. Any building that receives a grant or federal funding can't be altered without specific permission. It saves a lot of places from people who might want to make 'improvements' and end up destroying something important, sometimes through their own ignorance. It's kind of sad."

I nibbled on my lip. "Federal grants, huh?" I tucked the book under my arm. It was worth a look.

Matthew lent me a pair of sweats and a T-shirt and drove me back to the shop on his motorcycle, and I held on to him tightly, enjoying the feeling of his body next to mine for a few more minutes. As soon as we reached the café, he helped me off the bike and pulled me into his arms. "Until tonight?"

"Yes," I said.

He gave me a kiss that rocked me to my core and grinned at the bemused expression on my face as he put on his helmet and drove away. Kate came to stand next to me. "I thought he was sexy when he played guitar, but Matthew on a motorcycle is positively orgasm inducing," she said.

Chad stood next to her but didn't seem at all upset by her comment. "Maybe I should get a bike."

She kissed him hard on the mouth. "You don't need one, baby."

Kate sauntered into the shop, and I laughed at the expression on Chad's face. "She just knocked your socks off."

Chad nodded, looking after her in adoration. "She always does."

CHAPTER 27

NEVER UNDERESTIMATE THE POWER OF A
GOOD SCRUBBING BRUSH. -AUNT FRANCESCA

After reading through Matthew's book and trying in vain to understand the section on federal grants, I spent the rest of the afternoon making tarts filled with homemade lemon curd and topped with fresh, juicy blackberries. I also made napoleons from puff pastry, layered them with fresh cream and strawberries, and then drizzled melted chocolate over the top.

I wore my normal uniform of shorts and a cami under an apron. Today my apron said "Kitchen Babe" in silver sequins. A ridiculous hot pink, but I liked it anyway. It was girly and pretty, and I felt girly and pretty today.

I decided to make mojitos for acoustic night, the perfect summer drink. Mom had plenty of fresh mint growing in the garden, but I needed lime. I stuck my head outside. Mom worked on the tables, trying to freshen them up for tomorrow.

"I'm going to run to the store. I'll be back soon."

"Can you grab a new scrub brush? These tables could use a good cleaning."

The old scrub brush was still in the evidence room at the police station, covered in Moses's blood. The thought of it made me swallow hard. I had to push it from my mind.

"Sure," I said, and grabbed some tote bags from the hook near the back door. I'd never been allowed to use the plastic grocery bags given out at the store. Mom had been eco-conscious long before it was trendy.

I bought limes and found a solid wooden scrub brush Mom would love. I paid for the order and walked home through the alley. I was smiling, thinking about Matthew, when someone shoved me sharply from behind. I tripped and fell forward, barely stopping myself before hitting the ground. I turned around in surprise.

"Harrison?"

He looked unsteady on his feet, his eyes bleary. "Long time no see." He grabbed my arm. I tried to wriggle my arm out of his grasp, but he held on tight.

"What do you want?" I asked. My heart thumped in fear. I was certain he wanted to confront me about breaking into his apartment.

He squeezed my arm so hard it hurt; I twisted it to break free. "I want to talk to you about Scott," he said. "You broke up with him."

I blinked in surprise. Maybe this wasn't about his apartment. "Why is it any of your concern?"

Harrison came closer. I smelled alcohol on his breath. "Scott is my friend and my business partner, and we're working on something big right now. If this goes through, we'll be set for life. Do you understand that? *For life*. I won't let you or anyone else screw this up."

He reached for me again, something cruel in his eyes, and I lost it. I screamed my head off, flailing my arms, scratching his face, and kicking him as hard as I could. I must have made contact with something because he doubled over, holding himself between the legs. I took one of the totes and whacked him on the head. I heard a solid *clunk* as the scrub brush hit his skull, and he fell over. I took off running full speed down the alley. I didn't look back, and I didn't stop until I reached the café and locked the door behind me.

Mom walked in from the garden, her arms full of fresh flowers. She froze when she saw me. "What happened?"

"Harrison . . . Scott's partner . . ."

Suddenly I couldn't breathe. I sank into a chair. The tote bags had gotten wrapped around my wrists. She put down the flowers and gently untangled them.

"Who is Harrison, and what exactly did he do to you?" Her voice stayed calm, but I heard the cold anger behind her words. She believed in peaceful solutions to conflict, but she was also fiercely protective when it came to anyone hurting me.

I told her what happened, my teeth chattering as I spoke, and she called the police. Officer Miller, who'd been patrolling the neighborhood, showed up minutes later. He took a quick look in the alley and then sat down at the kitchen island to question me. I told him about what had happened, calmer now, and showed him the dark bruises on my arm. Mom poured him a cup of coffee and got him a plate of cookies. She was pale, but she held it together. I had a feeling she knew if she lost it right now, I'd lose it too.

"Why exactly would Mr. Harrison . . ."

"Philips." I filled in the last name for him. I could breathe again but still felt unsteady. My arm was bruised and sore. No one had ever hurt me like that before.

Officer Miller wrote it down. "Why would he attack you?"

I opened my mouth, and the whole story came out in a rush. I couldn't tell him about breaking into Harrison's apartment, but I told him about Anderson and the way they'd pressured us. "Harrison is Scott's business partner, and Scott was the one spying on us."

He raised an eyebrow at that. "Your boyfriend?"

"Ex-boyfriend."

He shook his head. "And this is all about a parking garage?"

"Harrison called it the deal of a lifetime. I think that was what he was talking about."

"Do you want to press charges?"

"Yes." I didn't hesitate. I wanted Harrison to pay for what he did to me.

"I'll do it as soon as I get back to the station." He gave me a steady look. "Be careful, Miss Campbell. I don't like the way these people are acting. Don't go out alone, even in the daytime. Mr. Philips sounds like a desperate man, and desperate men often make poor decisions."

"I will."

Mom shook her head. "First Moses gets attacked, and now Fiona . . ."

I sat up straight, staring at her. "You're right. First Moses and then me. Both times with the scrub brush."

She pushed my hair out of my eyes, her face concerned. "Yes. You bought the scrub brush at the market. What happened? Did you hit your head, honey?"

"No. You don't understand. The old scrub brush. You kept it behind the door of your office. Moses saw someone looking through the papers on your desk . . . in your office. The letter from the historical society must have been in the pile of mail you hadn't opened yet."

She sank into her seat, comprehension dawning in her eyes. "And Harrison had that letter."

I nodded. "He's the one who did it. He hit Moses with the scrub brush from your office, and I hit him with the new scrub brush. It's like you always said. Karma. I can't believe I'm saying this."

She smiled at me. "Karma."

Officer Miller scratched his chin. "It's a nice hypothesis, but we have no way of proving Mr. Philips hurt Mr. Richards. Or he stole your letter."

"Yes, we do."

I told him about the fingerprints all over it the envelope. "We thought it was dirt, but now I'm not so sure."

Mom covered her mouth with her hand and gasped. "Blood," she said. "The prints were brown. I assumed it was dirt, but it could have been dried blood."

I nodded. "Moses's blood. I think that's what's on the envelope. Along with Harrison's fingerprints."

"And your lawyer already has this letter?" he asked.

"Yes, sir."

"I have one more question."

"What?"

"Are you planning to solve all the cases in the South Side today or only this one?" he asked, giving me a little wink.

I grinned at him. "I think I'm done for the day."

He wrote everything down in his notebook and thanked Mom for the coffee and cookies. "I'll call Officer Belfiore right away. We'll take care of it. Don't worry, ladies. Be safe," he said, shaking his head. "All this fuss over a parking garage. Who would have thought?"

When he left, Mom sat down next to me, putting her head in her hands. "He's right. Is it so important?"

"What?"

"The parking garage." She lifted her head. "First we found out Matthew worked for Anderson. Later we found out Scott betrayed you because of them. Now Harrison threatens you over them, and it looks like he was willing to kill poor Moses because of it. It's all about money, isn't it?

Maybe I should sell the café and give them what they want."

I shook my head. "I won't let you. And Matthew doesn't work for Anderson. He told me last night."

"Who does he work for?" Her brow wrinkled in confusion.

"I have no idea."

The door to the kitchen opened, and Matthew flew inside. He pulled me into his arms, lifting me out of my chair and holding me against the solid warmth of his body. I wrapped my arms around his neck. He wore a white shirt with the sleeves rolled up and faded blue jeans. I clung to him, needing to feel safe again.

"I saw Officer Miller. He told me someone tried to hurt you. What happened?"

My eyes met Mom's. When she nodded, I knew I should tell him. "Scott's friend accosted me in the alley. I'm okay, but he scared me."

A muscle twitched in Matthew's jaw as he processed that information. "Is this because you broke up with Scott?"

I nodded. "But there's more. We think he might be the one who hurt Moses."

"He hurt Moses? And he hurt you?" His eyes went to the bruises on my arm, and his face darkened. "Where is he?"

I touched his cheek. "I'm filing charges. Officer Miller will take care of it. All we can do is wait."

He growled. "I would like to discuss this matter with him personally."

"So would I," Mom said.

I rolled my eyes. She wouldn't kill flies, and now she wanted to beat up Harrison. "No one is going to do anything. We'll get through today and tomorrow and deal with this after the council meeting is over."

We had a record number of people show up for acoustic

night. They filled the shop, the garden, and the sidewalk out front. Chad and I were constantly busy making smoothies. We made one Chad called Java Junkie that tasted like coffee-flavored ice cream. We also had several fruity ones, including mango, raspberry, and peach.

The frozen mojitos were a big hit, but looking at the limes brought back what happened in the alley. What would have happened if I hadn't gotten away from Harrison? I liked to imagine he wanted to scare me or that he'd just been drunk, but I knew deep inside it was more than that. I couldn't understand the rage or the reason behind it. I also couldn't understand the fear I'd seen in his bloodshot eyes.

By the time acoustic night ended, I was sticky and tired, but I'd been able to listen to Matthew play, and that made it wonderful. Sally and Ralph brought Moses, and he played a few songs on his sax, to the delight of the crowd. He couldn't stay long, and Sally kept checking on him, asking him if he'd eaten and making sure he wasn't getting too tired.

"She treats me like royalty," said Moses with a laugh. "She won't let me lift a finger. I could get used to all this pampering, Miss Sally."

"You deserve it, Moses," she said with a smile. She bustled off to get some soup I'd left in the kitchen for Moses. He turned to me.

"Can I talk with you alone for a moment?" he asked.

"Sure."

I wheeled him out to the garden, and we sat by the fountain. "Officer Miller stopped by to visit today. They think they know who hurt me."

I wasn't sure how to respond. "Did he give you a name?"

He shook his head. "No, but he told me they figured it out because of you. He credits you with solving the whole case." I opened my mouth to speak, but he reached for my hand and gave it a squeeze. "Don't tell me who it was, sweet child. We have to do this the right way. They'll bring the man into custody. I'll identify him. He'll go to jail. And it will mean the world to me to put this all behind me and move on with my life. Thank you, Fiona, for all you've done."

I blinked away tears. "I'd do anything for you, Moses."

"I know you would."

"Until they bring him in, be careful, okay?"

"I will," he said, giving me a megawatt smile. "Not that Sally would let anything happen to me. She's like a mama bear guarding her cub."

As if on cue, Sally came out into the garden and clucked about Moses getting too tired. "See what I mean?" he asked with a grin.

"Are you all ready for your speech tomorrow?" asked Sally. Ralph stood next to her, looking dapper in his bow tie and round tortoiseshell glasses.

I wrinkled my nose. "I guess so."

"Your mom told us about the national registry," Sally said in a whisper. "That is fabulous news."

"I hope it is. I wish I knew more about applying for federal grants. I borrowed a book about it from Matthew, and it's so complicated, but even if we're in the process of applying for a grant, it gives us more protection. Sadly, I don't even know where to start."

Ralph stood up a bit taller and straightened his bow tie. "Well, I do."

Sally put a hand on his arm, her eyes glowing with pride. "That's what Ralphie does, or at least part of what he does."

"I work for the university," he said. "I usually apply for research-related grants, but it can't be too different. Do you have copies of the paperwork from the national registry? If so, I can start the process tonight."

I thought I might burst into tears. "Would you?"

"Of course. Any friend of Sally's . . ."

I gave him a giant hug. I hugged Sally and Moses too. For the first time, I felt like everything might turn out okay.

I gave Ralph copies of all the paperwork, and he promised to get right to work on it. Sally put a hand over her heart. "Ralph. You've never been so sexy as you are right now. Do you realize that?"

His cheeks turned instantly pink. "I feel that way about you, Sally. Every minute of every day."

Now I put my hand over my heart. I'd never seen Sally so happy. I waved goodbye to all of them and went back to the kitchen. I made three frozen mojitos and brought them out for my mom, Matthew, and me. Matthew's face lit up as soon as he saw me.

"Do you want to go and sit outside?" He took my hand, leading me out to the garden.

We sat side by side on the bench by the fountain, my head resting on his shoulder. The mojitos were refreshing and had enough rum to make me relax. Matthew wrapped an arm around me, and I sighed. I didn't know what tomorrow would bring, and I lived in the moment in a way I'd never been able to before. I had finally learned my mom's lesson. I would not wait too long like Aunt Francesca had or hide my true feelings like my mother. I wanted to tell Matthew exactly how I felt, to share everything with him. Even if my mother thought Campbell women were cursed to only love once, it didn't necessarily have to be a bad thing.

"You're what matters most to me, Matthew. You mean more than anything."

He kissed me, a smile playing on his lips. "Really? And how did you finally figure this out?"

I put my hand on his cheek. "I loved you, but I thought you embodied all of the things I'd been trying to avoid my whole entire life, and that scared me."

"When did it change?"

"When your heart spoke to my heart, and I listened."

"It was that simple?"

I nodded. "To my great surprise, actually it was."

And with that, I broke the curse of the Campbell women, once and for all.

CHAPTER 28

IN THE COOKIES OF LIFE, FRIENDS ARE THE
CHOCOLATE CHIPS. -AUNT FRANCESCA

After the Sunday tea party, I showered and dressed in my Chanel suit and slid into nude pumps. The suit fit me beautifully. I wore a silk sleeveless shell underneath and pulled my hair up into a tight chignon. The final touch was a strand of pearls that had belonged to Aunt Francesca with matching studs in my ears.

I packed my things carefully, including the files I'd copied when I'd broken into Harrison's apartment—just in case. I was about to leave when I saw the garbage bag in the corner of my room, the one holding Scott's shoes. I'd forgotten about them completely.

I looked inside the bag at the elegant leather shoes, now stained and dirty. I still didn't understand why Harrison would have stolen his shoes. It didn't make sense.

My mom came into my room, putting on her earrings. "Are you almost ready?" she asked. "What's in that bag?"

I showed her the contents. "Do you remember how Scott complained about losing his five-hundred-dollar shoes?"

"Yes," she said. "And the other pair got ruined by the fountain."

I cleared my throat. "Well, Mindy and I may have found his missing shoes."

Her eyes widened. "When you broke into Harrison's apartment?"

I nodded. "I thought it was kind of weird, so I, uh, took them."

She let out a sigh of pure exasperation. "You mean you *stole* them. Why didn't you say anything earlier?"

"I kind of forgot about them. What should I do?"

She thought about it. "Bring them to the meeting. Even if Harrison is a no-good bastard and Scott is a slimy weasel, we should return them to their rightful owner."

I blinked in surprise. "A bastard and a slimy weasel? What about all that love and peace stuff?"

"That was before they hurt my baby."

We walked to the meeting in silence. The weather had turned oddly cool as the sun sank low in the sky. The entire South Side felt quiet. Every Sunday it seemed like the whole neighborhood was a little hungover and recovering from the weekend.

"Is Matthew coming?" asked Mom.

I swallowed hard. "I don't know. We didn't talk about it."

"That's probably for the best. Even if he doesn't work for Anderson, we don't know who he works for, and there could be a conflict of interest. It's far more sensible just to keep things completely separate."

Mom took a deep breath and let it out slowly. With her ivory-colored suit and pumps and her hair pulled up in a bun, she looked more like the president of the PTA than a former stoner hippie chick. Claire was a complex creature. Although I knew she was most comfortable in jeans or a long, soft skirt, every once in a while, bits of her early upbringing peeked through. She'd grown up wealthy and pampered as the only child of a prominent family. Pumps and pearls were as much a part of her as kombucha and mandalas.

I slipped my arm through hers. "Janet thinks we'll be okay. We won't lose the café."

Her eyebrows came together in a worried frown. "This has gone so far beyond the café. And what about our friends and their shops? I won't breathe easy until it's all over."

I'd hoped to see our friends and some of our neighbors at the town hall, but when we got there, the entrance looked deserted. A sick feeling grew in the pit of my stomach. We were all alone. The city council meeting was normally held in a conference room upstairs, but when we walked into the building, we saw a sign saying the meeting place had been switched to the auditorium in the back of the building. The clicking sound of our high heels echoed as we walked through the empty marble hall.

We paused in front of the large ornate doors. My hands shook. Mom clasped my hand in hers. "Whatever happens, Fiona, we've done our best."

She was right. I gave her a quick hug as the door to the auditorium opened and Auntie Mags stepped out. "Here you are. We've been waiting for you."

We looked past Auntie Mags and into the room. It was packed. People even stood in the back and against the walls. When we walked in, the entire crowd turned to look at us. Several people smiled and waved.

"I saved you a seat up front," said Auntie Mags. "We got here early. We knew there would be a crowd."

"How did you know?" Mom looked a bit shell-shocked.

Auntie Mags put an arm around her shoulders. "Because as soon as word got out about how you were being harassed by the Anderson people, the calls came in. They all wanted to help, even people who don't live in the South Side. This has become bigger than they ever expected, Claire."

"Will that make any difference?"

Auntie Mags shrugged. "It won't hurt."

As we walked down the long aisle to the front of the auditorium, people called our names and reached out to shake our hands. It was surreal, like a visit with every person I'd known since childhood. Even the tea ladies were there, still wearing their hats and gloves.

The city council members, all of them looking decidedly nervous, sat on the stage at a long table. My eyes scanned the crowd, hoping to catch a glimpse of Matthew's face. The Anderson people were in the front. He wasn't with them, but Scott and Harrison were, and it made me sick to my stomach to look at them.

I sat between Mom and Auntie Mags. Sally and Ralph sat behind us. Ralph handed me an envelope and gave me a wink.

"I got the ball rolling," he said. "It's up to you now, little miss."

I opened the envelope and looked inside. He'd applied for a grant to restore the garden and return the café to its previous glory. I grew teary as I read the words. It was a start, complete with an application date and some official-looking numbers, and it might be what we needed to sway the council to our side.

"Thank you, Ralph. This is perfect."

Moses sat next to Mom, still in a wheelchair. Officer Belfiore and Officer Miller approached from the back of the room. Mindy was with them in a tiny black skirt. Her legs looked about fifty miles long. She gave me a little wave when she saw me but stayed near the exit.

"Mr. Richards, can we have a few words?"

Moses looked up at them in surprise. "Of course."

Officer Belfiore knelt beside the wheelchair and spoke quietly to Moses. I saw Moses's eyes widen in surprise. "Thank you, Officer." He looked back where Mindy stood. It was hard to see her in the crowd. "And thank that young lady for me too. It's a brave thing she's doing."

They walked to the back of the room, and Moses leaned over so Mom and I could both hear him. "I think you might already know this, but the person who attacked me is here. Tonight."

"What happens now, Moses?" I asked.

"They want me to ID him after the meeting." His eyes scanned the room. "I hope I can. It was so dark in that office."

"You'll do fine." I patted his hand, trying to soothe him, but my own stomach was tied in knots.

The chairman called the meeting to order at exactly seven o'clock. The head of the council, a man with a thick white moustache, leaned forward to speak in the microphone. "Ladies and gentlemen, I am Mr. Meers. Tonight, we are here to decide on whether or not we should, according to the laws of eminent domain, purchase the 1600 block of the South Side for the purpose of allowing Anderson Solutions to build a much-needed multilevel parking structure."

A loud cry of outrage went up from the crowd, and Mr. Meers's cheeks turned an unhealthy shade of red. He held a gavel in his hand and slammed it on the table. "This meeting will be conducted in a civilized and respectable manner, or all of you will be asked to leave the room." He slammed the gavel again, and the councilwoman next to him jumped.

The Anderson group, a row of dark suits in a sea of long-haired, tie-dyed bohemians, didn't look nervous. They looked smug, in fact.

Scott's eyes met mine briefly before he looked away, an angry flush coloring his cheeks. I studied him for a moment, looking at his elegant suit and his handsome face. I'd been so focused on my life plan, and Scott fit perfectly into the parameters of it. Knowing Matthew, however, made it seem shallow and wrong. I searched for Matthew again, but he was nowhere to be seen.

Mr. Meers called up the people from Anderson to explain their plans. They had a flashy PowerPoint presentation and quoted lots of facts and statistics about how the parking structure was desperately needed and would increase visitor traffic to the entire South Side. Several of the council members seemed to be on their side. They nodded in agreement as they watched the presentation. I looked down at my little stack of notecards, hoping my words would reach the ears of the people on the council and they would understand.

The spokesperson for the Anderson group was Mr. Smith, a dark-haired man with glasses. He spoke for about twenty minutes and then cleared his throat. "And, in conclusion, city ordinance 141 clearly states if the city council deems a construction project is in the best interest for the majority of our citizens, the council has the right to proceed with the project even if there are complaints or residents unwilling to sell. Mr. Alexander McAlister owns the majority of the 1600 block of the South Side. Even if he chooses not to sell his property, the council can still override. And as far as the remaining property on the 1600 block . . ." Mr. Smith's cold eyes fell ever so briefly on us. "That matter is also in the council's hands. City ordinance 244, passed this morning, says if there are more than five serious complaints against a property owner or business, the council has the right to close that property without prior notice."

My heart sank to my toes, and my gaze shot to Scott. He smiled triumphantly. He'd known about this all along.

Mr. Smith held up a stack of papers in his hand. He ticked them off one by one. "These are all complaints against the Enchanted Garden Café. Public nudity, two health-code violations, disturbance of the peace, noise pollution, and another complaint issued late last night. It appears the plumbing for the outdoor fountain is not up to code and poses a significant risk. This has become a matter of public safety, and it is well within the council's rights to close down the Enchanted Garden Café immediately."

The people from Anderson picked up their fancy equipment and went back to their seats. No wonder they had looked smug. They held some winning cards.

Mr. Meers called me to speak, and I looked at my mom in panic. Janet sat next to her, scribbling frantically in a notebook as she looked through the stacks of papers and files on her lap. Janet's face was pale and drawn. My mom took my cold hand in hers and gave me a little smile.

"You can do it, baby."

I stood up, looking at the faces of the people who had loved me my whole life. I didn't believe in their reiki or tarot cards or magic and had always been so different from them, but they loved me unconditionally. Time for me to pay a little bit of that back.

The view from the stage was scary. I wasn't sure of the exact capacity of the auditorium, but it looked like thousands of faces stared back at me. My heart pounded in my chest, and my hands trembled. I was terrified until I found mom's face in the crowd. I saw Kate sitting with Chad, and Sally with Ralph, and Madame Lucinda, Auntie Mags, and Janet. I wasn't here for Anderson or the council. I was here for them. I took a deep breath and spoke.

"The South Side is one of the oldest and most historical areas of our city. We recently learned the Enchanted Garden Café has been designated a national historic landmark, and suspect other buildings on our block would qualify for this status as well. These aren't a bunch of crumbling old buildings that should be bulldozed in the name of progress and convenience. These are irreplaceable treasures, and that is why we applied for a federal grant to repair the Enchanted Garden as soon as possible."

A cheer went up from my side of the audience. Mr. Smith and the Anderson people did not look pleased. They carried on a heated discussion with Scott and Harrison. Harrison's face got red, and Scott's gaze met mine. He understood at that moment I knew about his role in this. Whatever small bit of affection that may have still existed between us vanished forever.

"The South Side is the social hub that attracts visitors every weekend from all parts of the city. It's a mecca of bars, restaurants, and live music venues. It's not only a hangout for college students. It's a popular destination for people of all ages."

This caused another round of shouting and clapping from the audience. Mr. Meers had to pound his gavel several times to get them to settle down.

"Even more than the historical significance or the vibrancy of its nightlife, the South Side is a community, a group of artists, craftsmen, bakers, shop owners, alternative medicine practitioners, and musicians. Each person, each shop, each resident is a vital part of what makes up the magic of the South Side. And Anderson has used underhanded methods to try to destroy this, including spying, viciously attacking one person, and physically threatening another. Me."

I looked directly at Harrison and Scott and waited for a reaction. Scott sat up, a confused frown on his face. He obviously had no idea at all what I was talking about, but Harrison did. His color went from red to pure white. Mr. Smith rose to his feet.

"That's a false allegation. She's spouting lies."

"We've already filed charges with the police. And we have

concrete proof of the spying right here." I held up the papers from Harrison's file, looking directly at him as I did so. He slid down into his chair, his hands covering his face. Scott stared at me in shock.

My gaze went to my mom. She had no idea I held stolen documents. Her face glowed with absolute love and trust, but that was the way she always looked at me and at everyone. She had the best and most giving heart in the whole world.

"This is what the South Side is all about. Something more important and valuable than what can be calculated in dollars or shown on a spreadsheet. The people of the South Side are its greatest treasure, but tearing down those businesses for the sake of an ugly, utilitarian parking structure would be the worst sort of injustice."

I stepped down from the podium to hugs and people reaching out to touch me the whole way back to my seat. Mom waited for me with open arms.

"I am so proud of you, Fiona."

I kissed her soft cheek. "I don't know if it was enough. I didn't talk about alternative parking solutions or mention how much this has cost us in legal fees. I forgot so many things."

She patted my hand. "You spoke from your heart, my darling. They'll listen."

Sally gave me a big kiss on my cheek and whispered in my ear, "Your speech was perfect, and you look *divine.*"

We sat back down when Mr. Meers yelled for quiet again. "One more warning, and I will personally throw all of you out of here."

"I'd like to see you try," Kate muttered under her breath. She sat behind me. We both giggled so hard our shoulders shook. Stress induced but still pretty funny.

"If there is no one else left to speak, the council will adjourn to a private chamber to vote on this matter."

Mr. Meeks looked around the room. His mouth set in a hard line, and he was about to raise his gavel when I heard someone shout from the back of the room. "Wait. I have something to say."

We all turned around to see Matthew walking down the aisle. He wore a beautiful suit, and his hair was pulled back in a tidy ponytail at the nape of his neck. He looked less like a sexy French pirate and more like a cover model for GQ.

His eyes met mine as he passed our seats. He leaned over to whisper in my ear, "Don't worry. It's going to be fine."

I wanted to pull him aside and talk to him but couldn't. "I don't want you to get in trouble." My voice was a worried hiss.

He flashed me a smile. "I live for trouble. That's why I like you so much," he said, winking at me.

Mr. Meers glared at Matthew. "And who are you?"

"I'm Matthew Monroe, sir." Matthew's voice was deep and confident. He wasn't shaking. He didn't even seem nervous. "I would have been here sooner but was instructed to go to the conference room upstairs and got locked inside. Since I had no cell phone reception in this building, I couldn't call for help. Fortunately, I found a window and slipped out."

Mr. Meers seemed skeptical. "From the conference room . . . on the second floor?"

"Yes. There was a tree near the window. I used it to climb down."

"Who would lock you in that room and why?" asked Mr. Meers. He looked like he could use a drink.

Matthew's gaze went to the row of men from Anderson Solutions. Scott and Harrison slouched down even deeper in their seats, and I rolled my eyes. They'd locked Matthew in that room. The people from Anderson seemed to know it as well.

Matthew turned to me, a bunch of emotions flickering across his face. This was the moment of truth, and we both knew it. "People who didn't want me to speak," he said. "Because I'm here to represent Mr. Alexander McAlister. I'm his grandson."

CHAPTER 29

A WOMAN IS LIKE A TEA BAG. YOU NEVER
KNOW HOW STRONG SHE IS UNTIL YOU TOSS
HER IN HOT WATER. -AUNT FRANCESCA

I sat as still as a stone. Matthew's gaze stayed on my face, and he spoke directly to me. "My grandfather wanted to find out what was happening on his block, and he needed to hear about it from someone he trusted."

I nodded, even though I wasn't thinking clearly. Matthew gave me a little smile. Auntie Mags reached over me to grasp mom's hand. "Claire, he's Anna's boy."

"Anna?" I asked.

Mom got teary. "Our friend, the one who died in that car crash so many years ago."

"She was Mr. McAlister's daughter?"

Auntie Mags nodded. "That's why Matthew looked familiar to me. He's the image of his mom."

Mr. Meers's attitude toward Matthew changed immediately. I guessed that happened a lot when a person had a billionaire for a grandfather. That thought made me a little nauseated. I could handle the hippie musician I'd fallen in love with and the talented architect I'd gotten to know. I wasn't sure how to handle someone of Matthew's obvious wealth and status. It was way beyond my comfort zone.

"Has your grandfather made a decision yet, Mr. Monroe?" asked Mr. Meers, giving Matthew an extremely ingratiating smile.

"Yes, indeed he has, Mr. Meers." Matthew turned, and his eyes rested once again on my face. "The South Side has always held a special place in my grandfather's heart. This was where he came when he emigrated from Scotland. He raised his family here. He made his fortune here. But he left when my mom died because the memories were too painful for him."

This elicited another round of weeping from my mom and Auntie Mags. I gave each of them pats on their backs, trying to comfort them.

Sally cried too. "I can't help it," she whispered. "I've been so emotional lately. And this is better than a soap opera."

Matthew continued. "I've been in constant contact with my grandfather. I told him about what I've seen on the 1600 block, including the historical architecture and sense of community Ms. Campbell spoke so eloquently about." This caused me to blush yet again, and Matthew continued. "I also witnessed firsthand the relentless and undeserved bullying the Campbells have endured from the people at Anderson Solutions."

Mr. Smith stood up, veins bulging in his neck. "Those people have poisoned you with their lies."

"Those people had no idea who I was, Mr. Smith. They found out about a minute ago. I speak from my own observations, and I have every right."

Mr. Smith looked like he wanted to say a lot more, but Mr. Meers shut him down. "You had your chance to speak, Mr. Smith. The floor belongs to Mr. Monroe right now."

Matthew gave Mr. Meers a gracious nod. "I owed it to my grandfather to find out the real story. I promised him I wouldn't tell anyone, and I kept that promise, even when it was difficult. And thanks to all of you, I finally found out the truth."

He looked over the crowd. "The South Side has gotten a lot of bad press lately. It seems like people want to focus on the bars and the drinking and all the ugliness that can come from those things. But when I stayed in the South Side, I discovered so much more. It is a thriving artistic community. A place where holistic and alternative medicine practitioners offer their services, and vintage clothing can be purchased. It is a place with unique shops and wonderful restaurants." He winked at Rosie. "I had the most delicious pancakes at Pamela's, and the best coffee in the world is served at the Enchanted Garden."

Mom gave him a tremulous smile. Matthew grinned at her. "As Ms. Campbell told you, the Enchanted Garden is a designated historical landmark. I strongly suspect the other buildings on the 1600 block are eligible for that status as well."

This caused some grumbling from the Anderson group. Matthew held up a hand to silence them. "As an architect who has worked almost exclusively on restoring buildings of historical significance, I can attest I have carefully inspected these properties, and almost every single one of the buildings deserves historical landmark status. I plan to personally submit a petition to the National Park Service to create a historic district in the South Side that stretches from the 1400 block to the 1800 block so the entire area can be preserved for future generations."

This made the crowd jump to their feet. Mr. Meers didn't threaten them or ask them to sit down. He sat back in his chair and folded his hands over his stomach. It was Matthew who made the crowd quiet down, simply by raising a hand.

"And so, it is my honor to tell you that my grandfather will not sell these buildings to Anderson, and we are in the process of creating a trust so they cannot be torn down at any time in the foreseeable future."

My heart felt like it was going to explode in my chest. I rose to my feet with the crowd as they clapped and cheered.

Mr. Smith was not pleased. He rushed on stage and leaned forward to speak into the microphone. "What about the city ordinances? The Enchanted Garden will still be closed, and if the council decides the parking lot is necessary, it doesn't matter if your grandfather wishes to sell or not, Mr. Monroe."

Janet ran to the podium. She squeezed in between Mr. Smith and Matthew. She was so tiny her head barely reached Matthew's shoulder, and she had to stand on her tiptoes to reach the microphone.

"I am happy to say you are incorrect, Mr. Smith. The new ordinance you so blatantly tried to sneak past us is invalid in the case of any building that is a historical landmark because the National Park Service designates landmarks, not the city. Federal statutes, in this case, supersede local ordinances since Ms. Campbell had the foresight to apply for federal funding."

"But she doesn't even know if she'll get it . . ."

"It doesn't matter. As soon as the process begins, the status changes. As did the status of the Enchanted Garden Café. At exactly three o'clock this morning."

I looked at Ralph. "You were up until three applying for the grant? You're a rock star."

He wiggled his eyebrows at me. "Yes, I am."

Janet continued, her gaze on Mr. Smith. "I would think your lawyers would have told you that, especially after you attempted to hide the landmark status from my client."

Mr. Smith glared at her. "This is an outrage."

"That's one thing we can agree on." Janet took a deep breath. "Officer Belfiore. It's time."

Officer Belfiore came from the back of the room, all eyes on him. He whispered something to Moses, and Moses nodded, looking a bit perplexed. Officer Belfiore patted him on the shoulder and wheeled him out of the room.

As soon as the door shut behind them, Janet looked straight at Harrison. "Tampering with the US mail is a federal offense, and I am going to suggest strongly to my clients that charges be filed immediately, but I have a feeling there are other charges you should be worried about, Mr. Philips. Like assault and attempted homicide. You can take it from here, Officer Miller."

"Attempted homicide? What are they talking about?" Scott asked as Officer Miller approached from the back of the room.

Harrison was so pale the freckles on his cheeks stood out like polka dots. "Shut up, Lipmann, before you make it worse."

"You think this can get worse?"

Officer Miller stood at the end of their row of seats. "Come this way, gentlemen."

"Wait. Both of us?" asked Scott.

"Both of you," said Officer Miller, acting less than amused.

For a second, Harrison looked like he might run, but he soon realized there was no way out. He'd have to fight his way through a mob of hippies from the South Side to even get close to an exit. Scott's face grew positively green, and I thought he might throw up. It was painful to watch.

After they left the room, Mr. Meers looked at Janet and his fellow council members. "Well. That was an unusual council meeting. I think it's safe to say we've heard enough on this matter, and we should take a vote. Would you feel comfortable voting here?"

The ten members of the council nodded, and Mr. Meers asked them, "Should Anderson Solutions be permitted to buy the 1600 block of the South Side in order to build their parking garage?"

He called each member by name, and each stood up to say, "Nay." By the fifth vote, the Anderson people gathered together their things. By the eighth vote, they slithered out of the building. I ignored them. I only had eyes for Matthew.

He shook hands with Janet and each of the council members and then ran down the steps two at a time to reach me. He lifted me up into his arms and swung me around. I clung to him, my hands on his shoulders and my feet dangling above the ground. His strong arms were wrapped around my waist as I gave him little kisses all over his face.

He looked up at me, his eyes shining. "Tell me again."

I giggled and whispered in his ear, "I love you, Matthew Monroe."

"I love you too. And that was a brilliant move with the grant."

"I got lucky. Ralph, it turns out, is a professional grant writer. And you gave me the idea."

He kissed me so thoroughly I forgot we were in front of a room full of people. It wasn't until I heard catcalls that I realized we had an audience. Again.

Matthew laughed and spun me around once more before putting me back on my feet. He didn't let go, though. He kept me tucked close to his side. Right where I belonged.

Mom and Auntie Mags came over and kissed him on the cheek. "Matthew. Our hero. And we loved your mom so much . . ." Mom cried again and couldn't continue.

Auntie Mags tried to finish for her. "She would have been so proud of you today." Her face crumbled, but she took a deep breath and managed to stop it from becoming a complete weep fest.

Janet and her father, Paddy, came up to us. Paddy rolled his eyes. "Bunch of emotional women," he said with a thick

Irish brogue. He reached out to shake Matthew's hand. "Your mom worked with both of these sobbing ninnies to save my shop when you were just a wee babe. We would have lost everything if not for them, and we never would have been able to afford that fancy law school for our Janet."

Janet gave her father a punch on the arm. "What my dad is trying to say is years ago your mom saved our pub, and today you saved the whole district. Thank you, Matthew."

As they talked among themselves, I pulled Matthew's head down to give him one quick yet thorough kiss.

"What was that for?" he asked, his eyes bemused. The fire burning between us was constant. It only took a tiny spark to make it ignite.

"Nothing." I gave him another quick peck. "I can't seem to stop kissing you."

"Don't ever try," he murmured against my lips, and I grinned.

I grabbed the garbage bag with the shoes in it out from under my chair. Matthew looked at it curiously.

"What is that?" he asked.

"Um. Scott's shoes. He thought he lost them. I found them. Sort of. Harrison stole them."

"What are you talking about, Fiona?"

I winced, pulling him aside. "I may have broken into Harrison's apartment. Well, it wasn't exactly *breaking* in. We had a key."

His face darkened. "Was this before or after he attacked you?"

"Before. But I don't think he has any idea it was me. I'm not stupid. I didn't give my name or anything."

He looked inside the bag. "But you stole a dirty pair of shoes?"

I tucked a lock of hair nervously behind my ear. "They

had my mom's letter. I wanted to see if they'd taken anything else. I found these by accident. Are you mad?"

His mouth was set in a grim line. "Furious. The idea of you going into that apartment . . . what if he'd been in there, waiting for you?"

I reached up to stroke his cheek. "He wasn't and I'm fine, but I'll stick to baking from now on and leave the crime solving to the proper authorities. Although it was kind of fun, the whole breaking and entering thing." He gave me a sharp look, and I giggled. "I'm kidding."

We walked out of the town hall hand in hand. When we got outside, we stood next to Mom and Moses. Harrison was being read his rights, and Scott stood next to him, his back to us, running a shaking hand through his hair. Moses stared first at Harrison, but soon his gaze went to Scott.

"Officer Belfiore," he said. "May I please have a word?"

"Certainly." Officer Miller waited with Harrison, and Officer Belfiore came over to speak with Moses. "What is it, sir? We're nearly finished here. I need your statement before I take Mr. Philips down to the station."

Moses sat up straight. "There is a little problem with that plan," he said softly. "Mr. Philips isn't the man I saw in Claire's office. He is."

He pointed straight at Scott, and Scott's eyes widened in surprise. "Me? I wasn't even there that night. It's not possible."

"You were there all right," said Mindy. "And as drunk as a skunk. You both took off and left me standing in front of the café alone. I had to get a cab home."

"You're a liar, Mindy," said Scott.

"No, she's not." They swung their heads to look at me. Suddenly, it seemed so clear. All the puzzle pieces had come together. "And I have proof." I held out the garbage bag and handed it to Officer Belfiore. As soon as Harrison saw it, he got so pale I thought he might faint.

"What is that?" asked Scott. He had no idea what was going on.

"Ask Harrison," I said. "He knows."

Scott looked at him, and Harrison shook his head. "I have no idea what she's talking about. I've never seen that bag in my life."

Officer Belfiore opened the bag and showed Scott the contents. He frowned in confusion. "My shoes? Why would you have my shoes, Fiona?"

"Harrison stole them from you. I have a feeling you were too drunk that night to even notice."

Scott ran a shaky hand through his hair. "Why would Harrison steal my shoes?"

"To cover your tracks. And his. Do you remember when you lost them? It was the night Moses was attacked."

Harrison's face turned so red it was nearly purple. "You little . . ."

He couldn't finish his sentence. Officer Belfiore pulled him away. Office Miller cuffed Scott, pulling his hands behind his back.

"It looks like this is a twofer," he said with a chuckle.

"Wait," said Harrison. "Why am I still being taken in? He said he saw Scott, not me."

Officer Belfiore took notes. He answered Harrison without looking up. "Mr. Richards saw Mr. Lipmann in Claire's office, but that doesn't mean Mr. Lipmann is the one who hurt him."

Harrison spluttered. "He said it was Scott. You heard the old man. We all heard him. And his blood is on Scott's shoes, for God's sake."

We all froze. "It's interesting you know what's on his

shoes, Mr. Philips," said Officer Miller. "Considering we never showed you what is in the bag."

Harrison's eyes widened in panic. "That doesn't prove anything. You have no right to take me in. I'm calling my lawyer."

"Go ahead," said Officer Belfiore. "But we have enough cause to bring you in with or without the shoes. They are the icing on the cake."

"What do you mean?" asked Harrison.

"Mr. Lipmann stood at the desk. Mr. Richards was hit from behind. Unless Mr. Lipmann can be at two places at once, I'd say he's the thief and you're the assailant."

A vein pulsated in Harrison's neck. Not a pretty sight. "You have no proof of that either."

"Actually, we do," said Officer Belfiore with a smile. "We have bloody fingerprints on the stolen letter. Now I'm sure Mr. Lipmann's fingerprints are all over that envelope, but I'm a pretty good guesser, and I'd bet money on the fact the bloody ones are yours. And thanks to Ms. Campbell, we also have a pair of expensive, valuable, blood-splattered shoes to prove both of you were at the scene."

Harrison was silent as they helped him into the police car. Scott's gaze met mine. "Can I talk to you for a moment, Fiona?"

Matthew's grip tightened on my hand. "Whatever you have to say to her, you can say to both of us."

Scott's eyes narrowed. "It's a personal matter."

"I don't care." Matthew's entire body was tense. If they had been rams, they would have locked horns by now. Perhaps primitive of me, but Matthew's little show of protectiveness turned me on. I didn't even think of pulling away.

"Just talk, Scott," I said.

"I was drunk that night, Fi. I thought I went home and passed out."

"Did you know about the letter?"

He pursed his lips. "I knew he had it. I didn't know how he got it. I didn't ask."

"That makes you guilty too."

"Stop talking, Lipmann," shouted Harrison from the back seat. "Shut up. Now."

Scott's blue eyes scanned my face. "You said he attacked you. Is that true?"

"Yes. I fought him off with a scrub brush, ironically enough."

He blew out a sigh. "I never imagined it would end up like this. It sort of snowballed. I didn't date you because of a parking garage. No matter what you might think, I loved you."

"Only words, Scott. They don't mean a thing."

Officer Miller led him to the car, and Scott's eyes filled with panic. "None of this is my fault. It isn't fair."

"It's called karma," I said with a wave. "And it keeps the universe in balance, especially for people like you. Have fun in jail, Scott."

We turned and walked away as Scott was loaded into the police car next to Harrison. I felt like I'd dodged a bullet. If karma hadn't intervened and sent Matthew to me, I might have ended up the miserable wife of an alcoholic meatpacker. I may have even started eating processed cheese. I shivered just thinking about it.

Matthew watched him go with a wary face. "I don't think that is the last we'll hear from him."

I went up on my tiptoes to kiss him. "Who cares? As long as I have you, nothing else matters."

Matthew put his hands on my cheeks, his thumbs caressing my skin. "Do you mean that?"

"Yes, even if you do keep surprising me. Learning you're an architect is one thing. Learning you're the grandson of Mr.

McAlister is quite another. It explains all of the photos of you online wearing a tux with a supermodel on your arm."

I kind of snarled the last few words, and Matthew chuckled. "The only girl I want on my arm from now on is you." He kissed me softly.

"There you go again. Trying to kiss me into submission."

He grinned. "I'll use whatever tools available to me. From the moment I saw you standing in your shop all sweaty and annoyed, you were all I wanted."

"Really?" I was breathless and out of focus from his kisses, and Matthew apparently could tell.

He gave me a look of pure male satisfaction. "You held a stone phallus in each hand; I knew you were the girl for me."

I wrinkled my nose at him. "You had to bring those up, didn't you?"

"Those were some lucky fertility charms." He gave me a saucy wink.

"Oh, please. Stop."

He caressed my cheek, staring deep into my eyes. "You loved me without knowing who I was, and I found it refreshing."

"Refreshing? I was mean to you. Was that refreshing as well?"

He bit his lip and gave me a sexy smile. "You were challenging but so worth it."

He took my hand and led me back to the shop. People already packed the place, and someone had decided to block off part of the street so we could have an even bigger party. I changed into a comfortable dress and flats, and we danced and sang and drank and laughed until the wee hours of the morning.

Later, Matthew and I sat alone by the fountain. "I don't know what I'll do when you leave."

He raised a dark eyebrow at me. "What are you talking about?"

My lips quivered. "You said last night would be your final acoustic night . . ."

"I said I won't be *hosting* it anymore. Frankie called me. He's coming back from India in a few days. He wanted it to be a surprise."

"Oh." I frowned at him. "You aren't going back to Philly?"

His lips twitched. "Do you *want* me to go back to Philly?"

I shook my head, unable to speak, unable to breathe properly. I wrapped my arms around him and held him close.

He sighed. "How could you think I would ever leave you voluntarily?"

"We never made any promises. I was trying to appreciate each moment. For the first time in my whole life, I didn't even attempt to plan for the future."

"I want it all, Fiona, present and future. I would take the past, if I could. I am yours. That's my promise. And I intend to keep it. For always."

CHAPTER 30

GOOD THINGS COME TO THOSE WHO BAKE.
-AUNT FRANCESCA

The next morning was Monday, and Mondays were always my favorite, but this Monday started exceptionally well. I woke up to Matthew's naked warmth in my bed, and we made love softly and sweetly in the morning light. Afterward Matthew dozed as I showered, and then he got up to shower too. He tried to pull me into the shower with him, but I giggled and slipped away. As I went downstairs to get the paper, grab some coffee, and help Mom, there was a bubble of pure joy and happiness in my chest. I no longer had to concentrate to find my heart center. It practically glowed from the inside out.

Matthew wasn't leaving. He planned to stay here and work on his idea of turning the South Side into a historical district. Mr. McAlister was on the mend and promised to come out to visit as soon as he felt a bit better. Mom would not lose her shop, and my friends were not going to lose their businesses. Moses was finally well enough to return to his apartment, where he'd be surrounded by his beloved books and have his saxophone by his side. Janet told him last night the lawyers from Anderson had already approached her about a settlement. It looked like Moses's hospital bills would be covered, and Janet felt fairly certain he'd never have to worry about money again. I felt like I was floating.

Mom grinned. "Good morning, dearest. It suits you, you know."

I wore an old T-shirt and a pair of khaki shorts. "What does?" I asked, looking at my clothing in confusion.

She kissed my forehead. "Being in love."

Matthew padded down the steps, and I handed him a cup of coffee. Mom kissed his cheek. "Good morning sweet, darling, magical boy."

She went into the garden, and we both stared after her. "That's a little different from the last time we had a sleep-over," said Matthew.

I eyed him over the rim of my cup. "She didn't find my panties next to a used condom in the garden this morning."

I almost fell off my chair at the expression on Matthew's face. He was horrified. "You never told me."

"I knew you'd be embarrassed."

We heard my mom coming back, and Matthew looked a bit panicked. "I'll get the paper."

I took out ingredients for cookies as my mom started making breakfast, humming a little song as she worked. Matthew strolled back in, his brow wrinkled in concentration and his eyes on the paper.

"What's so interesting?" I asked.

Matthew turned the newspaper to show me the cover story. "Secret River Found Beneath the City of Pittsburgh."

"What does it say?" asked Mom.

My eyes scanned the page. "They were digging to put in a new subway line, and discovered a hidden river running deep underground. Some people insist it was one mentioned in an ancient Mayan prophecy. A geologist interviewed by the reporter said the area closest to the surface is directly under the South Side, and several older properties have plumbing systems connected directly to this river."

We all stood still for a moment before racing out into the garden to look at our fountain. It gurgled happily in the dappled morning sunlight falling through the trees, not looking very mystical or mysterious at all.

"I knew it was magic. Every time I made a wish, it came true," said Mom, her lovely blue eyes growing sad. "Well, almost every time."

The bell hanging on the front door rang, and we looked up in surprise. "Are you expecting anyone?" I asked.

She shook her head. We heard a big booming voice call out a greeting. "Hello, hello. Where are my girls?"

Mom grinned. "Frankie? Is that you? We're out in the garden."

Frankie stuck his head out the back door. His dark curly hair hung to his shoulders in a mix of black and gray, and he had on a long, embroidered tunic he must have purchased in India. His glasses were round and tortoiseshell, and he had an earring in one ear. He walked over to Mom and she gave him a hug.

"When did you get back?" she asked.

He kissed her cheek and wiggled his eyebrows at us. "Hello, young ones." He reached out to shake Matthew's hand and turned back to my mom. "I came straight from the airport. I have a surprise for you, something from India."

The door to the garden opened, and a tall, dark-haired man appeared. In that moment, it was like time stopped. We stood absolutely still, staring, and even the fountain seemed to fall silent. The sun shone down upon us, and I realized I held my breath. Something monumental was about to happen, something I'd remember forever.

"Hello, Claire de Lune."

The color drained from Mom's face. "Simon? Is that you?"

"I have been searching for you, my darling Claire, for so many years. I was about to give up when I walked into a café in Rishikesh and saw Frankie." He turned and looked at me, his green eyes intense as he searched my face. "Is this Fiona? *Our* Fiona?"

I nodded, giving him a wobbly smile and a little wave. When he smiled back at me, I knew my mom was right. We did have the same dimple in our cheek.

Mom looked flustered, and it was the first time I'd ever seen her like this.

"I waited for you," she said. "You never came."

He walked slowly toward her, and I noticed he had a slight limp. "I was in an accident, *ma cherie.* It happened as I was on my way to meet you. I stayed in the hospital for weeks, and it took months before I could walk again. By the time I got out, you'd already gone, and I had no way to contact you."

"You were hurt?"

He nodded. "I never would have abandoned you on purpose, and I never once stopped loving you. Not for one day. Not for one moment. Can you forgive me?"

He opened his arms to her, and she didn't hesitate. She ran to him, and he held her close.

"Uh, who is Simon?" asked Matthew, his voice a whisper.

I found it hard to keep my composure. "My father."

Frankie looked on proudly. "Mission accomplished," he said. "Let's give them a little privacy, kiddos."

"You know what this means, don't you?" asked Matthew as we walked back into the kitchen. I shook my head, and he grinned. "It means your mom was right all along. That fountain is magical."

I slid my arms around his waist. "I certainly got what I wished for."

He kissed the top of my head. "Me too."

Frankie winked at us. "I see the two of you are getting along well. This worked out even better than I planned."

Matthew put his arm around my shoulders and pulled me close. I tilted my head and looked at Frankie. "There is one thing I'm a little confused about. How did the two of you know each other in the first place?"

Frankie grinned. "Moonbeam is my godson. His daddy was my best friend in the whole wide world."

"Moonbeam?" I asked, trying very hard not to laugh.

"Shush," said Matthew with a smile. "My parents were . . . unique. Like your mom."

"Your parents were more than unique, Moonbeam," said Frankie. "They were two of the best people I've ever met. Like your parents, Fiona." He touched Matthew's yin and yang necklace. "I'm glad to see you still wear your old man's necklace."

"I never take it off." Matthew shook his hand and then turned to me to explain. "Frankie has always been there for me, from the time I was just a little guy. He even taught me to play the guitar. That's why I am such a *decent* guitarist."

Frankie's wide face wrinkled into a frown. "*Decent*? Who would call you *decent*? That is outrageous. That is like calling Michelangelo a *decent* painter. You are the best guitarist I've ever heard, and I've spent some time around the greats, my man."

I put my hands up. "I said you were pretty cute too."

Matthew gave me a saucy wink. "I'll take that."

Frankie scratched his chin. "Who would have thought that one day Claire's little girl and Anna's little boy would hook up? We did a lot of weed in our day, but we never would have come up with something like that. It's amazing. It's like fate or something."

"Not fate. Magic," I said softly.

Frankie's face lit up, and he nodded. "It is indeed."

Even though I couldn't see it, count it, or calculate it, I knew I was right. Magic had brought Matthew to me, and it brought Simon back to my mother.

I held Matthew close as the secret river rushed silently under our feet and the fountain gurgled softly in the garden. I looked out the window, and for a second, I thought I saw something silver shimmering in the water. Was it the magic of the fountain or the spirit of dear Aunt Francesca, coming back to make sure my mother and I not only found our true loves but also somehow managed to keep them? I couldn't be certain. It felt like she was still with us, though, watching over us with a smile on her lips and the bright summer sun on her face.

"What are you thinking about?" asked Matthew.

"Something I read in Aunt Francesca's journal," I said. "*In the end, we only regret the chances we couldn't take, the decisions we took too long to make, and all the wonderful things we did not bake.*"

He smiled. "It would have to be about baking."

"Of course," I said, and as I pulled him closer to give him a kiss, I thought I heard the faint strains of bubbling laughter coming from the fountain, as effervescent as a glass of champagne. Before I could be certain, however, a soft breeze blew through the crumbling old walls of the Enchanted Garden Café and carried the sound right up to the summer sky.

Piña Colada Smoothie

2 cups good coconut milk (Fiona would not use the cheap stuff)

2 cups pineapple juice

2 cups fresh pineapple (canned will do)

1 shot of rum (or more, if you're trying to get a handsome stranger to share his secrets with you)

Put everything in a blender, add ice, and puree until smooth. This recipe makes 2 or 3 good-size smoothies, perfect for a romantic night in the garden.

Moses's Favorite Snickerdoodles

1 cup butter, softened
   2 cups sugar
   2 eggs
   1 teaspoon vanilla
   3 cups flour
   1/2 teaspoon cream of tartar
   1/2 teaspoon baking soda
   For rolling:
   4 tablespoons sugar
   2 teaspoons cinnamon

Cream the butter with an electric mixer and then add the sugar. As soon as it's incorporated, add the eggs one at a time and the vanilla. Mix together the flour, cream of tartar, and baking soda in a small bowl. Slowly add the dry mix, beating it on low speed. Cover and chill.

Mix the 4 tablespoons of sugar with the 2 teaspoons of cinnamon and place in a shallow bowl. Form the cookie dough into 1-inch balls and roll the balls in the cinnamon/sugar mix. Place on an ungreased cookie sheet and bake in a 375-degree oven for 10 minutes (or until slightly golden and brown around the edges).

This makes about 4 dozen cookies, but it won't be enough, especially if you enjoy them as much as Moses does. Consider doubling the recipe.

Aunt Francesca's Secret Sugar Cookie Recipe

- 3 cups of flour
- 1 1/2 teaspoon baking powder
- 1/2 teaspoon salt
- 1 cup of sugar
- 1 cup butter
- 1 slightly beaten egg
- 3 tablespoons cream
- 1 teaspoon vanilla

Preheat oven to 400 degrees. Sift together flour, baking powder, and salt. Mix sugar into the dry ingredients. Cut in butter with a fork or a pastry blender until particles are fine. Add beaten egg.

Add cream and vanilla. Mix well and refrigerate dough. Roll out into 1/8-inch thickness. Cut cookies using cookie cutters. Place on a parchment-lined baking sheet. Bake for 8–10 minutes or until golden. Cool before decorating.

Aunt Francesca would say the magic is in the baker's hands, not the ingredients, but a nice heavy cream makes these cookies extra tasty.

ACKNOWLEDGMENTS

A big thank you to all the people who helped turn the idea for this book into a reality, especially my wonderful editor Lara Parker and my fantastic cover artist Najla Qamber. I'd be lost without the two of you.

Thanks also to my readers, including Malissa Close, Annie Amsden, Katie Ernst, Anne Lippin, Colleen Myers, and Andrea Durnell. You saw this book at various stages and used your own unique talents to make it into something special. I owe each of you a big glass of wine and lots of chocolate.

Also, a big thank you to my own fairy godmother and dear friend, Francesca Carinci. Aunt Francesca is based on you, and the fact that you allowed me to share your magical sugar cookie recipe in this book is a special privilege. Love you!

ABOUT THE AUTHOR

National award winning author Abigail Drake has spent her life traveling the world and collecting stories wherever she visited. She majored in Japanese and Economics in college and worked in import/export and as an ESL teacher before she committed herself full time to writing. Abigail is a trekkie, a book hoarder, the master of the Nespresso machine, a red wine drinker, and a chocoholic. She lives in Beaver, Pennsylvania with her husband and three sons. A Labrador named Capone is the most recent edition to her family, and she blogs about him to maintain what little sanity she has left.

For more information
www.abigaildrake.com
abigaildrake@comcast.net

CPSIA information can be obtained
at www.ICGtesting.com
Printed in the USA
LVHW110733230819
628457LV00006BA/738/P

9 781987 703511